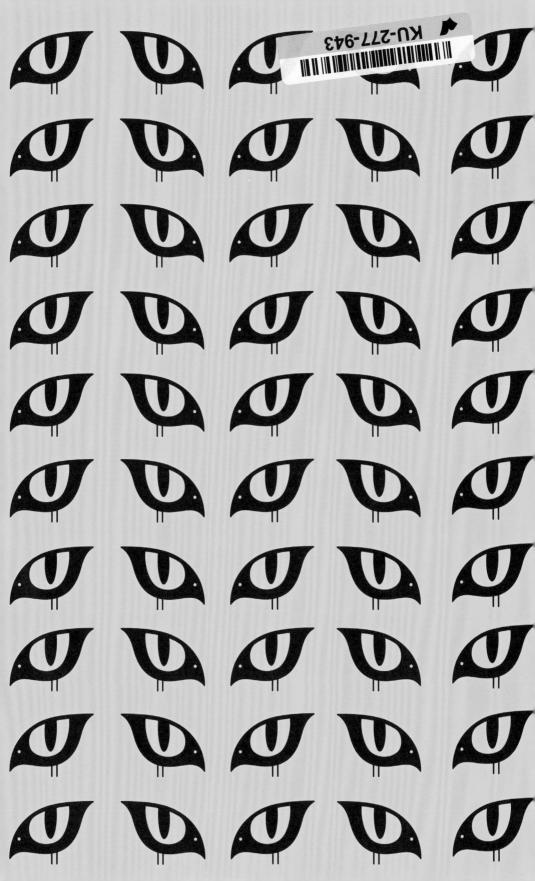

OLD BABES IN THE WOOD

You Are Happy

Selected Poems: 1965–1975

Two-Headed Poems

True Stories

Interlunar

Selected Poems II: Poems Selected and New, 1976–1986

Morning in the Burned House

Eating Fire: Selected Poetry, 1965–1995

The Door

Dearly

NON-FICTION

Survival: A Thematic Guide to Canadian Literature

Days of the Rebels: 1815–1840

Second Words: Selected Critical Prose

Strange Things: The Malevolent North in Canadian Literature

Negotiating with the Dead: A Writer on Writing (republished
as On Writers and Writing)

Moving Targets: Writing with Intent 1982–2004

Curious Pursuits: Occasional Writing

Writing with Intent: Essays, Reviews, Personal Prose 1983–2005

Payback: Debt and the Shadow Side of Wealth

In Other Worlds: SF and the Human Imagination

Burning Questions: Essays and Occasional Pieces 2004–2021

FOR CHILDREN

Up in the Tree

Anna's Pet (with Joyce Barkhouse)

For the Birds

Princess Prunella and the Purple Peanut

Rude Ramsay and the Roaring Radishes

Bashful Bob and Doleful Dorinda

Wandering Wenda and Widow Wallop's Wunderground Washery

GRAPHIC NOVELS

Angel Catbird

The Handmaid's Tale

War Bears

Old Babes in the Wood

Stories

MARGARET ATWOOD

Chatto & Windus

LONDON

5 7 9 10 8 6

Chatto & Windus, an imprint of Vintage, is part of the Penguin Random House group
of companies whose addresses can be found at global.penguinrandomhouse.com

Penguin
Random House
UK

Copyright © O. W. Toad, Ltd. 2023

First published in the United Kingdom by Chatto & Windus in 2023

penguin.co.uk/vintage

Owing to limitations of space, all acknowledgements to reprint
previously published material appear in the 'Acknowledgements'
section at the back of this book

A CIP catalogue record for this book is available from the British Library

HB ISBN 9781784744854

Printed and bound in Great Britain by Clays Ltd, Elcograf S.p.A.

The authorised representative in the EEA is Penguin Random House Ireland,
Morrison Chambers, 32 Nassau Street, Dublin DO2 YH68

Penguin Random House is committed to a sustainable future
for our business, our readers and our planet. This book is made
from Forest Stewardship Council® certified paper.

For my readers.

For my family.

For friends and absent friends.

For Graeme Gibson, as always.

CONTENTS

✦

I

TIG & NELL

II

MY EVIL MOTHER

III

NELL & TIG

I

TIG & NELL

FIRST AID

✦

N ell came home one day just before dinnertime and found the front door open. The car was gone. There was a trail of blood splotches on the steps, and once she was inside the house, she followed it along the hall carpet and into the kitchen. There was a knife on the cutting board, one of Tig's favourites, Japanese steel, very sharp—and beside it, a blood-stained carrot, one end severed. Their daughter, nine at the time, was nowhere to be found.

What were the possible scenarios? Desperadoes had broken in. Tig had tried to defend himself against them, using the knife (though how to explain the carrot?), and had been wounded. The desperadoes had made off with him, their daughter, and their car. Nell should call the police.

Or else Tig had been cooking, had sliced himself with the knife, had judged that he needed stitches, and had driven himself to the hospital, taking their daughter with him to avoid leaving her by herself. This was more likely. He must have been in too much of a hurry to leave a note.

Nell got out the bottle of carpet cleaner and sprayed the blood spots: they would be much harder to get out once they'd dried.

Then she wiped the blood off the kitchen floor and, after a pause, off the carrot. It was a perfectly good carrot; no need for it to go to waste.

Time passed. Suspense built. She was at the point of phoning all the hospitals in the vicinity to see if Tig was there when he came back, hand bandaged. He was in a jovial mood, as was their daughter. What an adventure they'd had! The blood was just pouring out, they reported. The tea towel Tig had used for wrapping the cut had been soaked! Yes, driving had been a challenge, said Tig—he didn't say dangerous—but who could wait for a taxi, and he'd managed all right with basically just one hand since he'd needed to keep the other one raised, and the blood was trickling off his elbow, and they'd sewn him up quickly at the hospital because he was dripping all over everything, and anyway, here they were! Luckily not an artery, or it would be a different story. (It was indeed a different story when Tig told it a little later, to Nell: his bravado had been an act—he hadn't wanted to frighten their daughter—and he'd been worried that he would pass out if the blood loss got out of control, and then what?)

"I need a drink," said Tig.

"So do I," said Nell. "We can have scrambled eggs." Whatever Tig had been planning to do with the carrot was no longer on the agenda.

The tea towel had been brought back in a plastic bag. It was bright red but beginning to brown at the edges. Nell put it to soak in cold water, which was the best way to deal with bloodstained fabrics.

But what would I have done if I'd been here? she wondered. Not a Band-Aid: insufficient. A tourniquet? She'd had perfunctory instruction in those at Girl Guides. They'd done wrist sprains too. Minor emergencies were her domain, but not major ones. Major ones were Tig's.

———

That was some time ago. Early autumn, as she recalls, a year in the later 1980s. There were personal computers then, of a lumbering kind. And printers: the paper for them came with the pages joined together at top and bottom, and had holes along the sides, in perforated strips that you had to tear off. No cellphones though, which was why Nell hadn't been able to text or call Tig and ask him where he was, and also what had caused the blood?

How much waiting we used to do, she thinks. Waiting without knowing. So many blanks we couldn't fill in, so many mysteries. So little information. Now it's the first decade of the twenty-first century, space-time is denser, it's crowded, you can barely move because the air is so packed with this and that. You can't get away from people: they're in touch, they're touching, they're only a touch away. Is that better, or worse?

She switches her attention to the room the two of them are in right at this moment. It's in a nondescript high-rise on Bloor Street, near the viaduct. She and Tig are sitting in chairs that are something like schoolroom chairs—there is in fact a whiteboard at the front—and a man called Mr. Foote is talking. The people in the other chairs, who are also listening to Mr. Foote, are at least thirty years younger than Tig and Nell; some of them perhaps forty years younger. Just kids.

"If it's a motorcycle crash," says Mr. Foote, "you don't want to take off the helmet, do ya. Because you don't know what's gonna be in there, eh?" He moves his hand in front of him, circularly, as if cleaning a window.

Good point, thinks Nell. She imagines the glass of a helmet, smeared. Inside, a face that is no longer a face. A face of mush.

Mr. Foote has a talent for conjuring up such images. He has a graphic way of speaking, being from Newfoundland. He doesn't tiptoe around. He's built on a square plan: wide torso, thick legs, a short distance between ear and shoulder. It's a balanced shape, with a low centre of gravity. Mr. Foote would not be easy to upend. Nell expects that's been tried, in bars—he looks as if he'd know his way around a bar fight, but also as if he wouldn't get into any of those he couldn't win. If pushed too hard he'd throw the challenger through a window, calmly—"You needs to keep calm," he has already said twice—then check to make sure there were no bones broken. If there were, he'd splint them, and treat the victim for cuts and abrasions. Mr. Foote is an all-in-one package. In fact, he's a paramedic, but that does not come out until later in the day.

He's carrying a black leather binder and wearing a long-sleeved zip-fronted sweatshirt with the St. John Ambulance logo on it, as if he's a team coach, which in a way he is: he's teaching them first aid. At the end of the day there will be a test and they will each get a certificate. All of them are in this room because they need this certificate: their companies have sent them. Nell and Tig are the same. Thanks to a family connection of Tig's, they're giving talks on a nature-tour cruise ship, birds for him, butterflies for her: their hobbies. So they are technically staff, and all staff on this ship have to get the certificate. It's mandatory, their ship contact has told them.

What hasn't been said is that the majority of the passengers— the guests—the clientele—will not be young, to put it mildly. Some of them will be older than Nell and Tig. Truly ancient. Such people can be expected to topple over at any minute, and then it will be certificates to the rescue.

Nell and Tig are unlikely to be doing any actual rescuing: younger people will leap in, Nell's counting on that. In a pinch, Nell will dither and claim she's forgotten what to do, which will be true. What will Tig do? He will say, Stand back, give them room. Something like that.

It's known—it's been rumoured—that these ships have extra freezers on them, just in case. Nell pictures the distress of a server who opens the wrong freezer by mistake, to be confronted by the appalled, congealed stare of some unlucky passenger for whom the certificate has not proved sufficient.

Mr. Foote stands at the front of the room, running his gaze over today's crop of students. His expression is possibly neutral, or faintly amused. Bunch of know-nothing softies, he's most likely thinking. City people. "There's what to do, and there's what not to do," he says. "I'll be telling you both. First, ya don't go scream-ing around like a headless chicken. Even if buddy's minus his own head."

But headless chickens can't scream, Nell thinks. Or she assumes they can't. But she takes the meaning. Keep your head in an emer-gency, they say. Mr. Foote would add, "If ya can." He would defi-nitely want them to keep their heads.

"You can fix a lot of things," Mr. Foote is saying. "But not if there's no head. That's one thing I can't teach ya." It's a joke, Nell guesses, but Mr. Foote does not signal jokes. He's deadpan.

"Say you're in a restaurant." Mr. Foote, having dealt with motor-cycle crashes, has moved on to asphyxiation. "And buddy starts choking. The question you needs to ask is: Can they talk? Ask them if you can hit them on the back. If they say yes in words, it's not too bad because they can still breathe, eh? But what's likely— a lot of people are embarrassed, they stand up, and what do they do? They go to the washroom, because they don't want to be mak-ing a fuss. Calling attention. But you got to go in there with them, you got to follow them, because they can die. Right on the floor, before you even notice they're gone." He gives a meaningful nod. He has known instances, the nod says. He's been there. He's seen it happen. But he got there too late.

Mr. Foote knows his stuff, Nell thinks. The exact same thing has almost happened to her. The choking, the going to the washroom, the not wanting to make a fuss. Embarrassment can be lethal, she sees now. Mr. Foote has nailed it.

"Then you got to bend them forward," Mr. Foote continues. "Five whacks on the back—the glob of meat or the dumpling or the fish bone or whatever can shoot out of them right then and there. But if not, you got to do the Heimlich manoeuvre. Thing is, if they can't talk, they can't exactly give you permission, plus they might be turning blue and passing out. You just got to do it. Maybe you'll break a rib, but at least they'll be alive, eh?" He grins a little, or Nell assumes it's a grin. A sort of mouth twitch. "That's the endgame, eh? Alive!"

They run through the Heimlich manoeuvre and the right way of hitting someone on the back. According to Mr. Foote, the combination of these two things would almost always work, but you had to get in there soon enough: in first aid, timing is everything. "That's why it's called first, eh? It's not the effing tax department, excuse my French, they can take all day, but you got maybe four minutes."

Now, he says, they will have a coffee break, and after that, they will do drowning and mouth-to-mouth, followed by hypothermia; and, after lunch, heart attacks and defibrillators. It's a lot for one day.

Drowning is fairly simple. "First, you need to get the water out. It'll pour out if you let gravity be your friend, eh? Turn 'em on the side, empty 'em out, but fast." Mr. Foote has dealt with numerous drownings: he's lived near water all his life. "Turn 'em on their back to clear the airways, check for breathing, check for pulse, make sure someone calls 911. If there's no breathing, you needs to do the mouth-to-mouth. Now this gadget I'm showing you, it's a CPR barrier guard, it's for the mouth-to-mouth, 'cause sometimes they'll throw up, like, and you don't need to have that in your own mouth. Anyways, there's the germs, eh? You should carry one a these on you at all times." Mr. Foote has a supply of them. They can be purchased at the end of the day.

Nell makes a mental note to get one. How has she managed to live without a mouth barrier guard until now? How feckless.

In order to practise the mouth-to-mouth, the room is divided into pairs. Each pair is given a red plastic torso with a bald white tip-back head and a yoga mat for kneeling on while they bring their shared torso back to life. Pinch the nose shut, cover the mouth with yours, give five rescue breaths, letting the chest rise each time, then perform five chest compressions. Repeat. Meanwhile, the other person calls 911, after which they take over with the chest compressions. These can get tiring, it's hard on the wrists. Mr. Foote stalks the room, checking everyone's technique. "You're gettin' there," he says.

Tig says now that he's down on the mat, Nell will have to call 911 to get someone to lift him back up again, considering the state of his knees. Nell giggles into the plastic mouth, sabotaging her rescue breath. "I just hope nobody drowns on our watch," she says. "Because they'll probably stay drowned." Tig says he understands it's a relatively painless way to go. You are said to hear bells.

When they've all brought their plastic torsos back to life, they move on to hypothermia and shock. Both involve blankets. Mr. Foote tells an amazing story about a man on a ski trip who went out the door of a cabin to take a leak, without a flashlight, through deep snow, and fell into a melt well around the base of a tree, and couldn't get out, and wasn't found until morning. He was stiff as a board and cold as a mackerel, said Mr. Foote, not a breath in him, and as for his heart, it was silent as the tomb. But someone else in that cabin had taken the CPR course, and they worked on the possibly dead person for six hours—six hours!—and brought him back.

"You keep going. You don't give up," says Mr. Foote. "Because you never know."

They break for lunch. Nell and Tig find a little Italian restaurant tucked into one of the soulless high-rise buildings, and order a glass of red wine each, and eat quite good pizza. Nell says she's going to have a wallet card made that says "In Case of Accident Call Mr. Foote," and Tig says they should run Mr. Foote for prime minister, he could give the whole country mouth-to-mouth. He thinks Mr. Foote has been in the navy. Nell says no, he's a spy. Tig says maybe he's been a pirate, and Nell says no, he's definitely an alien from outer space, and being a first-aid instructor called Mr. Foote is a perfect front.

They're both feeling silly, and also incompetent. Nell is sure that if confronted with any of these emergencies—the drowning person, the one in shock, the frozen one—she will panic, and everything Mr. Foote has taught them will go right out of her head.

"I might do snakebites, though," she says. "I learned a little about that in Girl Guides."

"I don't think Mr. Foote does snakebites," says Tig.

"Bet he does. But only in private sessions. It's niche."

The afternoon is exciting. Real defibrillators are handed out, and their paddles are applied with precision to the red plastic torsos. Everyone gets a turn. Mr. Foote tells them how to avoid defibrillating themselves by accident—your heart could get confused and decide to stop. Nell murmurs to Tig that death by self-defibrillation would be very undignified. Not as undignified as sticking a fork in a wall socket, Tig murmurs back. True, Nell thinks. You had to beware of that with small children.

Then comes the test. Mr. Foote ensures they all pass: he broadly hints at the answers, and instructs them to raise their hands if they don't understand a question. They will receive their certificates in the mail, he says, closing his black leather binder, with relief, Nell expects. One more batch of no-hopers off his hands, and pray to God none of them is ever involved in a real emergency.

Nell purchases one of the CPR mouth barrier guards. She wants to tell Mr. Foote that she's enjoyed his stories, but that might sound frivolous, as if this was merely entertainment, as if she doesn't take him seriously. He might be insulted. So she says a simple thank you, and he nods.

Once she and Tig are home—once it's the next day, or possibly the day after that—she totals up all the life-threatening experiences the two of them have had, or experiences she'd feared might have been life-threatening. How prepared had she been for any of them?

The time the metal chimney set fire to the inside of the roof, and Tig climbed up into the crawl space in clouds of choking smoke and poured buckets of water on the fire. What if he'd blacked out in there, from smoke inhalation? After that incident, Tig bought a fire blanket, and every floor of any house they were living in had to have a fire extinguisher. He worried about hotels too, and always checked to make sure he knew where the stairs were, just in case. Also the windows: Did they open? Increasingly, windows in hotels were sealed shut, but you could break the glass, maybe, by wrapping your arm in a towel first. That would be no use if the window was too high up.

The time Tig set off all the fire alarms in a thirty-storey hotel by smoking a cigar in the hall underneath one of the sensors, and the two of them climbed down all the flights of stairs and exited through a lobby filled with firemen, pretending they hadn't done it. That event wasn't life-threatening. It wasn't even very embarrassing, since they hadn't got caught.

The time a lumber truck ahead of them on the highway lost its load: wooden boards peeled off it, flying through the air and bouncing all over the asphalt, narrowly missing them. On top of that, it was in a blizzard. Knowing CPR wouldn't have helped.

The time they were canoeing on one of the Great Lakes and their canoe was tipped by a freak wave from a passing ocean steamer. Not life-threatening: they were close to shore, the water was warm. They'd got wet, that was all.

The time Tig came roaring up on the ATV towing a trailerful of wood he'd been cutting with his chainsaw, blood pouring down his face from a scalp wound he didn't know he had. That wasn't life-threatening: he hadn't even noticed.

"There's blood pouring down his face," Nell said to the children, as if they couldn't see.

"There's always blood pouring down his face," one of them replied with a shrug. As far as they were concerned, he was indestructible.

"I must have a lot of blood," Tig said, grinning away. What had he skinned his head on? Something unimportant. Next minute he was unloading the wood, the minute after that he was splitting it: it was already dry, he'd been harvesting dead trees. Then bang, he was filling up the woodbox. In those days they'd lived in fast-forward.

The hikes they used to take, before there were cellphones: they hadn't considered them risky. Had they even packed a first-aid kit? Maybe some moleskin for blisters, antibiotic ointment, a couple of painkillers. What would have happened if one of them had sprained an ankle, broken a leg? Had they even told anyone where they were going?

One autumn, for instance, in a national park. Rough weather: early snow and ice.

Marching along through the yellow and gold beech forest with their enormous packsacks, poking iced-over ponds with their hiking poles, consulting trail maps and having differences of opinion about them. Eating squares of chocolate, then pausing for lunches: parking themselves on logs, devouring mini-cheeses, hard-boiled eggs, nuts and crackers. Rum in a flask.

Tig was already having trouble with his knees, but he went on the hikes anyway. He tied his knees up with bandanas, one above, one below. "Why are you still walking?" a doctor asked him. "Basically, you don't have a knee." But that was much later.

That year there was an urban legend about hiking danger making the rounds, to the effect that male moose in season—the fall season, the one they were in—were sexually attracted to Volkswagen Beetles. They'd taken to leaping off cliffs on top of them, squashing both car and driver. Nell and Tig thought this was BS, but they'd added "probably" because strange things could happen.

They set up their tent in a likely spot, made supper with their WhisperLite single-element gas burner, slung their food packs into a tree at some distance in case of bears, and crawled into their gelid sleeping bags.

Nell lay awake, reflecting on the fact that their dome-shaped tent strongly resembled a Volkswagen Beetle. Would a male moose come along in the middle of the night and jump on top of them?

And once it had discovered its mistake, would it become enraged? Male moose were notorious for becoming enraged in mating season. They could be a serious hazard.

In the clear light of morning, the moose-squashing possibility seemed remote. Not a life-threatening experience, therefore, except in Nell's head.

The next year, a couple taking the exact same trail they'd been on had been killed in their tent by a bear, and partly eaten. Tig liked to think of this as a narrow escape. He took to reading out loud to Nell, at night, from a book called *Bear Attacks*. There were two kinds of attacking bears, it claimed: bears who were hungry, and mother bears protecting their young. The way you should react was different for each, but there was no immediate method for telling the difference. When to play dead, when to ease away sideways, when to fight back? And with what kind of bear: black or grizzly? The instructions were complex.

"I'm not sure we should be reading about this just before going to sleep," said Nell. They'd come to a story about a woman who got her arm chewed off, though she'd finally managed to deter the bear by hitting it on the nose.

"She must've had nerves of steel," said Tig.

"She must've been in shock," said Nell. "It can give you superhuman powers."

"She survived, anyway," said Tig.

"Just barely," said Nell. "No pun intended."

Did any of this stop them from going on more of their underequipped hikes? It did not. Tig bought some bear spray, however. Most of the time they remembered to pack it.

Revisiting all of this—because revisiting sets in, after a time, after many times—Nell is now wondering, Would the instructions of

Mr. Foote have made a difference in these situations, if push had come to shove? Maybe with the chimney fire: if Nell had been able to haul an unconscious Tig out of the crawl space, she could have given him some rescue breaths while the house was burning down. But eaten by a bear or squashed by a moose? No salvation there.

Mr. Foote was right: no one can guess. No one knows the final outcome, though why is it called an outcome? No one comes out, eventually. "We aren't going to make it out of here alive," Tig used to say as a joke, although it wasn't one. And if you did guess, if you could foresee, would that be better? No: you'd live in grief all the time, you'd be mourning things that hadn't happened yet.

Better to preserve the illusion of safety. Better to improvise. Better to march along through the golden autumn woods, not very well prepared, poking icy ponds with your hiking pole, snacking on chocolate, sitting on frozen logs, peeling hard-boiled eggs with cold fingers as the early snow sifts down and the day darkens. No one knows where you are.

Had they really been that careless, that oblivious? They had. Obliviousness had served them well.

TWO SCORCHED MEN

✦

John has shot himself in the radiator," said François. He laughed his pink-cheeked, silent laugh. "But you mustn't tell him that I told you."

"What do you mean, 'in the radiator'?" I asked. François was not always self-evident.

"He meant to shoot himself," said François, "but he changed his mind and shot the radiator instead." He paused, giving me time to say *Really?* with the required lift of the eyebrows.

"Yes! I think so," he continued. "There is water all over the floor. He has called a plumber. He is in quite a rage."

"Oh dear," I said. John had been our landlord over the winter, although Tig and I were in another rented house by then. John had been in the habit of coming down from Paris to see how we were getting on, he said, though I suspect the real reason was to have an audience, apart from his skeptical French wife. He'd stay in a room he kept for his own use, emerging to shamble around the grounds, argue with various handymen employed to fix things, and share the odd meal with us.

I was thus familiar with the rages, which could be unleashed at any time. I also knew where that radiator was located: in a back hallway off the kitchen. That was where John cleaned his gun, or guns. I was uncertain as to the number. What did he shoot with it, or them? Wild boars, possibly, once. The hills were swarming with them; they rooted up the vines, plus you could make sausages out of them. But surely no boar hunting recently, for John: he was no longer in good enough shape for it.

"In the radiator! It is so funny," said François, making more laughing expressions. "But you mustn't reveal that you know. His feelings would be hurt."

This is how the two of them went on. Laughter on the one hand, rages on the other. They were close friends: one lanky, explosive Irishman; one short, roundish, genial Frenchman. It was an unlikely pairing. However, although John's rages could be directed at anyone or anything, they were never directed at François. And François was as solicitous about John's emotional state as if he'd been a stray kitten, of which François had adopted several.

Here is the clue: they'd both been in the war.

They're dead now. A thing that happens increasingly: people die. This radiator incident took place in the early 1990s, when the two of them must have been—what? I'm counting backwards. John had been in the British navy, let's say he was eighteen, nineteen, or twenty in 1939. Therefore, at the time of the radiator shooting he must have been in his early seventies, more or less. François was three or four years younger.

Both of them presented me with their stories that year. Since they knew what sort of creature I was, they also knew—indeed they trusted—that I would someday relate their lives for them. Why did they want this? Why does anyone? We resist the notion that we'll become mere handfuls of dust, so we wish to become words instead. Breath in the mouths of others.

Gentlemen, the time has come. I will do my best for you. Are you listening?

———

I must now set the scene, the scene in which I came to know the two of them.

John's house—the one Tig and I rented that winter—was in a Provençal proto-village: a few houses scattered around a cross-road, most of them on working farms. There were straying pigs (rages about the pigs). There was a lot of mud on the roads (rages about the mud). There were neighbours in thick knitted cardigans and filthy overalls (rages about the neighbours). John's house, however, was not part of a working farm. It must have belonged to gentry once, and John qualified as a modern-day version of that: a spacious flat in Paris, near the church of Saint-Germain; a retirement income that allowed for indulgences, such as trips and dining out; the country house we'd rented.

The house was two-storey, stone, eighteenth-century, with the vertical shutter-trimmed windows of that time and place. It had an ironwork fence and gate, a garden inside that, a portico facing south, its pillars twined around by wisteria. It had one of the most beautiful interiors either Tig or I had ever seen. Despite its beauty, this interior always seemed indistinct, as if it were being viewed through smoke: the colours a little faded, the outlines a little hazy. The furniture was neither comfortable nor convenient, but it was authentic. John made sure we knew that, though the exquisite taste was his wife's, not his. (He never threw rages about this unseen wife, or not when we were around.)

During the war the house had belonged to an Englishman of ambiguous loyalties. Just as the war was ending he was found murdered, on the porch with the pillars and the wisteria, in the lovely garden, in the sunlight. Bullet in the head. No gun in sight, so not suicide.

"Why?" I asked John. A shrug, followed by a mini-rage about the criminality and secretiveness of the region. Nobody knew why. Or rather, someone must have known but nobody would say. That's what it had been like then, said John; it was still like that, under the surface. You never could tell when vengeance might strike, over some dirty piece of political backstabbing or sod-off insult, or a scuffle over some syphilitic wench, or over a land tug-of-war, there was always that, or over the two big ones: theft of snails—lay hands on another man's snails and he'd garotte you—and truffle poaching, which would earn you castration with a rusty paring knife.

And serve you right, said John, for being so sodding stupid.

The woods were full of signs threatening traps or poison, to deter potential miscreants and their truffle-sniffing dogs. Once, when hiking in the hills, we'd come upon two huge raw bones, cow bones they must have been, wired into the shape of a St. Andrew's Cross and dangling from a tree. Was it a hex sign of some kind? A warning, but about what, or to whom? We were off the main trail; nobody came there. "Don't touch it," said Tig, but I wouldn't have anyway. There were already flies, and a stench of rotting meat.

We told John about the bone arrangement, which generated another rant about the dark doings in these parts. Evil peasants, dead ignorant, witless mud-wallowers, *emmerdeurs,* smugglers, thieves. No respect for civilization, or the law either, such as it was.

But maybe this was because of historical memory, I said. The distrust of authorities. Over the centuries there had been many waves of Nonconformists in this area: the Cathars, the Vaudois . . . (I was a reader of tourist guides in those days.)

John let out a bellow. The Cathars! What tripe had I been dabbling in? Stuff the Cathars, thought they were perfect, holier than thou, nobody gave a toss about them except for the peddlers of cheap souvenirs made in China and crapulous handicrafts reeking of lavender; and stuff the Vaudois too, pretentious Bible-kissing po-faced hypocrites! The two of them—just two more examples of the kind of pious dog-fucking that went on whenever religion entered the picture.

But they'd been horribly persecuted, I said. The Cathars. Wasn't it Simon de Montfort who'd incinerated Carcassonne—everyone inside its walls, including women and children—and said, "Kill them all, God will know his own"?

At this point Tig slid off to the kitchen to pour himself a Scotch. He was not much interested in thirteenth-century dualism, or heresies in general, or massacres; unlike me. At that time I was a collector of the many excuses people had come up with for butchering one another.

John, however, was well versed in heresies. No, he said, it wasn't Simon de Montfort, the lip-ripping eye-gouger, it was some drivelling Catholic abbot; and it wasn't Carcassonne, it was Béziers: a wall-to-wall cut-and-slash orgy and human barbecue, the stink must've been foul. If I was going to mess around in French history—which he didn't recommend, it was one bloodbath and charnel heap after another—I should at least get it straight. Anyway, stuff their persecution! They were heretics, it was their choice, what did they expect? They'd have been disappointed if no one had persecuted them, they were all masochists anyway, rolling around in their pain and getting off on it, fuck them, so three cheers for the Catholics, they were good at the persecuting, he'd say that for them.

Not that he himself was a Catholic. Stuff the Catholics, and most especially the Irish ones! He reserved a special circle of hell for his native country, and never tired of relating anecdotes about the venality of the politics, the perviness of the clergy, and the dumb-cluckery of the average Irish peasant. The valet polishing his shoes two different colours in a rundown grand hotel in Dublin, back in the day, or the garage man filling up the oil in his car and saying, "What will that be then?" Didn't know their arse from a hole in the ground, most of them.

I wasn't willing to let go of the heretics. But the Nonconformists, I said, attempting to herd him back to the topic. Especially in the south of France. Their refusal to toe the line. Surely that had something to do with the strength of the French Resistance down here during the war? Such as the Maquis, who'd hid out in the mountains and snuck down at night to assassinate the occupying Germans and blow up the railway lines?

What kind of brain-dead North American twat was I? said John. Did I know how many innocent villagers had been lined up and machine-gunned in retaliation for that useless and selfish Maquisard playacting? None of their heroics had made a blind bit of difference, it was just throat-slitting for cheap thrills. Stuff the Maquis!

After running out of groups to denounce, he'd shut himself in his room and (I suspected) weep. Underneath the bluster he was a sentimentalist, like many of the enraged. He must have had an idea once—possibly he still did have one—of how things ought to have been in a better world than this, but I never found out what it was.

I wasn't sure exactly what John had done during the war, but whatever it was, it hadn't been fun. He'd been in the Pacific, where a huge number of Royal Navy ships had gone down and fifty thousand men had died. Had his ship been torpedoed? Had he almost drowned? He didn't talk about the war very much except in the form of invective against the Americans, who'd taken all the credit for the South Pacific. It was hardly remembered at all that the Brits had been in it.

As for *South Pacific*, the musical, which he'd been dragged off to by a woman when he'd been too drunk to resist, it made him spew. Stuff dancing sailors! Stuff that shop-soiled bottle blonde washing a man right out of her hair! None of those warbling jokers had ever had a fellow standing next to them all in one piece and the next minute, *boom*, no head, just a bleeding . . . Stuff it!

After the war he'd gone into advertising, and had made a triumph of it; hence the retirement income. This was in New York (stuff New York, everyone was a crook) and also in Toronto (stuff Toronto, timid prudish provincial mud puddle), during the great days of the hard-drinking admen, stab you in the back as soon as look at you, they were all pirates and he didn't exempt himself.

The really successful products for ads then were cigarettes and booze; also anything to do with soap, because the war had been so grimy and filthy everyone wanted to scrub themselves blue afterwards. Sparkling clean, a new start, that's what they'd wanted. He himself had specialized in shampoos. That and home permanents—a big thing in those days, torturing your head in the name of beauty—and hair dyes. He claimed to have been the author of a well-known slogan: "Only your hairdresser knows for sure." Sheer brilliance, that was: a wink at a shared secret, plus a hint of the sexually illicit. What had been going on behind the scenes to produce that blissful smile on the woman in the ad, that roguish sideways look? Sneaking around with the hairdresser! Hanky-panky in the change cubicle, the little slut.

There was a lot of innuendo in those ads; and, among the men who composed them—they'd all been men, no bossy, ball-crushing career spinsters to tut-tut and ruin everything—a lot of sneaking around. Much of the sneaking around had been done by John, according to him. Oh, if he were to tell all, we would scarcely believe it! He'd been handsome—he didn't say so, but photos were produced. High times and never a thought for tomorrow. Bed-hopping, lots of takers for that, bored housewives aching for it, cheating on their hubbies, an extra thrill for them, throwing caution to the winds on the spur of the moment, little pink tongues hanging out, with him standing by, pun intended, always happy to help.

Could this have been exactly true? I wondered. It couldn't have been that carefree. It was the 1950s, then the early 1960s: no birth control pill yet. Those impromptu flings must have smelled of rubber, from the various gizmos that would have been inserted into one body part or slid onto another. They must have involved assorted foams and jellies and creams now as antiquated as whale-bone corsets. The housewives allowing themselves to be seduced by John on the spur of the moment—with a semblance of reluctance, naturally—must have been much better prepared than he'd suspected. But I said none of this.

Like ninepins, he said. That's how they'd gone down. All the while he was making piles of money at the ad game, spending it just as fast, drinking his lunches. Then drinking his dinners. Then drinking his breakfasts. Then the doctor told him that if he didn't stop drinking he would die.

He and an alcoholic pal checked into a drying-out clinic, but before their first day they climbed over the back wall and buried half a dozen bottles of Scotch on the grounds, in case of dire need. He told this as if it had been a caper, a prank, and we'd laughed dutifully; but as I'm revisiting this escapade now, I frame it otherwise. Clambering over a wall in the dark, staring into a future in which there was nothing visible, the self you'd constructed out of shreds and performances crumbling around you, a man with no head standing always behind your shoulder; then a sheer drop. Terror.

"Took me three tries and two years, but I finally got off the stuff," he said. "Saved my life." Now he wouldn't touch even a dessert with a drop of liqueur in it: one stumble and he'd be done.

What happened after that? There was an interlude, either overlapping with his alcoholic period or after it, during which he'd had a sailboat—was it a yacht? I was the wrong person to be impressed by boats, as I knew next to nothing about them—and was entangled with a stunning young woman—a witch with red hair, he said, from Denmark, or was it Sweden? A wanton. He actually used that word.

I was embarrassed for him during these parts of his recitals, partly because of the vocabulary, so faded and shabby, but also because the whole thing was like some juvenile wet-dream fantasy out of *Playboy* magazine. Today he'd be called a misogynist as a matter of course, but it seemed to me that his rages against women—cheaters, prudes, witches, wantons—were a subset of his general misanthropy. Mankind, including womankind, was a wreck.

Except for his French wife, of course, who seemed to be a kind of supernanny. And except for François.

François lived in a town that was an hour's walk from John's village. Tig did that walk every day. In later years he would say that he could remember every detail of it, and often walked it with his eyes shut before falling asleep. Though I went less frequently—it was an effort to keep up with Tig, he was a marcher—it's the same with me: I know each twist and slope.

Out the gateway of John's house. Turn right along the gravel road. Past the T-junction, pigs and mud. More pigs and mud until the first right. Through some open fields. At that time of the year, say February or March, not a great deal was growing in them, or not officially. There would often be an old woman there, a shawl wrapped around her head, rubber boots on her feet, tending a herd of goats with two dogs to help her. The goats would graze while she gathered what we assumed were edible wild plants and stuffed them into a burlap sack; the dogs would guard the goats. Once, she'd set the dogs on Tig, most likely to see what he'd do. They hadn't attacked, but they'd come very close to him, ears laid back, growling and barking. What worked with the dogs in the countryside was to bend over as if you were picking up a stone, said Tig. Then they'd back off. They must have had prior experiences with stones.

Recalling this old woman who must be long dead, I'm close to tears. But why? I'd barely registered her at the time, but now I can call her up exactly, as if she were a feature of the landscape. She's part of what's gone, of everything that's been swept away. I might be the only person left who remembers her. I used to believe that having a good memory was a blessing, but I'm no longer so sure. Maybe forgetting is the blessing.

Anyway, the mind invents things. What colour was her shawl? Did she even have one?

Beyond the field was a wood: tall trees, filtered sunlight. Once you were inside this wood, the road dipped down into a ravine with a stream at the bottom of it, crossed by a wooden bridge. Several times there'd been people down beside the stream, with camper vans. Not tourists, said Tig. They'd never stayed long.

Then the road climbed again and came out of the wood and curved to the right. Here it passed a large rectangular cistern made of blocks of cement—not much used, judging by the algae—in which lived a large colony of frogs. You could hear them croaking from a distance, but no matter how quietly you walked up to them they would always know you were coming and would fall silent, only to start up again once you'd gone past. Over the months I put some time and thought into trying to defeat these frogs—I wanted to see them in action—but I never succeeded.

Past the frogs were some old fig trees. Many shrivelled figs lay squashed on the ground. I had not known at first what they were, and had asked François.

"What are those things that have fallen off the trees onto the road and been squashed, and look disgusting?" I'd said.

Possibly we were having a coffee at an outdoor table, Tig and François and me, listening to people yelling at their dogs, who'd be tearing around with red and blue handkerchiefs tied around their necks. *Jane! Jane! Viens ici! Bob! Bob! Fais pas ça!* The dogs all had English names.

This question had delighted François. "Yes! The things that fall off trees, and are squashed, and look disgusting!" he'd exclaimed. "Mysterious! I, too, have seen them! What could they be?" Speculation followed. A species of reptile? A fungus? It took a while to get him to reveal that they were figs.

Past the fig trees the houses of the town began, with their irises in rock gardens, their geraniums in pots. (Stuff the irises! Stuff the geraniums! John would fulminate. Stage sets, all of it! You can't even paint your house in this fraudulent carnival without a certificate from some sodding postcard company pretending to be the government!)

Next came a fountain—a river god with water pouring out of his mouth. Limestone buildup and moss had partly obscured his features and given him a green beard. His expression was ambiguous: Was it a roar of outrage, a challenge? Was he being stifled, was the gurgling of the fountain a drowning sound, a last gasp? His eyes were blind, the pupils long since eroded away.

These are the sorts of details I can recall, though past the fountain I have no clear image of the road. It meandered off into narrow streets, with little shops and cafés; and also a four-star hotel, and a restaurant that served lavender profiteroles, where we sometimes had lunch with François.

I would encounter François when we were both shopping, each of us with our woven-straw leather-handled baskets.

"François, there are some wonderful big sardines today," I opened on one occasion. I'd been told this by the proprietress of one of the more expensive shops, who was in the habit of confiding such news to me slyly and in whispers, and who'd once sold a truffle to me with furtive glances, as if it had been a stolen state secret.

"Oh no, I cannot look a sardine in the eye," said François, rolling his own eyes upward.

"Really?" I said, inviting the expanded version I knew was waiting.

"You see," said François, "in the internment camp it was nothing but sardines. We boiled them, we fried them, we toasted them. We made tiny lamps with their oil. Everything stank of sardines, sardines, sardines, morning and night! We ourselves, we could not get the smell of them off our skin. So, for me, sardines have ceased to be possible." He gave a little shudder.

The internment camp had been in Spain, which had stayed neutral in the war. François had been put into this camp when he'd escaped through the Pyrenees after having almost been convicted of treason. "We were in the Resistance, we were very young and enthusiastic," he said. "I was seventeen, can you imagine? We were distributing sheets of propaganda by slipping them into newspapers. This was in Marseilles, and I was observed."

"Oh no!" I said. "That must have been terrible!"

"It was not droll. But the regime then was Vichy, they claimed to be France, so they had to have a trial, they could not simply shoot me. The newsagent was the only witness against me, but the Resistance accosted him ahead of time and warned him that if he identified me he would be a dead newsagent. So he stood up in court and said I was the wrong François. It was a different François they needed, a bad François."

"That was lucky for you," I said.

"Indeed, it was useful to have a bad François, one who could never be found. But they knew it was me; sooner or later they would have eliminated me. I left that very night and walked through the mountains, as many did. I did not make a convincing Spaniard, needless to say, so my unauthorized presence in their worthy domain did not go undetected by the authorities for long. Thus it was that I kept my rendezvous with the sardines."

"Ah," I said, nodding. "The evil sardines."

"The British rescued me from these malevolent fish. They traded me for a sack of flour."

"A sack of flour?"

"Yes, a sack of flour. However, attention please! It was a very *large* sack!"

François had then worked with General de Gaulle and the barely existent Free French, in London. He'd lived in a decaying flat in Earl's Court with several other French refugees, and learned English. He'd witnessed the Blitz and had the greatest admiration for a certain kind of cold-blooded British bravery, or possibly idiocy: in the world of François the two were similar. He did not consider himself a hero in the matter of the Resistance—rather a fool, for having been caught.

"There we would be," he would say, spreading his arms as wide as they could go, "in London, and all around us the bombs would be falling! The *bombs* would be *falling!*" He pronounced both of the Bs in *bombs.* "And out on the sidewalk, there would be an

Englishman"—pause for effect—"playing the piano!" A cheru-
bic smile, a glance upward to indicate the falling bombs, a shrug.
What ridiculousness had been enacted on those sidewalks! But
what defiance!

François had been assigned a position in Free French Intelli-
gence, tracking train movements around France. Many train work-
ers had been in the Resistance, and it was they who'd snarled up
the trains during and after D-Day. They'd prevented German rein-
forcements from reaching the Normandy landing beaches quickly;
in retaliation, they'd been shot. But in the early days of the war
these men had merely supplied information: risky enough in itself.

François and his young train-tracking friends had followed the
fate of a guillotine being shipped to a city where it was to be used
in an execution. The train had been sidelined, it had been sent
backwards, it had been stalled; it never did reach its destination.

"Was that on purpose?" I asked.

"Who knows?" He spread his hands and lifted his shoulders. "In
those times there were many accidents. Bad accidents, but also
good." A pause. "How do we know what is our purpose?"

After the war François had been part of the upsurge of artistic
and intellectual activity that had made Paris such an international
star in the 1950s and early 1960s. Sartre, de Beauvoir, and Camus
were holding court at the Dome; in the theatre, Jean Genet and
Beckett and Ionesco and the Theatre of the Absurd were making waves. François had been a playwright in the fringe theatre
of those times. In one of his plays, he told me, a large cockroach
climbed up the side of the stage, across the ceiling, and down the
other side. Another play consisted of a rocking chair, which was
rocking quickly as the curtain rose and then rocked slower and
slower until it stopped.

"They sound very short, your plays," I said.

"Oh yes, they were," said François, making his laughing face. "Very short!"

Had these plays ever been produced? I wasn't sure. François had never said explicitly that they had, and it would have been rude to ask.

One reason John was so tolerant of François, I came to believe, was that he felt the life of François had been unluckier than his own. In fact it had been tragic. François had married, someone he really loved, said John, but the wife developed a mental illness and killed herself. There had been a daughter, who inherited the same illness; I gathered that she, too, was dead. Whereas John, after a period of sowing wild oats with the greatest abandon, ended up in the ironic but forbearing hands of his altogether too sane wife, living in the centre of the universe, which was Paris as far as he was concerned.

François did not complain about the sadness of his life, however: a mark of his saintliness. (John would have complained very loudly, and he knew it.) It was not fair, said John. Why should François have been doomed in this way? Why should he have nobody to care for him? I suspected John of various attempts at matchmaking, but if there had been any they hadn't succeeded, and François lived alone with his semi-wild stray cats, who came and went through his upstairs window as it suited them.

Several years after that winter, François had open-heart surgery. We learned about this from John, by email—email had been invented by then, but not yet social media, so the world was spared the experience of John letting loose with his rants on Twitter, as he would have done had he lived that long. He was upset by the heart operation—why François, who was younger than John? If anyone ought to have a rotten heart it should be him! He appeared to expect us to do something, or to be in some way responsible. His tone was reproachful: How had Tig and I allowed this to happen?

Perhaps his grip on reality was already slipping. Had it ever been altogether firm? According to him it had. Reality was shite! Stuff reality, he could see it plainly, and the rest of us, living our banal, tawdry little lives and enjoying ourselves with our snouts in the trough, were wearing rose-coloured blinkers. Stuff enjoying yourself! He had more serious concerns, he was writing a novel. Why weren't we doing anything about François?

François recovered from his operation. We'd sent him several get-well cards and notes, so he had our address, and eventually we received a package. In it was a letter saying that he'd found the whole enterprise—the enterprise of his near death and his heart repair—very curious. Accompanying the letter was a manuscript—not long enough to be a novel but longer than a story. He said it was based on his experiences while under general anaesthesia. It was the longest thing he'd ever written, he added. As he was aware that I could read French, perhaps I would find it amusing?

The novella was called *L'Endormi se ment,* the sleeping man lies to himself. It was a pun on the word *l'endormissement,* or going to sleep—François was fond of puns. It began with the narrator lying on a billiard table in a green room, surrounded by people dressed in green: smocks, gloves, masks. Surgeons, he guessed. Was he dead?

"And now," one of them whispers to him, "you're going to make love."

"With a giant frog, I suppose, doctor?" he replies, in reference to the green outfits.

"Not at all! With a real woman!"

Cries of encouragement from the onlookers. A real woman does appear, but she dissolves in his arms and he finds himself floating gently in the sea. Along comes a ship named *L'Ana-Lise*. The Analysis.

"Do you know how to play with words?" a man on deck asks him.

"It's not that I know how to, it's that I'm obliged to, because words lie. Ailments, on the other hand, don't lie." This is a jeu de mots—"le mot ment, en revanche les maux ne ment pas"—it makes little sense when translated into English.

The novella went on like that, with one untranslatable double meaning after another. The narrator is expected to write a daily essay on subjects provided by the captain, who will judge the essays of all on board, and failures will be tossed to the sharks.

The first subject proposed is "le contraire d'une chaise." The opposite of a chair. So begin the games with words, lightly enough. But things quickly become darker. The captain is very hard to please, the subjects proposed are impossible—"If I erase the word *eraser* with an eraser, what remains?"—and the other passengers are unpleasant.

The captain's mistress, a statuesque Norwegian blonde, arrives to seduce the narrator. They wander into a complex philosophical argument about whether one makes love only with one's penis. No sexual act takes place. She leaves, calling him "a poor little guy who takes himself for a genius."

Alone, he admits to being a poor little guy—isn't everyone with any degree of self-knowledge an insignificant person?—but denies taking himself for a genius. What does it mean, anyway, to *take oneself*? Surely in such a case of false self-identification one should say *mistake oneself*. Ah, those lying words.

The next day many of the passengers and the entire crew float away in the only lifeboat, and the captain jumps overboard.

Only three passengers remain on *L'Ana-Lise*. They kill time by drinking all the available liquor. The ship is destroyed in a tempest, and the narrator saves himself by climbing onto a floating billiard table.

It's the same table on which he'd begun his journey. The doctors in green approach him, then turn away, and he realizes he will not wake up. This doesn't bother him. As he floats gently on his raft, he can hear in the distance a single voice, singing children's songs from long ago.

Did François really dream all this while under general anaesthesia? Unlikely. The verbal embroidery was far too complex. Some fragment of a reverie may have inspired his novella, but it must have taken him considerable time and effort to write the whole thing down. The subject—his own possible death—must have engaged him sufficiently for that. Why had he sent this booklet to Tig and me, of all people? Or rather to me, since Tig did not read French. What was I supposed to do with it?

In any case, the story was prophetic, for shortly afterwards François actually did die. Words lie but illnesses don't, and the illness of François had told the truth.

It may have been a coincidence, but after that John's situation took a downward plunge. He sold his beautiful country house, then regretted it. He sent us his novel in progress, which was about the protagonist's repetitive sexual exploits and was moderately awful. Tig, who was more tolerant of John than I was by then—I was getting tired of his invectives, especially when they were directed at me—took on the task of replying. He was as tactful as possible, but it was probably not enough.

John's language began to melt. Garbled emails would arrive: denunciations of everyone and everything that segued into word salad. The replies we sent, expressing concern—was he all right, what was happening?—would be met with silence.

But this is a sad ending. Since I can—since I am the only one left who can—let me dial time backwards so we can spend a happier moment together. The four of us: John and François, and Tig and me. Already we're looking younger, as you can see.

Let's say it's spring. The two of them come to us in some excitement. "We have a surprise for you," says François. "We have made a discovery!" He's beaming. John, too, seems unusually mirthful. Is he chuckling? No, John does not chuckle.

"What is it?" says Tig.

The two of them are so pleased with themselves we can't refuse the promised treat, whatever it may be. "You will see. It is extraordinary," says François. "You will like it!"

The surprise involves taking us to lunch. We get into a car (ours? John's? François doesn't have a car) and wind up a narrow road, past houses and olive terraces and into the dry brown hills. It must be a sunny day—I don't remember rain—but I'd insist on sunniness in any case. The destination is one of those farms that contain an ancient Old World barn. High wooden beams holding up the roof, rough brick walls. A smell of elderly cheese and fresh dung. We're ushered in by a man acting the part of the farmer, though most likely he is the farmer, and are seated at one of the tables overlooking a sawdust ring of the kind used for exercising horses or auctioning animals. In the middle of it is a small dirt mound.

The lunch begins to arrive. The hors d'oeuvres, the entrée, the main course . . . "Everything's made of cheese," I whisper.

"Yes! Everything is made of cheese!" cries François, clapping his hands. The all-cheese menu appeals to his sense of the absurd:

it's like the sardines of his youth, only with cheese. "But it is inventive, the cheese, yes? They have found so many different ways of presenting it!"

"Made on the premises," rumbles John. "Not phony muck from some jumped-up snob shop. Next comes the cheesecake."

"Is that the surprise?" I ask, trying my best to look pleased. "The cheese menu?" Tig pours himself another glass of wine.

"No, no, you will see," says François. He's almost giggling.

"There's a floor show," says John, grinning. "Not the usual. No wenches."

"See! It begins!" says François, pointing to the left.

A group of sheep runs into the ring, baaing loudly. They are whiter than run-of-the-mill sheep: they've had a shampoo. Following them—chasing them perhaps—are six or seven well-kept goats, a couple of sheepdogs nipping at their heels. Then three donkeys, and after them two cavorting ponies, their tails tied up with red ribbon. Finally, there's a llama: it appears to be the driving force, the one all the others are fleeing, llamas being notoriously aggressive and bad-tempered.

François is radiant with glee. John is actually laughing: this in itself is a surprise.

Round and round the ring gallop the animals, as fast as they can go, in a cacophony of baas and bleats and whinnies and hee-haws. After the third circumlocution, the llama canters to the centre of the ring and climbs onto the mound. It stands there, triumphant, king of the castle. The others stop, gazing up at it. The audience of diners applauds.

"There's politics for you," says John. "He's the sodding prime minister."

"Like a theatre!" says François. "Isn't it marvellous? Are you entertained?"

"Yes!" I say. "Thank you!" But I'm failing to grasp the point.

Perhaps there isn't a point. Perhaps that's the point. Is it like the cockroach walking up one wall and down the other?

I don't want François to be disappointed in me. "It's fantastic!" I add, as fervently as I can manage. Tig is silent, though he smiles and nods sagely. Once we're alone, however, he will say, "What the fuck was that?"

François is no longer laughing. "They do what they can for us," he says. "We should not expect more. Shall we go?"

MORTE DE SMUDGIE

✦

G rieving takes strange forms.

When Nell and Tig's cat Smudgie died, Nell dealt with her disproportionate sense of loss by rewriting Tennyson's "Morte d'Arthur," with Smudgie in the leading role, supported by a full cast of noble cats in medieval robes and chain mail. This was a deeply frivolous thing for her to do, and the results were not felicitous:

> *A paw,*
> *Clothed in white samite, mystic, wonderful . . .*

Nevertheless, she laboured painstakingly over her transliteration, tears dropping onto the keyboard. Those Victorians, so adept at death, she thought, wiping her eyes, slowing her breathing. No wonder, since so many of them did in fact die. They dropped like flies, of consumption, of brain fever, of wasting away, of who knows what? It was their lack of sanitation, their ignorance about germs, and their hopeless ideas about what to feed people, especially young children. They felt it was wrong to give the kids anything that wasn't white. White bread, sugar, milk pudding, mashed potatoes, rice. Vegetables and fruits were too rough for their infant digestions, meat dangerously increased the animal spirits. The poor things were practically transparent—greenish and rickety—and if they cried, a hefty dose of gripe water laced with opium would soothe them to sleep, often permanently. Then they'd become little angels, watching silently from the silvery daguerreotypes that might have been taken of them, though only for more affluent parents.

Funerals were a major art form back then. One London merchant, anticipating the period of extravagant mourning that would follow Queen Victoria's death, cornered the market in black velvet and made a fortune.

Black velvet sent Nell into a convulsion of sobs. Smudgie, so black and velvety! So deep, so dark, so moonlit! Why was she being this idiotic about him? He was only a cat.

There is no "only a," she told herself. Nothing and no one is "only a." In any case, he'd been the sole entity who could read her innermost mind, a location she kept sealed away from everyone else, even Tig. Especially Tig; he would have been frightened by it. But Smudgie would sit on her lap, gazing up into her eyes with his own round yellow eyes, tail twitching slightly, communing with her secret self: so fanged, so taloned, so intent on prey. It was a good thing for the world, she often thought, that she'd succeeded in controlling this daemon of hers. If she'd let it out, think what carnage would have followed.

So all day long the noise of battle roll'd
Among the mountains by the winter sea;
Until King Smudgie's Table, cat by cat,
Had fallen in Lionnesse about their Lord,
King Smudgie: then, because his wound was deep,
The bold Sir Cativere uplifted him . . .

In reality Smudgie had not been much of a valiant knight type. Birds had harassed him, squirrels had taunted him when he dozed on the backyard picnic table; Nell had seen one of them jump on him, daring him to chase it. He'd never caught any prey, to her knowledge; nor did he win fights with other cats. She'd once found him cowering and shivering in a window well, avoiding the front door because one or a number of tomcats had sprayed on it, challenging him to a duel. Then there was that time he'd come back to the house with another cat's claw stuck in his nose.

But despite his lack of heroic spirit, Smudgie knew things about her. Significant, dangerous, arcane things. Surely he did, him with his penetrating yellow eyes. More of a Merlin than an Arthur, then: more of a sorcerer, more of a diviner . . .

Sentimental rubbish, she told herself. True, Smudgie did know things, but those things were limited to who opened the cat food tins and which cupboard they were kept in. Though he did seem fully aware whenever it was his day to be taken to the vet. How many times had she crawled around under large pieces of furniture, attempting to retrieve him? It usually took the two of them, Nell squeezing beneath the bed with a broom, Tig to intercept Smudgie as he shot out from under.

"Come here, you swine!" Tig would shout, and then he would shout some more as Smudgie dug his claws into Tig's hands. "Throw a towel over him!" "Quick, open the door!" This last, of the cat carrier.

"Aw, sweetie, it will be all right," Nell would say falsely as Smudgie growled and drooled, glaring at her through the bars. Traitor! How could she entrap him like this?

At the vet's, however, it was all right: it was just some shots and a peek inside the ears for mites. Though once back at the house, Smudgie would not speak to her for days, and might poop in the bathtub as a punishment. That was how intelligent he was: he didn't poop on the floor, gauging rightly that a slip on a cat turd might push Tig's patience over the edge. Bathtubs were easy to clean.

Though maybe Smudgie had been clairvoyant after all, because a vet had indeed been the finish of him.

"My end draws nigh; 't is time that I were gone.
Make broad thy cat carrier to receive my weight,
And bear me to the vet place; yet I fear
My wound hath taken cold, and I shall die."

"Feline diabetes," said the vet. "You can treat it, but you'd have to give him a needle every day, and also take a urine sample."

Nell and Tig were away at the time, in Ireland, doing whatever they used to do on such trips. The person talking to the vet was Nell's baby sister, Lizzie, who was holding the fort in respect to cats. She called Nell long distance—this was before email or cellphones—to report the bad news.

"How many times do you think he'd let anyone give him a needle?" said Lizzie.

"Never mind a urine sample. Excuse me, Smudgie, could you just pee in this bottle? He's very prudish, he never lets anyone watch him when he's peeing," said Nell.

"Once," said Lizzie. "If that. For the needle. Then he'd run away."

Nell couldn't bear to think of Smudgie cowering under a bush in the rain because he was afraid to go home. Getting sicker and sicker, suffering more and more, alone in the dark. Forlorn. Dwindling unseen. Should she fly home to be with him? But with him for what?

"I should come back," said Nell. She knew what Tig would have to say about that. *Are you sure it's the right decision?*

"Don't be silly," said Lizzie. "I can handle it."

"Can you? Will you be all right?" Lizzie had an overly empathetic temperament, and was a spider rescuer.

"Of course," said Lizzie.

But she wasn't all right. The next day there was another phone call: Lizzie again, crying so hard she could barely speak. "It's Smudgie," she said. "He's dead! I took him to the vet, I stayed with him the whole time. He growled. He knew, he knew, he knew what was happening!"

"Where is he?" Nell asked. Usually the vet would just slide in the needle and then dispose of the corpse. She'd had cats before.

"I thought you might want to . . . you might want to bury him yourself, in the backyard," Lizzie sobbed. Nell did not particularly wish to do that, but she said, "Yes, of course."

"So I wrapped him in a piece of red silk brocade and, and, and, I put him in the freezer!"

It was typical of Lizzie to have a spare piece of red silk brocade on hand. She liked to shop for remnants in fabric stores and then consider what she might make out of them, but she'd probably never anticipated dead-cat-wrapping for the brocade. Cerements, thought Nell. How Egyptian. Or more like a preserved saint, freeze-dried and put on show in a cathedral. Would there be holy relics of Saint Smudgie distributed or sold? Would there be pilgrimages? Would there be miracles?

"With the hamburgers?" Nell asked. Lizzie had two roommates: Nell hoped Lizzie had informed them. She didn't like to think of one of them pawing through the frozen packages in search of dinner and coming upon red-brocaded Smudgie unexpectedly, fur-covered, stiff, with white incisors showing between his shrivelled lips. *What the fuck is this?*

How helpless the dead are, Nell thinks. What humiliations occur to them. Not that they care.

Saying "With the hamburgers" had been tactless. She should have said "Thank you."

"Thank you."

"Was that okay?" Lizzie asked anxiously. "To save him for you? I didn't know what else to do."

"It's perfect," said Nell. When she got back, she might dig a hole somewhere in the perennials. But there were skunks: they were likely to unearth Smudgie and strew him about. That should not be allowed to happen. What, then? Tiptoe along the street and around the corner carrying the frozen packet, slip it into someone else's garbage bin? Was there a law against that?

After this phone call she'd told Tig about Smudgie being stashed in the freezer, wrapped in a majestic red robe and nestled among the peas and sausages. Tig had been delighted, and had laughed quite a lot. He had an almost Mexican way of making fun of death. Or not making fun, exactly. Acknowledging that death was part of life. Little painted clay skeletons dressed in the clothes they wore in life, going about their occupations: gambling, playing musical instruments, sitting at office desks. Tig and Nell had some of those in their bathroom, collected on one of their excursions. Their possibly too frequent escapes from real life.

"So long as he doesn't end up in the oven," Tig had said.

Nell had laughed too. She was still in shock, she hadn't yet entered her full mourning phase. The veils, the weepers, the black velvet.

But even then she'd thought, It can't be a garbage bin. Some ritual was surely required, something more respectful. Some ceremony else.

Maybe that was why she was rewriting Tennyson, though as she moved slowly through the text, transmuting a word here, a phrase there, she became more unsure of the therapeutic value of what she was doing. Was this an act of commemoration or simply a mutilation? Not that there was always a difference.

And on a sudden, lo! the level lake,
And the long glories of the winter moon.

Then saw they how there hove a dusky barge
Dark as a funeral scarf from stem to stern,
Beneath them; and descending they were ware
That all the decks were dense with stately Cats
Black-stoled, black-collared, like a dream—by these,
Three Pusses with crowns of gold—and from them rose
A meow that shiver'd to the tingling stars,
And, as it were one caterwaul, an agony
Of lamentation, like a wind, that shrills
All night in a waste land, where no cat comes,
Or hath come, since the making of the world.

Nell typed on, sniffling. King Smudgie was placed in the barge. He was lamented over, a lot, by the three mystical Cat Queens, who represented the Great Triple Goddess in her third avatar, the Queen of the Dead who came after the Maiden and the Mother. The Morrígan, wailer at the deaths of heroes, Nell added silently, for in those days Nell was up on her Irish pre-Christian belief systems as well as the Mediterranean stuff.

So like a shatter'd column lay the Cat;
Not like that Smudgie who, with tail at rest,
From claw to ears a star of [what to say here?
Smudgie was not much of a star at anything.]

Shot thro' the flowers at Catelot, and charged
Before the eyes of pusses and toms.

Then the Queens had stopped lamenting. Now for the King's big speech:

And slowly answer'd Smudgie from the barge:
"The old order changeth, yielding place to new,
And Cat fulfills Himself in many ways,
Lest one good cat food should corrupt the world.
Comfort thyself: what comfort is in me?
I have lived nine lives, and that which I have done
May Cat within Himself make fur! But thou,
If thou shouldst never see my face again,
Purr for my soul. More things are wrought by purrs
Than this world dreams of . . .
But now farewell. I am going a long way . . ."

At this point Tig came into the room. "I'm having a Scotch," he said. "Join me?" Then, after a pause, "What's wrong?" He wrapped his long arms around Nell and kissed the top of her head.

"Maybe we should get another cat," Nell snuffled into his shirt front. Scant hope of that. The cat box was usually Tig's chore, not one he enjoyed.

"We already have another cat," said Tig. Which was true: there was Smudgie's sibling, Puffball, who flirted with strangers and hadn't much of a brain to speak of. She was everyone's cat; whereas Smudgie had been Nell's, if anyone's.

"It's not the same," Nell sobbed. What was this mania of hers for having everything remain as it was? Why did she want to stop time, imprison them in some grotesque Brigadoon where nothing ever changed? Anyway, it couldn't be done, so why wish for it?

"Sorry," she said. "I'm just finishing something. I'll be down in a minute."

Long stood Sir Cativere
Revolving many memories, till the hull
Look'd one black dot against the verge of dawn,
And on the mere the meowing died away.

Tennyson had rewritten the ending later, though, in his *Idylls of the King*. The reduction of Arthur to a black dot must have been too doleful even for him. The second ending was almost greeting-card:

And the new sun rose bringing the new year.

Which was quite a different thing, Nell thought. Symbol of hope, et cetera. Not just a dwindling black dot. Though she couldn't decide which ending she preferred.

She printed out her transfigured poem. "Morte de Smudgie." Even the title was ridiculous. After a minute she tore it up and stuffed the pages into the wastebasket. It was terminally stupid, a futile thing to have done. Why had she bothered? She needed a drink, so she went downstairs to have one, with Tig. It was a thing they used to do before dinner, once the kids were no longer in the house.

Now here she is, in the present, revolving many memories. No cats now. The Tennyson rewrite thing had been, when? Twenty-five years ago, when she and Tig had still been young, though they hadn't thought back then that they were young. Middle-aged. Past the halfway mark. Countdown days. Already they'd been making jokes about creaky knees. What did they know about creaky knees back then? They could still go hiking, for heaven's sakes. When had that become impossible?

It hadn't really been about Smudgie. It had been about Tig. She must already have known on some level that he was bound to set sail first, leaving her stranded in the harsh frost, in the waste land, in the cold moonlight.

And now he's done it. He's no longer on the shore; he's moving away from her, over the water, diminishing, vanishing.

What about her? Will it be nothingness or sunrise? Or both, but in what order? And could they perhaps be the same?

And I, the last, go forth companionless,
And the days darken round me, and the years,
Among new men, strange faces, other minds . . .

Which about sums it up, she thinks. Tennyson was very skilful at that kind of thing. Aloneness. Forlornness. Tears from the depths of some divine despair. "O death in life, the days that are no more." Sugary woo-woo trash.

Though maybe, she thinks. Maybe she might get another cat.

Though maybe not.

II

———

MY EVIL
MOTHER

———

MY EVIL MOTHER

✦

Y ou're so evil," I said to my mother. I was fifteen, the talk-
back age.

"I take that as a compliment," she said. "Yes, I'm evil, as
others might define that term. But I use my evil powers only for
good."

"Yeah, tell me another," I replied. We were having an argument
about my new boyfriend, Brian. "Anyway, who gets to say what's
good?"

My mother was in the kitchen, grinding something in her mortar. She often ground things in her mortar, though sometimes she
used the Mixmaster. If I said, "What's that?" she might say, "Garlic
and parsley," and I'd know she was in *Joy of Cooking* mode. But if
she said, "Look the other way" or "What you don't know won't
hurt you" or "I'll tell you when you're old enough," I'd realize
there was trouble in store for someone.

She was ahead of her time with the garlic, I feel compelled to
mention: most people in our kind of neighbourhood hadn't found
out about it yet.

———

Our neighbourhood was on the northern margin of Toronto, one of many cities that were rapidly expanding over farm fields and drained swamps, wreaking havoc with the vole populations and flattening burdocks as they went. Out of the bulldozed mud had sprouted postwar split-levels in tidy rows, each with a pic-ture window—ranch style, with flat roofs that hadn't yet begun to leak in the winters. Those who lived in these houses were young moderns, with children. The fathers had jobs, the mothers not. My mother was an anomaly: no visible husband, no job exactly, though she did seem to have a means of support.

Our kitchen was large and sunlit, with a canary-yellow lino-leum floor, a breakfast nook, and a white dresser with rows of blue plates and bowls. My mother had a thing for blue in tableware; she said it warded off any evil eyes intent on ruining the food.

Her eyebrows were plucked into two incredulous arches, as was almost still the fashion. She was neither tall nor short, nei-ther plump nor thin. In everything, she took care to imitate the third choice of Goldilocks: just right. That day she was wearing a flowered apron—tulips and daffodils—over a shirtwaist dress with small white and pastel-green stripes and a Peter Pan collar. Cuban heels. Single strand of pearls, wild, not cultured. (*Worth it,* she said. *Only the wild ones had souls.*)

Protective colouration, she called her outfits. She looked like a dependable mother from a respectable neighbourhood such as ours. As she worked at the kitchen counter, she might have been demonstrating a jiffy recipe in *Good Housekeeping* magazine— something with tomato aspic, this being the mid-1950s, when tomato aspic was a food group.

She had no close friends in the vicinity—"I keep myself to myself," she'd say—but she performed the expected neighbourly duties: presenting tuna-noodle casseroles to the sick, taking in the mail and newspapers of those on vacations so their houses wouldn't be targeted by burglars, babysitting the occasional dog or cat. Though not the occasional baby: even when my mother offered, parents of babies hesitated. Could they have picked up on her invisible but slightly alarming aura? (Invisible to others; she claimed that she herself could see it. Purple, according to her.) Maybe they were afraid they'd return to find their infant in a roasting pan with an apple in its mouth. My mother would never have done such a thing, however. She was evil, but not that evil.

Sometimes women in distress—they were always women—would come over to our house, and she would make them a cup of something that might have been tea, sit them at the kitchen table, and listen, scanning their faces, nodding silently. Did money change hands? Is that how she made her living, at least in part? I couldn't swear to it, but I have my suspicions.

I'd see these consultations going on as I trudged upstairs to do my homework. Or homework was my cover story; I was just as likely to be painting red nail polish on my toes, or examining my mirrored face for flaws—too sallow, too zitty, too chipmunk-toothed—or applying a thick layer of deep-red lipstick and admiring my pouty reflection, or whispering to Brian over the hall telephone. I was tempted to eavesdrop on what my mother was saying, but she could always tell when I was doing it. "Big ears," she would say. "Off to bed! Beauty sleep!" As if mere sleep would make me more beautiful.

Then the kitchen door would close, and the murmuring would resume. I'm sure my mother gave these troubled women a chunk of advice, at the very least, though it might also have been a mysterious liquid in a jar. She kept a supply of such jars in the refrigerator. The goop in them was of different colours, and they were none of my business. Neither was the herb garden at the back of our house, in which nothing was labelled and everything was off limits, though I was occasionally allowed to pick flowers from the benevolent decoy ornamentals placed strategically here and there and to stick them into a vase. My mother had no interest in such frilly, girly decorations herself, but she was content to indulge me.

"That's lovely, my pet," she would say absentmindedly.

"You didn't even look at it!" I would whine.

"Yes, I did, my treasure. It's very aesthetic."

"I was watching! Your back was turned!"

"Who says you need eyes for seeing?"

To which I had no answer.

The percentage of husbands in our neighbourhood who developed coughs or broke their ankles, or who, on the other hand, were promoted at their offices, was probably no higher than elsewhere, but my mother had a way of hinting at her own influence on these events, and I believed her, despite the nagging doubts of common sense. I also resented her: she thought she was so clever! Nor would she tell me how she'd done it. "That's for me to know and you to find out," she'd say.

"Nobody actually likes you," I'd thrown at her during one of our standoffs. "The neighbours think you're a loony." I'd made this up while suspecting it was probably true.

"Tell me something I don't know."

"Don't you care what they say about you?"

"Why would I care about the tittle-tattle of the uninformed? Ignorant gossip."

"But doesn't it hurt your feelings?" My own feelings were frequently hurt, especially when overhearing jokes about my mother in the high-school girls' washroom. Girls of that age can be quite sadistic.

"Hurt, fiddlesticks! I wouldn't give them the satisfaction," she'd said with a lift of her chin. "They may not like me, but they respect me. Respect is better than like."

I disagreed. I didn't care about being respected—that was a

schoolteacher thing, like black lace-up shoes—but I very much wanted to be liked. My mother frequently said I'd have to give up that frivolous desire if I was going to amount to anything. She said that wanting to be liked was a weakness of character.

Now—now being the day of our fight over Brian—she finished grinding and scraped the contents of her mortar into a bowl. She stuck her finger into the mixture, licked it—so, not deadly poison after all—then wiped her hands on her flowered apron. She had a stash of such aprons, each with a seasonal theme—pumpkins, snowflakes—and at least five crisp, striped shirtwaist dresses.

Where had she acquired those flowered aprons and shirtwaist dresses and the string of real pearls? She wasn't known to go shopping, not like other mothers. I never knew how she got anything. I'd learned to be careful what I myself wished for, because whatever it was might materialize, and not in a form that fulfilled my hopes. I already regretted the pink angora sweater with the rabbit-fur collar and pompoms I'd received on my last birthday, despite having mooned over its image in a magazine for months. It made me look like a stuffed toy.

She covered the bowl of mushed-up garlic and parsley mixture with a little red plastic hat and set it aside. "Now," she said, "you have my full attention. Who gets to say what's good? I do. At the present moment, good is good for *you*, my treasure. Have you tidied your room?"

"No," I said sulkily. "Why don't you like Brian?"

"I have no objection to him as such. But the Universe doesn't like him," she said serenely. "She must have her reasons. Would you like a cookie, my pet?"

"The Universe isn't a person!" I fumed. "It's an it!" This had come up before.

"You'll know better when you grow up," she said. "And a glass of milk, for solid bones."

I still believed that my mother had some influence over the Universe. I'd been brought up to believe it, and it's hard to shake such ingrained mental patterns. "You're so mean!" I said. I was, however, eating the cookie: oatmeal raisin, baked yesterday, one of her staples.

"The opposite of 'mean' is 'doormat,'" she said. "When you're tidying your room, don't forget to collect the hair from your hair-brush and burn it. We wouldn't want anyone malignant getting their claws on that."

"Like who would bother?" I asked, in what I hoped was a contemptuous tone.

"Your gym teacher," she said. "Miss Scace. She's a mushroom collector, among other things—or she was in the old days. Some disguise! Gym teacher! As if I'd be fooled by that!" My mother wrinkled her nose. "It takes so much energy to keep her at bay. She flies around at night and looks in your window, though she can't get in, I've seen to that. But she's been poaching my mushrooms."

I wasn't in love with my gym teacher, a stringy woman with a chicken neck who was given to hectoring, but I couldn't picture her gathering toxic mushrooms by the light of the full moon, as I knew they ought to be gathered. She definitely had an evil eye—the left one, which wasn't entirely in sync with the right—but she lacked the heft of my mother. As for flying, that was bonkers. "Miss Scace! That old biddy! She's not even . . . She couldn't even . . . You're so crazy!" I said. It was something I'd overheard at school: *Her mother's so crazy.*

"Crazy is as crazy does," she replied, unperturbed. "Let's not duck the subject. Brian must go. If not off the planet, out of your life."

"But I like him," I said plaintively. The truth: I was besotted with him. I had his picture in my wallet, taken in a train-station photo booth, with a lipstick kiss covering his tiny, surly black-and-white face.

"I dare say," said my mother. "But the Universe doesn't care who we like. He was dealt the Tower. You know what that means: catastrophe!" My mother had read Brian's Tarot cards, though not with him present, of course. She'd made one of her pressure-cooker pot roasts and invited him to dinner—a suspect act in itself, which he must have known since he frowned the whole time and answered her perky inquiries in monosyllables—and saved an uneaten corner of his apple pie crust as the link between him and the Invisible World. The pie-crust corner was placed beneath an overturned tray; she'd laid out the cards on the tray bottom. "He's going to be in a car accident, and I don't want you in the death seat at the time. You need to cut him off."

"Can't you stop it? The car accident?" I asked hopefully. She'd stopped a couple of other looming disasters that had been threatening me, including an algebra test. The teacher had thrown his back out just in time. He was absent for three whole weeks, during which I'd actually studied.

"Not this time," said my mother. "It's too strong. The Tower plus the Moon and the Ten of Swords. It's very clear."

"Maybe you could mess up his car," I said. Brian's car was a mess anyway: third-hand and no muffler, plus it made strange clanks and bangs for no reason. Couldn't she just cause the car to fall apart? "Then he'd have to borrow another car."

"Did I say it has to be his own car?" She handed me the glass of milk she'd poured, sat down at the kitchen table, placed both her hands on it, palms down—drawing energy from the Earth, as I knew—and gave me the benefit of her direct green-eyed stare. "I don't know which car it will be. Maybe a rental. Now do as I tell you. The long and short of it is: if you dump Brian he won't die;

but if you don't then he will—and most likely so will you. Or else you'll end up in a wheelchair."

"How can you be so sure?"

"Queen of Hearts. That's you. You wouldn't want his blood on your hands. The lifelong guilt."

"This is nuts!"

"Go ahead, ignore my advice," she said placidly. She stood up, snapped her fingers to release the excess Earth energy, then took some hamburger out of the fridge along with a plate of mushrooms she'd already chopped. "Your choice." She spooned the garlic mixture into the meat, broke an egg into it, added dried breadcrumbs and the mushrooms: meatloaf, it would become. I wish now that I'd got the recipe. Then she began mixing in everything with her hands—the only proper way to do it, according to her. She made biscuit dough like that too.

"There is absolutely no way of proving any of this!" I said. I'd been on the high-school debating team that year, until Brian had said it was a brainy thing to do. For a girl, he meant. Now I pretended to disdain it, though I'd secretly taken up the study of logic and was keen on the scientific method. Did I hope for an antidote to my mother? Probably.

"You wanted that pink angora sweater, did you not?" she said.

"So?"

"And then it appeared."

"You probably just bought it."

"Don't be silly. I never just buy things."

"Bet you did! You're not the Easter Bunny," I said rudely.

"This conversation is over," she said with chilling calm. "Change the sheets on your bed, they're practically crawling, and pick those dirty clothes up off the floor before they fester. Panties are not carpets."

"Later," I said, pushing the limit. "I've got homework."

"Don't make me point!" She lifted one hand out of the bowl: it was covered with niblets of raw flesh, and pink with blood.

I felt a chill. I certainly didn't want any pointing going on; pointing was how you directed a spell. People used to get hanged for pointing back in the old days, my mother had told me—or else they were barbecued. Death by burning at the stake was very painful, she could testify to that. There were laws against pointing, once upon a time. If you pointed at a cow and it got sick, everyone knew you were neck-deep in the Black Arts.

I flounced out of the kitchen with as much defiance as I dared. I'm not sure I'd remember now how to flounce—it's an accomplishment, though not one you hear of teenage girls practising nowadays. They still pout and sneer, however, just as I did.

I moped off to my room, where I made the bed as sloppily as I could, then gathered up several days' worth of my shed clothes and stuffed them into the laundry hamper. We had a new automatic washing machine, so at least I wouldn't be put to work at the old wringer-washer tub.

I did collect the hair from my hairbrush and set fire to it in a red glass ashtray I kept for that purpose. My mother would be sure to conduct a hairbrush inspection, which would include the wastebasket, to check that I hadn't shirked. Until a year ago my mother had worn her long, red-gold hair in an elegant French roll, but then she'd cut it off with the poultry shears—the Kim Novak look, she'd said. There had been a conflagration in the kitchen sink—she did practise what she preached, unlike some parents—and the house had stunk like a singed cat for days. *Singed cat* was her term. I'd never smelled a singed cat, but she had. Cats regularly got singed in the old days along with their owners, according to her.

There was no sense in going toe-to-toe with my mother. Nor could I try sneaking around: she had eyes in the back of her head, and little birds told her things. Brian would have to be given up. I had a weep about that: goodbye, Old Spice shaving-lotion aroma and the scents of cigarettes and freshly washed white T-shirts; goodbye, heavy breathing in movie theatres during the dance numbers in musicals; goodbye, feeding Brian the extra fries from my hamburger, followed by greasy, potato-flavoured kisses . . . He was such a good kisser, he was so solid to hug, and he loved me— though he didn't say so, which was admirable. Saying it would have been soft.

Later that evening, I phoned to tell him our Saturday-night date was cancelled. He wasn't pleased. "Why?" he said.

I could hardly tell him that my mother had consulted some old cards with weird pictures on them and predicted he would die in a car crash if he went out with me. I didn't need to fuel any more school rumours about her; there were more than enough as it was. "I just can't go out with you," I said. "I need us to break up."

"Is there another guy?" he asked in a menacing tone. "I'll punch his face in!"

"No," I said. I started to cry. "I really like you. I can't explain. It's for your own good."

"I bet it's your crazy mother," he said. I cried harder.

That night I crept out into our backyard, buried Brian's picture under a lilac bush, and made a wish. My wish was that I would somehow get him back. But wishes made out of earshot of my mother did not come true. According to her, I lacked the talent. Perhaps I might develop it later—grow into it, as it were—but it could skip a generation, or even two. I hadn't been born with a caul, unlike her. Luck of the draw.

The next day at school there were whisperings. I tried to ignore them, though I couldn't help hearing the odd phrase: *Cuckoo as a clock. Addled as an egg. Crazy as a box of hair. Mad as a sack of ham-*

mers. And the worst: *No man in the house, so what can you expect?* Within a week, Brian was going out with a girl called Suzie, though he still shot reproachful glances in my direction. I comforted myself with versions of my own saintly unselfishness: because of me, Brian's heart was still beating. I'm not saying I didn't suffer.

Several years later, Brian became a drug dealer and ended up on a sidewalk with nine bullets in him. So maybe my mother had got the main event right, but the time and the method wrong. She said that could happen. It was like a radio: nothing amiss with the broadcast end, but the reception could be faulty.

No man in the house described our situation. Of course, every-one has a father—or, as they would say nowadays, a sperm pro-vider, fatherhood in the old sense of paternity having fallen into disrepute—and I had one too, though at that date I wasn't sure this father was still what you'd call "alive." When I was four or five, my mother told me she'd changed him into the garden gnome that sat beside our front steps; he was happier that way, she said. As a garden gnome he didn't need to do anything, such as mow the lawn—he was bad at it anyway—or make any decisions, a thing he hated. He could just enjoy the weather.

When I was wheedling her over something she'd initially denied me, she'd say, "Ask your father," and I'd trot out and hunker down beside the garden gnome—hunker just a little, as he wasn't much shorter than me—and stare into his jovial stone face. He appeared to be winking.

"Can I have an ice-cream cone?" I'd plead. I was sure that he and I had a pact of sorts—that he would always be on my side, as opposed to my mother, who was on her own side. It gave me a warm feeling to be with him. It was comforting.

"What did he say?" my mother would ask when I went back in.

"He said I can." I was almost sure I'd heard a gruff voice mumbling from within his grinning, bearded stone face.

"Very well, then. Did you give him a hug?"

"Yes." I always hugged my father when he'd allowed something marginally forbidden.

"Well done. It's nice to say thank you."

This fantasy had to be given up, naturally. Well before the time I was fifteen, I'd heard the other, supposedly real version: my father had deserted us. According to my mother he'd had urgent business elsewhere, though at school they said he'd run away, unable to tolerate my mother's craziness, and who could blame him? I was jeered at for his absence; it wasn't usual in that decade for fathers to be missing, not unless they'd been killed in the war. "Where's your father?" was annoying, but "*Who's* your father?" was insulting. It implied my mother had generated me with someone she didn't even know.

I brooded. Why had my father abandoned me? If he was still alive, why didn't he at least write to me? Hadn't he loved me even a little?

Though I no longer believed that my father was a garden gnome, I did suspect my mother of having transformed him in some other way. I'm ashamed to say that I went through a period of wondering if she'd done him in—with mushrooms or something ground in a mortar—and had buried him in the cellar. I could almost see her lugging his inert body down the stairs, digging the hole—she'd have had to use a jackhammer to get through the cement—then dumping him in and plastering him over.

I inspected the cellar floor for clues and found none. But that proved nothing. My mother was very clever: she'd have taken care to leave no traces.

Then, when I was twenty-three, my father suddenly turned up. By that time, I'd finished university and left my mother's house. My departure was not amicable: she was bossy, she was spying on me, she was treating me like a child! Those were my parting words.

"Suit yourself, my pet," she'd said. "When you need help, I'll be here. Shall I donate your old stuffed animals to charity?"

A pang shot through me. "No!" I cried. In our clashes I inevitably lost my cool, and a shard of dignity along with it.

I was determined not to need help. I'd found a job at an insurance company, on a low rung, and was sharing a cheap rented house west of the university with two roommates who had similar peasant-level jobs.

My father made contact by sending me a letter. He must have got my address from my mother, I realized later, but since I was in one of my phases of not speaking to her I didn't ask her about that. It seemed to me she'd been getting crazier. Her latest thing— before I'd put her on hold—had been a scheme to kill her next-door neighbour's weeping willow tree. I wasn't to worry, she'd said: she'd do it by pointing, at night, so no one would see her. This would be in revenge for something about running over a toad on a driveway, and anyway, the willow roots were getting into the drains.

Avenging a toad. Pointing at a tree. Who could handle that kind of thing, in a mother?

At first I was surprised to get my father's letter. Then I found that I was angry: Where had he been? What had taken him so long? I answered with a note of three lines that included the house phone number. We spoke, a terse, embarrassed exchange, and arranged to meet. I was on the edge of cutting him off, telling him I had no interest in seeing him—but this would not have been true.

We had lunch at a small bistro on Queen Street that served authentic French food. My father chose the restaurant, and I was impressed despite myself. I'd been intending to disapprove of him in every way.

My father asked if I would like some wine; he would not be having any himself, he said. Although I now considered myself a sophisticated young working girl and had taken to drinking at parties and on dates, I stuck with Perrier on this occasion; I needed a clear head and some self-control. Although I was very curious about my father, I was also furious—but I didn't want to upbraid and denounce him before I'd heard his excuses for the shabby way he'd ignored me.

"Where have you been all these years?" was my first question. It must have sounded accusing.

My father was a pleasant-looking older man, fairly tall, neither obese nor cadaverous—nothing out of the ordinary, which was a disappointment; when you've spent your infancy believing your father has been magically transformed, there are expectations. He had hair, though less than he must once have had. Some of it was grey; the rest was the same dark brown as my own. He was wearing a good suit and an acceptable tie, ultramarine with a small geometric pattern in maroon. His blue eyes were like mine, and so were his thickish eyebrows. He raised these eyebrows now, which gave him an open, candid look. He smiled tentatively. I recognized that smile, which was like my own. I could see why he might have felt overpowered by my mother.

"Part of the time I was in prison."

"Really?" I said. Suddenly he was more interesting. Whatever else, I hadn't expected prison. "What for?"

"Impaired driving. I almost killed someone. Not that I could remember doing it. I was blackout drunk." He looked down at the table, on which there was now a wicker basket containing thick slices of bread, both rye and white. "I'm an alcoholic." His voice was oddly neutral, as if he were talking about someone else. Was he sorry for the damage he'd done?

"Oh," I said. How to respond? By this time I knew several people who had problems with liquor, but none of them admitted it.

He must have sensed my nervousness. "That was a long time ago. I don't drink anymore. At all. I went through the steps."

"Oh," I said again. I wasn't sure what he was talking about. The steps? "But where do you live?" I asked. Did he have a home? Was he one of those people you sometimes saw on the street, collecting money in cups? HUNGRY SPARE CHANGE? No, because here we were in this tactful restaurant—his treat—preparing to eat a glamorous lunch. There was nothing homeless about his tie.

"I live here," he said. "In this city. I'm married; I have two children. Two other children," he added apologetically. He knew I would feel betrayed by this information, and I did.

He'd walked away from me, he hadn't looked back, he'd been living a whole other life. I felt instantly jealous of these half-siblings I'd never met.

"But what do you . . . But how do you . . ." I wanted to ask if he had a job, but wouldn't that be rude? What kind of a job could you get with a run-over person and a prison term on your record?

He guessed what I wanted to say. "I couldn't go back into my old job," he said. "I used to be in sales and marketing; now I'm in social work. I volunteer at prisons, as well. I counsel people like me—about being an alcoholic and how to pull yourself out of it."

I was relieved: not only would he not become a responsibility for me—someone I'd have to tend—but he was at least partly a virtuous person. I hadn't inherited a totally rotten set of genes.

"Mother told me she'd turned you into a garden gnome," I said.

"The one beside our front steps. To explain why you weren't there. That was her story when I was four."

He laughed. "She used to say I'd be better off as a garden gnome," he said. "I'd cause less harm and be more amusing."

"I really believed it. I used to ask you for ice cream and things."

"Did I give you some? The ice cream?"

"Yes," I said. "You always did." Foolishly, I began to sniffle. Inside my head I heard my mother's voice: *Never let anyone see you cry.*

"I'm sorry I wasn't there," he said. He extended his hand across the table as if to pat me, thought better of it, withdrew it. "When you were little. Your mother decided I should leave, and the way I was then, I'm sure it was the right choice. She said I had a weak character. Hopelessly weak."

"She says I have a weak character too," I said. "She says I have no backbone. She says I don't have the sense God gave a goose."

He smiled. "Two of a kind then. But I'm sure you have a backbone. You're out on your own, I see." Not with my mother was what he meant.

"You've got a backbone too," I said generously. "You were able to . . ."

"Stop drinking? I had a lot of help. But thank you."

All this time we'd been having our lunch. Foie gras to begin with—I'd never had it and was instantly seduced—and then omelettes. I'd never had a proper omelette before, either: only dry, overcooked ones.

"You did get the birthday presents I sent?" he asked, once we'd reached the choux à la crème. "And the cards? Once you were older—once I was on my feet again?"

"Birthday presents?" I said. "What birthday presents?"

He looked dismayed. "Well, for instance. The bicycle when you were eleven, and that pink angora sweater when you were, what? Fourteen? Fifteen? Your mother said you had your heart set on it."

"That was from you?" My mother was right: she hadn't bought it. But I was right too: she wasn't the Easter Bunny.

"She said you loved it." He sighed. "I guess she never told you it came from me. I suspected something like that because you never sent thank-you notes. She must have thought I'd contaminate you." He sighed again. "Maybe that was best. She was very protective of you, and she always had strong views."

I'd like to say that this lunch was the beginning of a warm, close relationship with my father, but it wasn't. It seemed I wasn't very good at warm, close relationships at that time. My boyfriends didn't last, even when they weren't nixed by my mother. I'd developed a habit of discarding them before they could do the same to me. I said I wanted to meet his other family—especially my two half-sisters, who were almost in their teens and had cute blond pigtails in the pictures he showed me—but he wasn't up to that. He'd never told his second wife about me, and he feared repercussions; he didn't want to upset the applecart, he said.

He especially didn't want my mother to encounter his new wife, and I didn't blame him: Who knew what she might get up to? I pictured her bringing a booby-trapped gift, something she'd ground up and put in a jar; or else she might point, and apples would fly off the applecart as if exploding, figuratively speaking. She'd have her reasons for whatever mischief she caused, of course—she'd be acting for the greater good, or for my good, or the Universe would have firm opinions about what was needed—but I no longer trusted her reasons. She wouldn't really care about the greater good, she'd just be showing off. Gratifying herself. That was my twenty-three-year-old view of her.

So over the next years we kept our distances, my father and I.

We had lunch once in a while, furtively, as if we were spies. "Don't let her get the better of you," he said once. *Her* always meant my mother.

"Why did you break up?" I asked him.

"Well, as I told you, she basically kicked me out."

"No, but really. Did you want to go?"

He looked down at the table. "It's hard living with someone who's always right. Even when it turned out that she was. It can be . . . alarming."

"I know," I said. I felt a wave of sympathy for him; "alarming" was mild. "Did she make you burn your hair?"

"Did she make me what-my-what?" He laughed a little. "That's a new one on me. What exactly . . . ?"

"Never mind," I said. "So why did you marry her? If you found her so difficult and scary?"

"Not scary, exactly. Let's say complex. She could be very enjoyable at times. Though unpredictable."

"But why did you?"

"She put something in my drink. Sorry. Bad joke."

My father died earlier than many. He'd had cancer—he'd told me about it, so at least I had advance warning. Still, it was a loss: now I would no longer have my own unique secret, a corner of my life that my mother hadn't managed to pry open and judge. I'd kept watch on the death notices, since I knew I wouldn't be notified by the family. The other family. The family that wasn't secret.

I went to the funeral, which was well attended by many people I didn't know, and sat at the back, far away from the official mourners. My mother came as well; she was dressed theatrically in black, which by that time nobody wore to funerals anymore. She even had a veil. I was married by then and had two children of my own, both daughters. My mother and I had had a major breach after the birth of the first one: she'd come to the maternity ward while I was in labour, bearing a gift of something orange in a jar for me to rub on my stretch marks, and announced that she wanted to cook the placenta so I could eat it.

"Are you insane?" I'd never heard of such a disgusting thing. It's old hat by now, of course.

"It's a traditional practice. It fends off malevolence. Have you been burning your hair combings, my pet—the way I taught you? That nasty old Miss Scace has been lurking around. She's always wanted to harm you, just to get back at me. I saw her just now outside the preemie window, pretending to be a nurse. She's addicted to disguises. In the old days she'd dress up like a nun."

"Miss Scace, my high-school gym teacher? That's not possible, Mother," I said carefully, as if explaining to a five-year-old. "Miss Scace died years ago."

"Appearances can be deceptive. She only looks dead."

You can see why I might have wished to keep my young children at a safe distance from their grandmother. I wanted them to have a normal childhood, unlike mine.

I'll say a word here about my husband, a lovable individual who has improved with time. I don't have to tell you that I held him at several arms' lengths from my mother during what I will quaintly refer to as our courtship period. I imagined him getting one earful of her and hightailing it for the nearest international flight, so alarmed would he have been. But that encounter had needed to take place sometime, since—through some means unknown to me but that may have involved Tarot cards—she'd become aware of his existence. The Universe had no objection to him, she'd told me: if anything, he was well aspected, with Jupiter looming large and the Kings of Cups and Diamonds prominent. She was looking forward to meeting him. "No hurry," she'd say to me, which meant there was.

I softened him up with anecdotes, which I packaged as light-hearted and jokey. The hair burning, the glop in the jars, the pointing, the cards, even my father as a garden gnome—these were harmless eccentricities. No one took them seriously, I said: not my mother, and certainly not me. My husband-to-be said my mother sounded like good fun and doubtless had a sense of humour. "Oh yes." I laughed, my palms sweating. "Such a sense of humour!"

You'll notice I said nothing to him about Miss Scace. That slice was truly wacko. I trusted him to be understanding, but not as far as airborne, mushroom-poaching Miss Scace was concerned. Life would be calmer if my mother and my significant other could at least tolerate each other.

Finally they met: tea at the King Edward Hotel in downtown Toronto, arranged by me. I didn't think my mother would kick up in such a genteel atmosphere, and she didn't. Nothing un-toward happened. My mother was polite, warmish, attentive; my husband-to-be was deferential, attuned, subdued. I did catch her sneaking a look at his hands—she'd want to get a peek at his heart line, to see if he was likely to go off the rails and start fornicating with secretaries—but she was discreet about it. Aside from that, she acted the part of a nice middle-class mother, of an outmoded variety. My husband-to-be was a little disappointed: he'd been led to expect something less orthodox.

My father's funeral took place during an interval of peace with my mother, so when I spotted her in her black dress and veil, I moved over to sit beside her. I was speaking to her again: speaking to her went in cycles. She would upset me, I would cut her off, I'd relent, there would be peace, then she'd cross the line once more.

"Are you okay?" I asked. She was crying a little, rare for her.

"He was my sweetheart," she said, dabbing at her eyes. "I drove him away! We were so much in love. Once upon a time." Mascara was running down her cheeks, and I wiped it away. Since when had she started wearing mascara? More importantly, when had she started crying in public? Was she getting soft?

It was true: she was indeed getting soft, but not in a good way.

Now that I'd been alerted to the possibility, I noted the signs with dismay—they were proliferating with unsettling rapidity, almost as if she were dissolving. The mascara phase was over nearly as soon as it had begun: outer beauty was no longer a concern, she said. Gone were the freshly ironed shirtwaist dresses. In fact, gone was the iron: my mother never ironed anything anymore. Taking the place of the starched dresses and the no-nonsense Cuban-heeled shoes was a succession of outsized T-shirts, not always clean, paired with jogging pants and an array of clumsy, orthopaedic-looking sandals. Her gnarled toes poked out the fronts of these sandals, their nails thickened and yellowish. I wondered if she was having trouble cutting them. Worse: I wondered if she was even remembering to cut them.

Was she still grinding things in her mortar? I wasn't sure. Several jars were growing whiskery mould in her fridge. By now I was conducting twice-weekly fridge inspections, to make sure she didn't give herself food poisoning from eating fermenting leftovers.

Her pressure cooker was long gone: she said she'd discarded it after Miss Scace had caused it to blow up. Her iron frying pans were rusting. Her pots had been cleaned—not very effectively—and stored away, though I found one in the backyard with three inches of algae-clogged water full of mosquito larvae. "It's a bird-bath," she said. The backyard itself was a jungle: no more neat borders, no more herbs. The prevailing weed was sow thistle.

I asked her why she wasn't cooking anymore.

She shrugged. "Too much trouble. And who would I cook for?"

I became increasingly worried about her. I'd phone her at suppertime to check that she was eating. "Are you having dinner?"

A pause. "Yes."

"What is it?"

Another pause. "Something."

"Is it in a can?"

"More or less."

"Are you sitting down?"

"None of your business."

So she was snacking—eating in bits and pieces, like a teenager foraging. I brought her a noodle casserole. "You can heat it in the toaster oven," I said.

"There was a fire." She didn't seem too worried about that.

"In the toaster oven?"

"Yes."

"When was it? Why didn't you tell me?"

"I put the fire out, so why would I tell you? It was that Miss Scace. She started it."

"Oh, for heaven's sakes!"

"Don't concern yourself, my pet. This time I'm winning."

I finally pried the full backstory out of her. She and Miss Scace had been at war for centuries, through several incarnations. They'd once been friends but had fallen out over a young man. Four hundred years ago, give or take, they'd begun to have battles in the air at night. Not on brooms, she added: that cliché about flying brooms was just a superstition. Then Miss Scace had ratted my mother out to the authorities for witchcraft, and the outcome had been fiery, and then terminal. According to my mother, her heart had refused to burn, so they'd had to incinerate it separately; the same had been true of Joan of Arc, she added proudly. Miss Scace had been at the bonfire and had jeered.

"I should have tattled on her first," she said. "But I thought it was dishonourable. A betrayal of our traditions."

"What happened to the young man?" I asked. There was no use talking to her about inventions or delusions: she would just clam up. And if I said I didn't believe her, there would be a fracas.

"Scace used him up," said my mother.

"What do you mean 'used him up'?"

"For her depraved sexual purposes," said my mother. "Night after night."

"Are we talking about the same Miss Scace?" I simply couldn't picture it. Miss Scace, in the gymnasium, coaching the girls' basketball team, with her umpire's whistle and her skinny legs below her pleated gym outfit. Flat-chested Miss Scace, in health class, scrambling for euphemisms while explaining the menstrual cycle. Sex was unmentionable then: officially it did not exist. "Surely not," I said firmly.

"She looked different in the old days," said my mother. "A lot more enticing. She had whalebone stays and cleavage. She painted her face with arsenic."

"Arsenic?"

"It was the style. Anyway, she wore him out. Sucked the marrow right out of his bones. Then, when he was exhausted, she stole his penis."

"What?" Penis theft was something new: that piece of lore hadn't come up when I was in high school.

"She must have been annoyed that it no longer worked. One

morning he looked down and it was gone. I expect she'd pointed at it when he was asleep. She was keeping it in a cedar box with some other penises she'd stolen; she was feeding them on grains of wheat. That's the usual method of tending penises."

I took firm control of myself. "Why was she doing that?" I asked cautiously. "Collecting penises?"

"Some people collect stamps, she collected penises. Many of us did in those days. Anyway, he consulted me—through a clairvoyant, of course, as I was no longer in that earthly incarnation. I told him to complain to the authorities, so he did, and she was forced to give the penis back."

"And reattach it, I suppose."

"Naturally, my pet. But that wasn't the end of it. She had to give all the other penises back as well—she'd collected the penises of some very important men, I can tell you! One of them was a baron. And then they burned her anyway. Served her right."

"And here you are," I said.

"That's true. Here we are. But there aren't any authorities anymore. Or not that kind."

"Do you mind me asking . . . Are you and Miss Scace still fighting in the air? At night?"

"Oh yes," she said. "Every night. That's why I'm so tired all the time."

The image of my mother in her baggy T-shirts and lumpy sandals wrestling in midair with Miss Scace, still possibly with her umpire's whistle around her neck, was too much for me. I was tempted to laugh, but that would have been cruel. "Maybe you should call it quits," I said. "Declare a truce."

"She'd never do that. Venomous old hag."

"It's bad for your health," I said.

"I know, my pet." She sighed. "For myself I wouldn't care. But

I'm doing it for you, as I always have. And the girls, of course. My granddaughters. I wouldn't want her to harm them. Maybe one of them has inherited the talent, so it won't be wasted."

It was high time we returned to so-called reality. "Have you paid your heating bill?" I asked.

"Oh, I don't need any heat," she said. "I'm immune to the cold."

Her decline was now rapid. Shortly after this, she broke her hip—falling out of the air onto a chimney, she whispered to me—and had to be taken to the hospital. I tried to consult with her about her future: after they fixed the hip she'd go to a rehab place, then to a nice assisted-living facility . . .

"None of that will be needed," she said. "I won't leave the hospital in this body. It's all been arranged."

The arrangements included congestive heart failure. Final scene: I'm at her hospital bedside, holding her fragile, thick-veined hand. How had she become so little? She was hardly there at all, though her mind still burned like a blue flame.

"Tell me you were making it up," I said. Now that I was asking directly and not in anger—a thing I'd never exactly done before—surely she would admit it.

"Made what up, my treasure?"

"The hair burning. The pointing. All of it. It was like my father being a garden gnome, wasn't it? Just fairy tales?"

She sighed. "You were such a sensitive child. So easily wounded. So I told you those things. I didn't want you to feel defenceless in the face of life. Life can be harsh. I wanted you to feel protected, and to know that there was a greater power watching over you. That the Universe was taking a personal interest."

I kissed her forehead, a skull with a thin covering of skin. The protector was her, the greater power was her, the Universe that took an interest was her as well; always her. "I love you," I said.

"I know, my treasure. And did you feel protected?"

"Yes," I said. "I did." This was somewhat true. "It was very sweet of you to invent all that for me."

She looked at me sideways out of her green eyes. "Invent?" she said.

And so I come to the end. But it's not the end, since ends are arbitrary. I'll close with one more scene.

My elder daughter is now fifteen, the talk-back age. A tug-of-war is going on: she wants to go running, in the dark, with some jock I've barely set eyes on. Running! Girls didn't used to run, except at track and field. They ambled, they strolled. To run would be undignified and lollopy; who knew about sports bras back then?

My daughter is wearing skin-tight pants and a stretchy top; her arms are bare, with three temporary tattoos on each, all of them birds and animals. She claims she'll make them permanent once she's eighteen. I've explained the difficulty of removal should one change one's mind later, but to no avail.

"No running in the dark," I insist. "It's too dangerous. There are prowlers."

"You're not the boss of me! There are fucking streetlights!"

No use at all to say *Vulgar language* or even *Potty mouth*. That horse bolted long ago. "Nevertheless. And with your, your friend . . . Boys can get carried away."

"Carried away, fuck! We'll be *running*! It's not like he's a rapist! I mean, he can be a bit of a dick, but . . ."

Bit of a dick? A mild diagnosis, in my opinion. "I'm saying no."

"You're such a bitch!"

"Don't make me point," I say. I'm beginning to get angry.

"What? Don't make you *point*?" She rolls her eyes, laughs. "Fuck my life! What's *pointing*?"

"It's a hex thing," I say, straight-faced. "You wouldn't like the results."

"Oh, for fuck's sake!" She sneers. "A hex thing! Are you insane?"

"Your grandmother was a witch," I say, as solemnly as I can.

This brings her up short. "You're shitting me! You mean, like, really?"

"Really," I say.

"Like, what kind of witch things did she do?"

She's not altogether convinced, but I have her attention. I drop my voice to a confiding whisper. "I'll tell you when you're old enough," I say, evading the immediate pitfall. "But no running at night, not until you're ready. Witches can see things at night that other people can't see. Dead people, for instance. If you're not instructed and prepared, it can be scary."

"I'm not a witch, though," she says uncertainly. She's considering the options.

"You may not realize it yet," I say. "Your grandmother believed the talent is passed on. It can skip a generation. I'm sure you'll grow into it. When that happens, you must be very, very careful. You mustn't abuse your power."

She hugs herself. "I feel cold."

She's thrilled. Who of her age would not be?

THE DEAD INTERVIEW

✦

MARGARET ATWOOD: *Good evening, Mr. Orwell. It's very kind of you to appear—or not exactly appear, since I can't see you. To manifest, or . . . It's very kind of you to have shown up for this interview.*

GEORGE ORWELL: Not at all. The kindness is yours. I so seldom have the opportunity to talk with someone still in their meat envelope.

My what?

I do beg your pardon. I didn't intend to shock. It's a local colloquialism. Let us say "still among what I once called 'the living.'"

You don't use that expression anymore? The living?

There are different ways of being alive.

True. Well, you've always been very much alive to me, even after you . . . after you were no longer in your meat envelope. (Nervous laugh) *It's such an honour to encounter you. You've been a huge influence on my own work!*

(Indeterminate snorting sound: exasperation?) **You're a writer? Selfish, lazy, and egotistical, like all writers, I suppose?**

Well . . . lazy, certainly.

I do not exempt myself from these criticisms. On the contrary. But I'm sorry—I haven't had the pleasure.

The pleasure of what?

Of reading your "own work." In fact, I don't have much idea of who you are. I can't see you.

Because Mrs. Verity has her eyes closed?

Correct. It would be more useful to me if these mediums could operate with their eyes open. As it is, this is like the telephone, with an undependable line at that. You're a female colonial, I understand from the voice?

Good guess!

Have they started writing?

Females, or colonials?

Ah, er . . . both.

Oh, they're writing up a storm these days! Though some colonials, and even some women, were writing when you were still . . . I guess you didn't read the women much.

(Coughs) I was very busy. Those were tumultuous times. Revolutions, dictatorships, wars . . . perhaps you've read about them. I did dip in a little, into the . . . how shall I put it . . . cheaper sensational and romantic products.

Like the mass-produced trash in Nineteen Eighty-Four? *(Dryly) "Women's books," they were called. But some women were writing serious literature, even then.*

(Clears throat) My dear girl, I hope I haven't offended you. Women do sometimes get their backs up over trifles.

Saying that kind of thing could get you in quite a lot of trouble these days. It would be called "trivializing." Women don't put up with so much anymore.

A thousand pardons. We men spoke that way without even thinking about it, I do realize that now. I was a man of my time. One can hardly be otherwise. (Pause) I take it you are not of my generation.

Not exactly, though we did overlap a little. I was ten when you shed the meat envelope. So by the time I actually wrote anything, there wasn't exactly any way I could get the publisher to send you some review copies.

Was that an attempt at humour?

(Feeble laugh) *In poor taste, I'm afraid.*

(Silence)

Please don't fade out! Am I losing you?

The connection comes and goes. It's like being on the BBC during the war. Almost everything was poor quality then, radios included. *The wireless* was the term. I seem to recall being on the wireless a fair bit.

Yes, you were. You presented some of your best short essays that way. (Pause) *I've attempted to contact you before, Mr. Orwell, but with no success. Possibly because I called you Mr. Blair. I got your father.*

Oh? I expect he was a fat lot of help.

He said he wished you'd been a diplomat, or else a lawyer. Made better use of the brains God gave you.

By God he meant himself, no doubt.

He said you'd thrown away your advantages.

Class advantages, he meant. The family silver. Schools for junior snobs and so forth. I did not consider those things advantages. Bundle of prejudices based on falsehoods. A muddying of the truth.

He said he was sorry you'd turned out such a damned Communist, and a sloppy dresser into the bargain.

I did not have the money to spend on tailors, and in any case a nice warm knitted waistcoat was of better use to me, considering the inadequate heating.

Is that the one in your picture? With the moustache and the haircut that looks done with a lawnmower, and the bemused expression? Under the tweed jacket? It seems to have a kind of smudge on it. Ink?

Yes. Possibly I did not wash it often enough. Or Eileen didn't. It would have taken too long to dry, especially in winter.

Eileen? Your wife?

My first wife. We accomplished so much together! I was smashed up when she died, and so suddenly. But she's fine now. She takes a great interest in gardening. Even at this distance.

But back to my father, whom I hardly knew, by the way. I was never a Communist! Democratic Socialism is not Communism. Imprecision in language . . . it's one of the things that preoccupied me, some said to a fault; but change the name of the thing, and in many cases you change the thing. Rewriting history . . . you could see it happening, on both sides of the fence, I might add. The English colonial record was hardly spotless. The Empire— humbug, balderdash, and claptrap, covering up naked greed and the lust for power.

People are realizing that more now, I think.

(Snorting sound) About time! When I was saying it, I was accused of disloyalty.

You'll be interested to know that the rewriting of history is still being attempted, especially in the United States.

I'm not surprised. The way they tried to paper over slavery, and then the Jim Crow laws . . . you can't have those kinds of inequities in a democracy. If indeed that country is one, or ever was.

There's a lot of disinformation being spread about.

You'd be amazed at what people can be manipulated into believing.

Actually, it may be even worse than in your day. At least Stalin didn't try to push blue bird-shaped aliens from outer space.

Ha! (Laughs) Taking lessons from that old blowhard, H.G. Wells, have they been?

Possibly his early fiction. But at least he believed in science. Not like a lot of anti-vaxxers today.

Anti-what?

It's complicated.

Wells was right about some things. But science will never be enough. And the one-world government he had in mind would be a tyranny, however disguised. Aldous Huxley made short work of that idea in *Brave New World*. Perhaps you've heard of it? He was my schoolmaster at Eton; taught me French, not very well.

Didn't he write you a letter? When Nineteen Eighty-Four *came out?*

(Coughs, laughs) Yes, he did. He said, "Whether in actual fact the policy of the boot-on-the-face can go on indefinitely seems doubtful. My own belief is that the ruling oligarchy will find less arduous and wasteful ways of governing and of satisfying its lust for power, and these ways will resemble those which I described in *Brave New World*."

You've taken turns being right. For instance, the United States came very close to a coup d'état, just recently. Invasion of the Capitol. Attempt to overturn the election results.

Sounds familiar. I lived in an age of coups, of one kind or another. Different slogans, but same idea. (Coughs)

And now many of them are trying to pretend it didn't really happen.

Down the old Memory Hole, eh? At least they have a free press. Independent voices allowed to speak up without being shot.

More or less. It's not perfect.

The perfect is the enemy of the good. (Coughs) Mind if I smoke?

It's very bad for you.

(Sound between a growl and a laugh) Not anymore. You only die once. Wasn't that the name of some shocking book? Or perhaps a shocking film. No, I'm confusing it with *The Postman Always Rings Twice*. Prole fodder, not that I didn't appreciate a good murder. (Sound of a match being struck)

I don't mind, myself. During my teen years—in the 1950s—people smoked a lot, so I'm used to the idea. But Mrs. Verity has a strict non-smoking policy. Some of her clients have asthma.

She won't notice. She's in a jolly old trance, isn't she? (Faint odour of tobacco)

May I ask you something? It's a delicate question.

Of course. I will try not to give a delicate answer.

I'm somewhat surprised to find you making use of the services of a spiritualist. Wouldn't that come under the heading of balderdash, claptrap, and humbug?

(Chuckles) **A change of state rearranges some of one's preconceptions. Rigidity is the symptom of a limited mind, and was far too typical of many in the so-called intelligentsia of my day. They mistook fixed ideas for thought.**

That habit has not gone out of fashion. But still, it's quite a leap from—

I have always tried to be practical. It's why I became a sort of pamphleteer—needed to pay the rent, and it was a quick way to an immediate readership. (Pause) **One must make use of the means to hand. Needs must when the Devil drives. So if Mrs. Verity is the means by which we can speak together, then Mrs. Verity it must be.** (Sound of a match being struck. Sound of a second match being struck)

You could use a lighter.

Snobbish contraptions. Monograms on them. (Sound of inhaling) Mrs. Verity's not her real name, you know. Verity— to inspire trust, I suppose. Better than "Dodge," her actual surname.

I've always been interested in alter egos. Pen names, pseudonyms, things like that. I've wondered about your own choice—"George Orwell." George: there were four Hanoverian kings named George—

Not those Georges! (Laughs) I needed a pen name, so as not to wound my mother unduly. She was horrified by some of my views. And my going about with the deeply and I must say squalidly poor, and then writing about it. So . . .

Let me guess. Saint George for England? Dragon-slayer?

Spare my blushes. I was young and enthusiastic. I didn't realize that dragons always grow new heads.

And "Orwell"—it's a river, but let's unpack it a little—

Excuse me? Unpack what? It's not a suitcase.

Sorry. It's a thing people say these days. Sort of like Lewis Carroll's "portmanteau words." Take it apart to see what it contains.

Oh, I see. (Coughs)

So, "Or," as in "on the other hand." Also, it's French for "gold." And "well"—people sometimes make you out to be Mr. Gloomy Pants because of the boot grinding into the human face forever in Nineteen Eighty-Four, *but I've never thought that: there's a note on Newspeak at the end, written in the past tense, so the totalitarian world in the book must be over.*

I'm glad you've grasped that. Many did not. I was attacked for pessimism.

They were wrong. Then there's "well," as in "All shall be well." Julian of Norwich. That's hopeful! And a well is also a well of inspiration, or a holy well . . .

That's stretching it, my dear. I have no pretensions to holiness. I wanted a river, yes, a natural feature; but an ordinary kind of river. Not a holy river, and not some damned private trout stream, bunch of aristocrats sticking their fishing rods into it.

I've always remembered something you—something Winston Smith says in Nineteen Eighty-Four, *when he begins writing his ill-fated journal on that beautiful cream-coloured paper. "For whom, it suddenly occurred to him to wonder, was he writing this diary? For the future, for the unborn . . . How could you communicate with the future? It was of its nature impossible. Either the future would resemble the present, in which case it would not listen to him; or it would be different from it, and his predicament would be meaningless."*

However, here I am, in my present but your future, and I believe I do understand Winston Smith's predicament. Or somewhat. Because you conveyed him so well! The horrible living conditions, the ugly clothing, the awful food, the fear of betrayal, the constant surveillance through two-way television—you couldn't possibly have known how close to reality that would become in this age, via the Internet!

The Internet? Is that some kind of political secret society? Like the Masons, or—

Not exactly. It used to be called the World Wide Web.

Like spiders?

No, more like . . . It's a way of communicating through wireless frequencies. Using certain devices. Different from radio, though. It started out with good intentions, as a way of sending rapid messages that were thought to be private, but governments have turned it into a spying device.

As usual. (Sound of a match being struck) Winston Smith would have used this Internet thing, I expect.

But he would have got caught, because the effect has been to collapse privacy and erode the notion of the individual. Though he still believed in the individual, somehow. Conscience and desire . . . Thus his attempted rebellion, and then the brainwashing, Room 101 . . . It was gripping! My young self was mesmerized!

Yes, yes. Not too badly done. I was attacked for that book by the Stalinist Left, of course. They were always attacking me. Capitalist stooge, toady to the status quo, poor little middle-class boy, that kind of thing. You won't believe this, but every time I'd mention Nature in one of my occasional pieces, I'd get hate mail telling me that a liking for Nature was bourgeois.

I love your praise of the toad. I'm very fond of toads.

Aha! Common ground! (Chuckles) I got attacked for the toad essay too. The joylessness of some of those on the Left was truly astounding. Any form of pleasure was off limits . . . good food, good sex, sunsets . . . those people were like the flagellants of the Middle Ages.

So the Junior Anti-Sex League and Winston's rigid, disapproving wife had a basis in reality?

Oh absolutely. Puritanical, they were. And if you didn't toe their party line, whatever it was at the time, you were banished to outer darkness. Excluded from decent society, namely theirs.

That's more than familiar. Things have become quite polarized. There are party lines now too, though the targets are different. And social banishments still happen, but they're called "cancellings."

Ha! Like a stamp, like a concert . . . good word choice! (Coughs) I became quite discouraged at moments, I must admit. What's the point of telling the truth if nobody wants to hear it? The Stalinists were well organized at that time. It was just after the war. Stalin was still good old Uncle Joe to many.

But your book was a huge success! You have no idea! And then, in 1956, after Stalin was dead, when Khrushchev made his "Secret Speech," revealing the atrocities that Stalin and his accomplices had perpetrated . . .

I did hear a rumour about that. It's not much of a comfort to have been right.

I think you'd like a film called The Death of Stalin.

Films are difficult for me. I have to view them through an intermediary and there's always a running commentary. Pause to get a beer, check their phones, go to the loo, that kind of thing. One doesn't wish to be such an inadvertent voyeur.

Must be annoying. You could watch it with me! I'd see it again!

A kind thought, but it wouldn't work. You wouldn't be able to let me in. You aren't a sensitive, I can tell. You aren't permeable enough. Egotistical writer, as I said.

(Laughs) *Many have told me that. "Not permeable enough." Maybe you could get Mrs. Verity to watch it with you. It's your kind of reality-based satire.*

Satire in extreme times is risky. Choose any excess, think you're wildly exaggerating, and it's most likely to have been true.

(Sympathetic murmur) *I know.*

I'd much have preferred it if the Soviet dream had turned out better. Without the wholesale deaths, the show trials, the murders . . . The original intentions were good. Or the intentions of some people were good. The idealists, who will of course go to any lengths for a cause they believe to be virtuous and in the common interest—they got carried away. Well, well. Successful revolutions are inevitably subject to corruption. Once power has been seized, those who have seized it want to hang on to it, by foul means or fouler. That was certainly what it was like during the years I was attempting to chronicle, in my own small way.

Many of us, including me, are so grateful that you did. You were very brave, and not only in Spain, during the Civil War. Much of what you said was unpopular at the time. Your work has really been invaluable, and you've been—how can I put this?—such an inspiration.

(Pleased murmur)

Though I should mention that when I first read a book by you, I wasn't old enough to understand it. I must have been eight or nine. The book was Animal Farm. *I thought it was a children's book, like* Charlotte's Web.

Charlotte's what?

It's about a pig. A good pig, though. And a message-weaving spider who saves his life.

Ah. Words matter, it appears. Even to pigs. (Chuckles. Sound of a match being struck)

I didn't know Animal Farm *was about the U.S.S.R. and the demonization of Trotsky. I had no idea who Trotsky was! I thought the animals were animals. The fate of Boxer the horse just destroyed me. I cried and cried!*

Oh dear.

Then I got angry. It was so unfair!

It was unfairnesses that drove me on the most, I suppose. The false accusations, the human sacrifices. More than anything, the injustices impelled me to write. Savage indignation, inflamed

by the betrayal of common human decencies. The betrayal of ordinary humanity.

Like Dickens? In your essay about him?

Yes. I suppose so. But I sense that Mrs. Verity is beginning to stir. Our time together is drawing to a close.

There's one more thing I'd like to tell you about. It's a book called Orwell's Roses, *by Rebecca Solnit. Her book takes as a point of departure your passionate interest in gardening, in growing things. Not many people know that about you. She makes you sound, well, kind of adorable. That photo of you with your adopted son, such a sweet child . . . You weren't Mr. Doom and Gloom at all! Enthusiastic about living, full of plans, until . . .*

Until the end, you mean. Don't worry. There must always be an end. As in novels. But one day at a time, eh? I did love it, the gardening. (Sighs) So wonderful . . . the hard work, the digging and so on, the fresh smells, even the smell of manure . . . then out of the dirt and the sweat, like a miracle, a beautiful thing growing . . . I suppose it's what I miss the most about the Earth. The beauty of it.

The rose bushes you planted at Wallington, in 1936 . . . You mention them in your journal. They flowered on the Day of the Dead. I thought you'd like to know.

So much I didn't know, at that date. So much was to come. The Spanish Civil War, the Second World War . . . so much horror and suffering!

Many of those horrible things ended, finally. Though they left scars, and the wars have a way of coming back.

I'm sorry to hear that.

Now we're facing a more insidious crisis. The Earth itself—the green planet as we have known it—the living Earth is threatened.

It began with the coal, I suppose. The coal furnaces, to drive machines. People don't want to know where their heat and light and luxuries really come from, or what gets crushed in the process. I wrote about that, I seem to remember. (Coughs) But what about the young people? Are they still hopeful?

I'm not sure. They're trying, though. Trying to reverse the damage we've done. Many of them are.

Mrs. Verity is waking up now. I fear I may have to—

Your rose bushes—the ones you planted in 1936—they're still alive! Still blooming, every summer. It seems kind of symbolic.

(Silence)

Hello? Hello? Oh, come back! Please, just a little longer . . .

(Sound of a yawn) Here I am, in the land of the living. Did your friend show up? Seems to me that he must've. I've been out like a light and now I'm dead tired. That's how it is when they're borrowing your head. They burn a lot of energy! Have a good chat, did you? Cup of tea? Anything wrong, dear?

IMPATIENT GRISELDA

✦

Do you all have your comfort blankets? We tried to provide the right sizes. I am sorry some of them are washcloths—we ran out.

And your snacks? I regret that we could not arrange to have them cooked, as you call it, but the nourishment is more complete without this cooking that you do. If you put all of the snack into your ingestion apparatus—your, as you call it, mouth—the blood will not drip on the floor. That is what we do at home.

I regret that we do not have any snacks that are what you call vegan. We could not interpret this word.

You don't have to eat them if you don't want to.

Please stop whispering, at the back there. And stop whimpering, and take your thumb out of your mouth, Sir-Madam. You must set a good example for the children.

No, you are not the children, Madam-Sir. You are forty-two. Among us you would be the children, but you are not from our planet or even our galaxy. Thank you, Sir or Madam.

I use both because quite frankly I can't tell the difference. We do not have such limited arrangements on our planet.

Yes, I know I look like what you call an octopus, little young entity. I have seen pictures of these amicable beings. If the way I appear truly disturbs you, you may close your eyes. It would allow you to pay better attention to the story, in any case.

No, you may not leave the quarantine room. The plague is out there. It would be too dangerous for you, though not for me. We do not have that type of microbe on our planet.

I am sorry there is no what you call a toilet. We ourselves utilize all ingested nourishment for fuel, so we have no need for such receptacles. We did order one what you call a toilet for you, but we are told there is a shortage. You could try out the window. It is a long way down, so please do not try to jump.

It's not fun for me either, Madam-Sir. I was sent here as part of an intergalactic-crises aid package. I did not have a choice, being a mere entertainer and thus low in status. And this simultaneous translation device I have been issued is not the best quality. As we have already experienced together, you do not understand my jokes. But as you say, half an oblong wheat-flour product is better than none.

Now. The story.

I was told to tell you a story, and now I will tell you one. This story is an ancient Earth story, or so I understand. It is called "Impatient Griselda."

Once there were some twin sisters. They were of low status. Their names were Patient Griselda and Impatient Griselda. They were pleasing in appearance. They were Madams and not Sirs. They were known as Pat and Imp. Griselda was what you call their last name.

Excuse me, Sir-Madam? Sir, you say? Yes?

No, there was not only one. There were two. Who is telling this story? I am. So there were two.

One day a rich person of high status, who was a Sir and a thing called a Duke, came riding by on a—came riding by, on a—. If you have enough legs you don't have to do this riding by, but Sir had only two legs, like the rest of you. He saw Pat watering the—doing something outside the hovel in which she lived, and he said, "Come with me, Pat. People tell me I must get married so I can copulate legitimately and produce a little Duke." He was unable to just send out a pseudopod, you see.

A pseudopod, Madam. Or Sir. Surely you know what that is! You are an adult!

I will explain it later.

The Duke said, "I know you are of low status, Pat, but that is why I want to marry you rather than someone of high status. A high-status Madam would have ideas, but you have none. I can boss you around and humiliate you as much as I want, and you will feel so lowly that you won't say boo. Or boo-hoo. Or anything. And if you refuse me, I will have your head chopped off."

This was very alarming, so Patient Griselda said yes, and the Duke scooped her up onto his . . . I'm sorry, we don't have a word for that, so the translation device is of no help. Onto his snack. Why are you all laughing? What do you think snacks do before they become snacks?

I shall continue the story, but I do counsel you not to annoy me unduly. Sometimes I get hangry. It means hunger makes me angry, or anger makes me hungry. One or the other. We do have a word for that in our language.

So, with the Duke holding on to Patient Griselda's attractive abdomen very tightly so she wouldn't fall off his—so she wouldn't fall off—they rode away to his palace.

Impatient Griselda had been listening behind the door. That Duke is a terrible person, she said to herself. And he is preparing to behave very badly to my beloved twin sister, Patient. I will disguise myself as a young Sir and get a job working in the Duke's vast food-preparation chamber so I can keep an eye on things.

So Impatient Griselda worked as what you call a scullery boy in the Duke's food-preparation chamber, where she or he witnessed all kinds of waste—fur and feet simply discarded, can you imagine that, and bones, after being boiled, tossed out as well—but he or she also heard all kinds of gossip. Much of the gossip was about how badly the Duke was treating his new Duchess. He was rude to her in public, he made her wear clothes that did not suit her, he knocked her around and he told her that all the bad things he was doing to her were her own fault. But Patient never said boo.

Impatient Griselda was both dismayed and angry at this news. She or he arranged to meet Patient Griselda one day when she was moping in the garden and revealed her true identity. The two of them performed an affectionate bodily gesture, and Impatient said, "How can you let him treat you like that?"

"A receptacle for drinking liquid that is half full is better than one that is half empty," Pat said. "I have two beautiful pseudo-pods. Anyway, he is testing my patience."

"In other words, he is seeing how far he can go," Imp said.

Pat sighed. "What choice do I have? He would not hesitate to kill me if I give him an excuse. If I say boo, he'll cut off my head. He's got the knife."

"We'll see about that," Imp said. "There are a lot of knives in the food-preparation chamber, and I have now had much practice in using them. Ask the Duke if he would do you the honour of meeting you for an evening stroll in this very garden, tonight."

"I am afraid to," Pat said. "He might consider this request the equivalent of saying boo."

"In that case, let's change clothes," Imp said. "And I will do it myself." So Imp put on the Duchess's robes and Pat put on the clothing of the scullery boy, and off they went to their separate places in the palace.

At dinner, the Duke announced to the supposed Pat that he had killed her two beautiful pseudopods, to which she said nothing. She knew in any case that he was bluffing, having heard from another scullery boy that the pseudopods had been spirited away to a safe location. Those in the food-preparation chamber always knew everything.

The Duke then added that the next day he was going to kick Patient out of the palace naked—we do not have this naked on our planet, but I understand that here it is a shameful thing to be seen in public without your vestments. After everyone had jeered at Patient and wastefully pelted her with rotting snack parts, he said he intended to marry someone else, younger and prettier than Pat.

"As you wish, my lord," the supposed Patient said, "but first I have a surprise for you."

The Duke was already surprised simply to hear her speak.

"Indeed?" he said, curling his facial antennae.

"Yes, admired and always-right Sir," Imp said in a tone of voice that signalled a prelude to pseudopod excretion. "It is a special gift for you, in return for your great beneficence to me during our, alas, too short period of cohabitation. Please do me the honour of joining me in the garden this evening so we can have consolation sex once more, before I am deprived of your shining presence forever."

The Duke found this proposition both bold and piquant.

Piquant. It is one of your words. It means sticking a skewer into something. I am sorry I cannot explain it further. It is an Earth word, after all, not a word from my language. You will have to ask around.

"That is bold and piquant," the Duke said. "I'd always thought you were a dishrag and a doormat, but now it seems, underneath that whey face of yours, you are a slut, a trollop, a dollymop, a tart, a floozy, a tramp, a hussy, and a whore."

Yes, Madam-Sir, there are indeed a lot of words like that in your language.

"I agree, my lord," Imp said. "I would never contradict *you*."

"I shall see you in the garden after the sun has set," the Duke said. This was going to be more fun than usual, he thought. Maybe his soi-disant wife would show a little action for a change, instead of just lying there like a plank.

Imp went off to seek the scullery boy, namely Pat. Together they selected a long, sharp knife. Imp hid it in her brocaded sleeve, and Pat concealed herself behind a shrub.

"Well met by moonlight, my lord," Imp said when the Duke appeared in the shadows, already unbuttoning that portion of his clothing behind which his organ of pleasure was habitually concealed. I have not understood this part of the story very well, since on our planet the organ of pleasure is located on top of the head and is always in plain view. This makes things far easier, since we can see for ourselves whether attraction has been generated and reciprocated.

"Take off your gown or I'll rip it off, whore," the Duke said.

"With pleasure, my lord," Imp said. Approaching him with a smile, she drew the knife from her richly ornamented sleeve and cut his throat, as she had cut the throat of many a snack during the course of her scullery-boy labours. He uttered barely a grunt. Then the two sisters performed a celebratory act of bodily affection and ate the Duke all up—bones, brocaded robes, and all.

Excuse me? What is WTF? Sorry, I don't understand.

Yes, Madam-Sir, I admit that this was a cross-cultural moment. I was simply saying what I myself would have done in their place. But storytelling does help us understand one another across our social and historical and evolutionary chasms, don't you think?

After that, the twin sisters located the two beautiful pseudo-pods, and there was a joyful reunion, and they all lived happily in the palace. A few suspicious relatives of the Duke came sniffing around, but the sisters ate them too.

The End.

Speak up, Sir-Madam. You didn't like this ending? It is not the usual one? Then which ending do you prefer?

Oh. No, I believe that ending is for a different story. Not one that interests me. I would tell that one badly. But I have told this one well, I believe—well enough to hold your attention, you must admit. You even stopped whimpering. That is just as well, as the whimpering was very irritating, not to mention tempting. On my planet, only snacks whimper. Those who are not snacks do not whimper.

Now, you must excuse me. I have several other quarantined groups on my list, and it is my job to help them pass the time, as I have helped you pass it. Yes, Madam-Sir, it would have passed anyway; but it would not have passed so quickly.

Now I'll just ooze out underneath the door. It is so useful not to have a skeleton. Indeed, Sir-Madam, I hope the plague will be over soon too. Then I can get back to my normal life.

BAD TEETH

✦

I was astonished," Csilla says, "to hear you had an affair with Newman Small. He had such bad teeth!"

"Who?" Lynne says. "I don't know anyone named Newman Small."

"Sure you do. He used to write book reviews for that magazine. You know the one. In the late 1960s. It folded after five years, and I was not surprised."

"What magazine?"

"It had beavers on the front. Doing undignified things. They were drawings, not real beavers."

"What undignified things?" Lynne asks. She doesn't recall the magazine—so many magazines have come and gone—but she's always intrigued by Csilla's notion of what might be classified as undignified.

"Oh, you know. Having sex. Wearing underpants."

"It's more undignified not to wear underpants," Lynne says. "Though maybe not for beavers."

They're having tea in Csilla's backyard. It's the second COVID summer; otherwise they would be in a restaurant—or not in one, outside on a patio—but at their age you have to be careful. Csilla spreads raspberry jam on a scone, adds whipped cream, takes a bite. "But how could you stand those teeth?" She gives a little shudder. "Wasn't it like being kissed by a crumbling stone wall?"

"You're hallucinating," says Lynne. "No such kisses took place."

Csilla's own teeth are childishly small, geometrically even, blamelessly white, and all accounted for, though she must be pushing seventy. She never tells her age, whereas Lynne flourishes hers. Clock up enough years, she's in the habit of saying, and you can dance on a table provided you can still clamber up there. You can have sex with the mailman and nobody will care. You can flush away your push-up bras—not literally, you wouldn't want plumbers involved, asking how the bra got into the toilet—but you get the idea. You don't have to hold in your stomach anymore. You can make six kinds of a fool of yourself because you're a fool just for being old. You're off the hook for almost everything.

Lynne is definitely older than Csilla, so she's more off the hook. But how old is Csilla, actually? Lynne calculates: the Hungarian Revolution took place in 1956, when Lynne herself was sixteen. Csilla was definitely alive then, since she'd been yanked out of Hungary by her velvet-gloved but nerves-of-steel mother. They'd been just two of the two hundred thousand people, give or take, who'd seized the chance to skedaddle to the lands of superior shopping malls and daytime-TV game shows. Lynne once met this legendary mother when she was still on the planet and being catered to hand and foot by Csilla. She'd had a gang of other perfumed, flinty-souled Hungarian mothers with whom she'd played card games and exchanged war stories about their respective escapes, plus grumblings about the thankless children they'd saved from the Communist salt mines. Lavender on the outside, meticulous about their coiffures and manicures and eye shadow, but pure adamant within.

Lynne has created various fantasies for this mother. She'd been the mistress of a leading apparatchik but had cheated on him and fled from his jealous temper. She'd been selling contraband American rock 'n' roll records and was on the verge of being arrested. She'd been a member of a secret resistance cell and the Stalinists were onto her. Thousands of suspected resisters had been caught and murdered, let's not forget! In one of these fantasies, the mother had seduced a border guard so that she and Csilla could gain egress. In another version, she'd shot him. In a third, she'd done both.

But according to Csilla, her mother hadn't been at all political. No secret resistance cells for her! She'd merely been nostalgic for foods of yore—some kind of Merry Widow Austro-Hungarian cuisine that had possibly existed in her youth. Schnitzels. Paprika. Goulash. *Proper* goulash. Whipped cream, Csilla would add—*real* whipped cream. All the good stuff. So she'd grabbed a suitcase and Csilla along with it, and hightailed it for the border.

The question is: What age had Csilla been then? She's been coy about that. Old enough to talk, anyway. She still has an accent. Csilla has frequently adjusted the age she was at the time of her primal uprooting: as she herself gets older and older, young Csilla grows younger and younger. Her children tease her about that. "Wait a minute, last year you were ten, now you were five?" "So, maybe you weren't even born?"

Csilla is impervious to both questioning and mockery. She simply pretends she hasn't heard, changes the subject, and forges ahead on whatever twisting narrative path suits her at the moment. She's a strategic liar, being a memoirist. She likes to roll the dice, try things out on people, see how far she can go. In another life she would have lost millions at the roulette table in Monte Carlo, then won it all back while wearing a backless silver lamé gown and white evening gloves and toting an ebony cigarette holder, with a sequined bag tucked under her elbow containing a pearl-handled . . . Rein yourself in, Lynne tells herself. Csilla has never smoked, in any life. Otherwise she wouldn't have such perfect teeth. Her teeth would be yellow and sporadic, her gums would be receding.

She'd gone in for suntans though, and it's showing. A little crepe, some furrows. Glamour must be paid for eventually, Lynne silently tsks. She's always been a shade umbrella person herself. Reading books out of the direct rays while others rubbed lemon juice into their hair to turn it blond and basted themselves with baby oil so they could toast to a deep golden brown.

Csilla had no need of lemon juice, being blond by rights, but she's continued to opt for a tan. It sets off her pearly teeth. If asked, she would have said, Why not enjoy the ride? It's going to end sooner or later, so better to go out with a tan. Look good in your coffin.

Underneath the fluff and schmaltz and the baroque fantasiz-ing and the picture-perfect smiling, she's a melancholy fatalist. "Naturally," she'd said to Lynne when Lynne had called her on this a few decades ago. "Don't you know about Hungarian gloom? It's built-in."

"Have another scone," she says now. "I baked them myself."

Unlikely, thinks Lynne. Csilla is a takeout queen, not a baker. "Thanks," she says. "How're the grandkids?" Csilla has four of these, whereas Lynne has only three. Despite their youthful flight-iness, expressions of disinterest in washer-dryers, and spouting of near-prehistoric feminist slogans ("A woman needs a man like a fish needs a bicycle" and so forth), both Csilla and Lynne had got married, after all—both of them more than once. They'd reproduced. They'd lullabied. They'd navigated diapers. They'd fallen back on casseroles, even frozen ones: made from scratch by Lynne, grabbed from the supermarket by Csilla.

Csilla dodges the grandkid diversion by not hearing it. "So, I'm doing a little archaeology on Newman Small," she says, as if thinking. "After the magazine with the sexy beavers, he got a contract job with the federal government. Advising them on some culture thing. There was more money in the culture-advising business back then, you'll remember, and Newman always knew where the blood was, he knew how to suck out a few choice clots for himself. Soviet bureaucracy, Canadian bureaucracy, it's all the same. There's a system and you work it, that was Newman Small. He denounced the system too, of course. That's the Canadian way: high-handed accusations but cash under the table. You couldn't have done such a thing with the Soviets, they'd only liquidate you."

"We like to be inclusive," says Lynne. "We like to acknowledge all viewpoints. Correction: we like to pretend to acknowledge them."

Csilla laughs but plows ahead with her fable. "Newman kept on with the book reviews though, for other outlets. Those reviews weren't bad either; he knew the right buzz words. I guess that's how you met him: the two of you got together over your book reviews."

"Csilla, I did not get together with Newman Small," Lynne says.

"Your reviews were better, though. Maybe that's why Newman Small wanted to slide into your bikini bottom. He wanted to conquer your book-reviewing power by seducing you. Maybe he thought your mastery of the form would rub off on him via his dick."

"I have never worn a bikini in my life," says Lynne indignantly. She finds this the most shocking thing Csilla has said about her so far. She's always been a strict one-piecer. Though not out of prudery, she claims. It's just that girls with short waists should not wear bikinis. For girls, read women. The four horizontals make them look oblong, even more oblong than they are. This is a hard truth, but a truth nonetheless.

"Your flannel PJs, then. The ones with the teddy bears on them."

Lynne regrets having ever shared this personal nightwear information with Csilla. Teddy-bear flannel PJs are far beyond anything Csilla would consider wearable. They were a sort of joke, having something to do with getting cold feet as one entered the golden years. It's underhanded of Csilla to use these pyjamas against her in such a ruthless manner, but Csilla has always been ruthless.

"Wrong decade," Lynne says. "Anachronism. Those PJs date from the twenty-first century."

"Or whatever you were wearing then," says Csilla, not missing a beat. "Slenderella, remember them? In their lacy fake-satin period. I had the two-piece thing with the little jacket. The point is, how could you?" She raises her eyebrows, widens her eyes. "I know it was the 1960s and we were all doing dumb things, but Newman Small! He must have had a lot to offer in some other way to make up for his bad teeth. Was he well endowed?"

"Well endowed?" says Lynne with a laugh. "That's rather formal. What century are we in?"

"Okay, hung like a donkey."

"Csilla," says Lynne, pronouncing her words distinctly, "I did not fuck Newman Small. He's a blank in my life. I've never set eyes on him."

"Well, your first ex says you did. He remembers it very well. It's etched, he says. It was agonizing for him. It gave him recurring nightmares. Have a grape, I washed them."

"Jason? He told you that?" Lynne feels a chill run down her spine. She hasn't spoken to Jason for a while—when, exactly? At least a year. What would make him remember an event that never happened? Has some unknown grief unsettled him? Has he fallen victim to a brain malady? Does he have Parkinson's, does he have Alzheimer's, does he have a tumour? Surely none of these things has happened: she would have heard. So why is he telling tales about things she never did, transgressions she hadn't actually committed? It's hard even for her to remember all of her actual transgressions; has Jason too got mixed up about them? Or is he just being amusingly malicious? It's not out of the question.

She pours more tea, stirs milk into it, making little circles with the teaspoon, buying time. When she's sufficiently in control of herself, she says, "Jason would never have said such a thing. It just isn't true. Why were you even talking to him?"

Lynne suspects why. Csilla is writing a book about the 1960s. She has a series going on: the social history of Canada, decade by decade. Picture books with commentary. Fashions of the era, public uproars, politicians, sports triumphs, pop stars, minor celebrities. Jason is a minor celebrity, or he was; he'd once had a radio show on which he'd interviewed other minor celebrities. Lynne too had been a minor celebrity, which is how they'd met. She'd been an award-winning poet in her extreme youth, by which she means twenty-seven. *Poet* by its nature is minor, and *award-winning* is now a common adjective: it might be applied to a beer or a cow. Many of the major celebrities of the 1960s are dead, and Lynne can barely remember who they were, let alone the minor ones. After a while everything that was once major is minor.

"Another scone?" Csilla asks. "I talk to him a lot. Jason loves a good gossip. He's been a terrific source, he's a walking encyclopedia, he's got the dirt on everybody. He knows where all the bodies are buried."

"Maybe so, but I'm not a body. He wouldn't have said that. He may exaggerate, but he doesn't lie." Unlike you, Lynne beams at her silently; then corrects, Unlike us. "Or he doesn't lie to that extent," she adds.

"There's a wasp on your plate," Csilla says. She waves her hands around.

"You shouldn't agitate wasps. Don't bother them and they won't bother you," Lynne says. A motto from her grit-your-teeth-and-don't-be-hysterical mother.

"Which happens not to be true," says Csilla. "I have been very nice to those wasps. Last week I gave them a piece of cake all to themselves and one of them stung me."

"Ingratitude is deplorable, especially in a wasp," says Lynne. "Most people would just massacre them. You take a paper bag and put it over the nest at dusk, then spray the shit out of them. So, when and where was this sordid liaison supposed to have taken place?"

"In 1967, in Ottawa."

"Well then. More and more improbable. Nobody has affairs in Ottawa."

"Oh, they do," said Csilla. "Civil servants have them all the time. They do it out of boredom."

"But nobody goes there from somewhere else to have them. Why would they even consider it?"

"Maybe if the other person was in a wheelchair and couldn't travel easily," Csilla says. "It would show devotion."

"Not even then," says Lynne. "I was living in Whitehorse in 1967. Just for half of that year: I had a grant. Jason used to come for weekends. So I would hardly be going to Ottawa for any reason."

"You must have told Jason it was something to do with your grant. I expect you flew to Vancouver," Csilla says. "Then you took the red-eye to Toronto and changed planes. You must have taken advantage of some cut-rate airline deal, being so young and penniless then. I admire your stamina! You must have been very keen to get there. Where did you meet Newman for your rendezvous, or is that rendezvouses? There must have been lots of them! Was it at the Chateau Laurier? Did he book you a room for when you staggered off the plane? Was he waiting there to clamp his decaying teeth onto your neck?"

"Csilla, this never happened. Never, not ever."

"You don't need to be so defensive. We all had flings then, yes? The pill had just come out. We were demonstrating our freedom. Sauce for the goose, tit for tat, all of that. Alcohol was involved, as I recall, not to mention pot. I had a miniskirt and white go-go boots. Remember?"

"I don't mind owning up to the affairs I did have," Lynne says. "And I am deeply ashamed of those flared jeans and the jacket with the Mao collar and the zip-front catsuit, if it's abject confession you're after. But I did not have an affair with someone called Newman Small. Double pinky swear, cross my heart and spit."

Csilla overlooks this reversion to childhood slang; possibly she doesn't recognize the vernacular. "Jason says you had a fight about it. He says you admitted it. He asked you if you were drunk or maybe on drugs because how else could you have even considered a man with such awful teeth? Newman Small! Jason says it fractured all aesthetic rules, and after that he no longer respected your intellect. He says it broke up your marriage."

"I'm going to call Jason. I can't believe he's been pushing this absurd story," Lynne says, levering herself out of her garden chair. "Thank you for the tea. The scones were delicious. You must tell me where you bought them."

"Oh, don't call Jason," Csilla cries. "If you make a fuss about it, he won't ever tell me anything else!"

———————

Lynne makes her way from the shady back garden, around the side of Csilla's house and through the forsythia bushes, which need pruning, then across the lawn, which needs watering, and then down the front steps to the sidewalk. Out here the sunlight is blaring. A few more degrees of warming and we'll go up in smoke, she reflects, but maybe not till after I'm dead. Her car is two blocks away. Despite the heat she must not hurry. That way fainting lies.

She's ruminating about teeth, the teeth of her youth. No fluoridation then, not even any dental floss. Only toothpicks. Then candy sprang up all over the place after the war, like sickly sweet weeds. Not to mention ice cream and chewing gum, and soda pop. It must have been a plot on the part of dentists, to create cavities; not that they'd needed any help. She remembers herself at eight, at nine, at ten, cowering in the dentist's chair, enduring the horrible drill—more like a jackhammer—worked in those days by a pedal. The grinding sound inside her head. The pain—did they even have anaesthesia yet? There must have been something, but it didn't work very well. Then the sound—a scrunching sound like walking on Styrofoam or twenty-below snow—as the filling was packed into the excavation. A number of those fillings, grey in colour and doubtless leaking mercury straight into her brain, are still embedded in her molars. Her front teeth, however, are caps: praise the lord for implants.

Why had Csilla escaped all that? Was it true—as Lynne's mother had proclaimed—that there were two kinds of teeth, soft teeth and hard teeth, and Lynne had unfortunately inherited the soft teeth from her father's side of the family, and what couldn't be cured must be endured? Or was it that the Stalinists had kept Hungary so short of the necessities of life, such as candy, that Csilla had been spared the corroding effects of the postwar sugar bonanza?

These thoughts occupy her until she reaches her own house and is able to rush to the bathroom to deal with the effects of so much tea. She then drinks a large glass of water to counter dehydration, and sits down to arrange her thoughts. What will she say on this call to Jason that she's about to make? Is it remotely possible that Csilla and Jason are right, and she did have an affair with the mysterious foul-toothed Newman Small for reasons no one can fathom, and was so traumatized by it, and by the ensuing scene and rupture with Jason, that she's forgotten all about it? That could have happened.

If only she'd been keeping a diary: she could consult it. But life was moving so quickly back then. She'd met Csilla when? In 1968 or so? At a cut-rate party thrown by a poetry publisher, in a cellar perhaps, but the cellar of what? Not a church. A tavern, long defunct. Csilla had been wearing a brightly coloured geometric miniskirt and a huge red and orange and blue wristwatch, and, yes, white go-go boots. How many male hangers-on in the subcultural scene were in love with Csilla—with her swinging blond hair and her golden-girl tan and her sexy European accent? Many. Lynne recalls the lovelorn—fellow poets, a lot of them—confiding in her over glasses of tepid white wine or equally tepid coffee, gazing at her with dark-circled eyes and bemoaning Csilla's cruelty, as evidenced by her refusal to sleep with them. Did Csilla ever have real feelings? Was she a heartless cockteaser? Was she an ice goddess? There had to be some unnatural reason for her resistance to them.

How many, on the other hand, were in love with Lynne? She'll never know. Csilla claimed to know, however. She used to have an extensive list of the supposed adorers of Lynne that she would trot out in order to jeer at them, since these suitors were each and every one of them deficient and ridiculous, and vastly unworthy of Lynne. But how did Csilla have access to their romantic feelings? There was no way of verifying that what she said was true. Lynne could hardly risk asking any of these young men, "Excuse me, but are you in love with me?" The word would have gone around that she was bats; even more bats than was normal, female poets being bats by definition. In any case, finding out would have been merely a matter for curiosity and ego gratification, since none of those on Csilla's list had interested Lynne: she'd read their poetry.

Some of the supposed suitors were married, older men with actual jobs, ducking out on their wives, thrill-hunting and slumming it among the counterculturals. The late 1960s was a time of big domestic breakups: the so-called sexual revolution, post-pill, pre-AIDS. Young bearded hippies everywhere, girls in maxicoats, then long flower-child skirts and granny boots, acid and weed freely available, plus—later—other substances. It was as if the 1950s ideal family had swelled up like a water balloon and then burst. Marriages were shattering like glass in a hailstorm. Men of fifty were ditching their tailored suits and throwing away their ties and denouncing the System and donning love beads, so embarrassing; while mothers of four were deciding they were really lesbians and had been all along, thus explaining their unsatisfactory sex lives. Everyone, it seems, was in search of their hidden inner identity and likely to go looking for it in bed after bed after bed. Jason included, Lynne included. So: Newman Small, sign of the times? Collateral damage? What exactly had Lynne been up to with him, him and his dental afflictions?

She lifts her landline phone—she's kept a landline, because what if extreme weather such as hurricanes or floods totals the cellphone towers, or the electricity goes off due to an ice storm and you can't recharge? Such things happen.

She opens the contacts on her cellphone and dials Jason's number. On a landline he's less likely to see that it's her. Will he pick up? Yes.

"Hello, Lynne," he says. "How are you?"

"Fine. You? Have you had COVID?"

"Not yet. You?"

"Not yet either." Lynne breathes in. "Jason." A pause. "I've just been talking to Csilla."

A pause on his end. "Yes?" he says cautiously.

"It's about this man called Newman Small."

"I expect it is," he says. Is that a laugh? Jason likes to laugh at foibles as long as they aren't his.

"Csilla says that you told her I had an affair with a man called Newman Small. In Ottawa. How could you? You know that's not true. I've never even met him!"

"I said nothing of the sort," says Jason.

"Then what did you say? You must've said something."

"Csilla told me a rambling story about some guy with bad teeth. I let her run on—she would have anyway, you know how she is—and then she asked me to confirm it."

"And did you?"

"No. I said nothing."

"She took that for a yes."

"She takes everything for a yes," Jason says. "When it suits her."

"Why didn't you tell her it isn't true?" says Lynne.

"No point," says Jason. "She believes whatever she likes, or says she does. Also, I could neither confirm nor deny. Who is this Newman Small? How do I know whether you slept with some unknown person I've never heard of? You can't disprove a negative."

"You mean you don't know who Newman Small is either?"

"Correct," says Jason. He is definitely laughing now.

"She's really out of line," says Lynne.

"This is new?"

"She wants to put it in her book. My affair with Newman Small. That series she's doing. Literati scandal of 1967."

"Tell her you'll sue her."

"I can't sue her!" says Lynne. "She's one of my best friends!"

"Still?" says Jason.

A week later, Lynne invites Csilla to her own backyard for tea, turn and turnabout.

She doesn't serve scones and whipped cream, however. She sticks to a more Protestant menu: sliced peaches with a dollop of vanilla yogourt, and date and oatmeal energy bites from the vegan bakery around the corner. It's another hot day so Lynne has moved a pedestal fan into the garden. Csilla looks as good as ever, in a pale flowered sundress with ruffled cap sleeves. Maybe not as good as ever, Lynne silently edits. As good as possible.

After they've gone through the politenesses—who among their mutual acquaintance has been infected, who's ended up in the hospital, who has died, who has died from other causes—Lynne tackles the main topic.

"I spoke to Jason," she says. "He claims he emphatically did not tell you I had a thing with Newman Small."

"Really?" Csilla raises her eyebrows incredulously. "He said that?"

"He also said he's never heard of Newman Small."

"He hasn't?"

"No." Lynne lets this sink in, though surely Csilla knows it already. "Was there ever any Newman Small?" she then asks. "Did you just make him up? Teeth and all?"

"Does it matter?" Csilla says, smiling her perfect smile.

"Yes!" says Lynne. "It does matter."

Csilla looks down at her teacup. "But it's such a great story," she murmurs.

"No doubt. But it isn't true," Lynne says. Her tone is reproachful, earnest, severe. How has Csilla managed to make her feel like a tedious, moralizing, beige-foundation-garmented Sunday-school teacher?

"A story isn't great because it's true," Csilla says. "It's great because it's good."

"How many people have you told this great story to?" Lynne asks. She doubts there will be a straight answer. She has a vision of herself, or a flat billboard image of herself, with the non-existent Newman Small's grinning, gap-toothed face glued onto her. She'll never get him off now. Once a story like that has been flung into the social pond, it's almost impossible to reel it back in.

"Not many. Just a few," says Csilla. A lie, without a doubt.

Lynne says nothing. She's feeling breathless. Is it rage or amazement? Why is Csilla so mendacious? Why does she invent these preposterous narratives? Because it isn't the first time. For the joy of creation? To make mischief, to stir things up for fun? To assert that life is a farce? Or for some deeper or more tenuous reason? She must know she'll get found out eventually. What does she want? A scolding? Proof that everyone's awful, including her?

"You didn't have to make him so repulsive," Lynne says. "You could have made him a hunk. But I assume you thought some sort of goblin was funnier."

"You're mad at me," Csilla says mournfully.

"Yeah, I'm sort of mad," says Lynne. "You've been making me look like an idiot. Was that the idea?"

"I guess you never want to speak to me again," says Csilla. She's looking down at the table, twiddling her teaspoon.

But how could Lynne be mad enough for that? Mad enough to never speak to Csilla again? She's too old for terminal scenes and door-slamming, she can't work up the self-righteous indignation. *You're dead to me* is what the younger generation might say. But Csilla is far from dead to her. Csilla is in fact part of her. The huge plastic watch, the white go-go boots, the outlandish fictions. The cheap white wine, the mediocre poets, the lovelorn swains. The two of them, tumbling around like kittens, happy to have bodies, believing they were free. Feeling and causing pain. Floating for just a moment beyond the grasp of time.

"I wouldn't blame you," says Csilla. "I don't know why I'm such a shit." She's adroit at this, whatever it is: repentance, self-abasement, wiggling out of consequences? Sabotage, then escaping? It helps to be beautiful.

"Remember the time you stole a month's worth of my birth control pills and said it wasn't you?" says Lynne. "In that aqua plastic dial-pack they had then? I had to go through crap for a new supply, they were hard to get then. You ruined two weeks of my dirty love life."

"Sorry to say, I sold them. On the black market, such as it was. Well, I needed the money, and I wasn't going to sell mine!" Csilla laughs, showing her child's teeth. "I'm a shit, like I said."

After a moment, Lynne laughs too. All those days with Csilla, all those years, turning to smoke, evaporating. So soon gone. "You're my very dear old friend, and I love you," she says.

Csilla smiles, her best, most innocent, most angelic pearly-toothed smile. "Do I hear a *but*?"

"No *but*," says Lynne.

DEATH BY CLAMSHELL

✦

HYPATIA OF ALEXANDRIA IS SPEAKING

But why clamshells? I had time to wonder, though not much time. Already I'd been pulled out of my carriage and had been dragged along the street—by my hair, some said later, but my arms and legs also came in handy to those doing the dragging. They must have brought the clamshells along on purpose. They certainly had a plan, they'd worked it out ahead of time. Why not just use knives? I ask myself now. So much more efficient.

But efficiency was never their first consideration. They were deeply concerned with symbolism. Therefore, the clamshells must have symbolized something to them, though I'm not sure what. Aphrodite was said to have been born from a bivalve of some kind. Two shells that open, revealing a pulpy, salty, but tasty interior. Make what you wish of that.

So, I was dragged along the street, a cobblestone street, by the way: very bumpy. All those doing the dragging were men, though there were some female bystanders, gazing at me in wonderment— wasn't I supposed to be the revered, trusted confidante of the rulers in this civilized, prosperous, vibrant, and tolerant queen city of the venerable Roman Empire? And if this could happen to me, how much more so to them? Fear, not pity or indignation, would have been their first emotion.

None of these bystanding women rushed to my defence. They drew their veils more closely over their faces and turned away, pretending not to see or hear. I don't blame them. They would simply have become casualties in their turn—collateral damage, as you say now. (And had I not similarly turned away from those being hauled through the streets to their doom? I had. But those spectacles were lawful, a voice within me protests. They were executions decreed for criminal acts. Still, I did turn away. It's a fine line. From some perspectives it isn't a line at all.)

Did I say that by this time I was screaming? Of course I was. The body screams whether you want it to or not. To prevent screaming under these circumstances you must practise the most extreme self-control, and from an early age. You must train for it. I had not done this: I had not walked on burning coals, lived in a cave with scorpions, driven hot needles beneath my fingernails. I was a mathematician and a teacher, not an ascetic. I hadn't seen the need for any scream-control exercises. Therefore I screamed. A lot.

But screaming is surely the point of such tortures, indeed of any tortures: the reduction of a person to the basics. *See? There is no so-called life of the mind. That was merely an affectation of yours. Your real identity is no more than this wedge of suffering flesh and what can be extracted from it: howls, pleas, liquids of several kinds.* The options in this playbook are limited by the nature of the human body; there are only so many things that can be done to it.

Altogether it was a noisy affair. In addition to my screams there was a great deal of harsh yelling. When participating in a homicidal mob, people egg one another on with enthusiastic shouts. You yourselves have witnessed as much at football games. "Foul abuse" is a standard way of describing what is shouted. In my case, the foul abuse consisted of aspersions on my virginity ("Degenerate whore!"), on my supposed religion ("Evil pantheist!"), on my inferred magical practices ("Filthy witch!"), and of brutal suggestions ("Tear her apart!").

I will spare you the details of what happened next, as it might be too distressing for you. Many in your world have the idea that there has been progress since my day, that people have become more humane, that atrocities were rife back then but have diminished in your era, though I don't know how anyone who has been paying attention can hold such a view.

Let me just mention that my garments were torn off. This is a banal rite at such fiestas, the violent removal of clothing; the point being humiliation. Then I was flayed alive with the clamshells, which were not very sharp, so the peeling off of my skin took longer than it might have done. This excoriation took place in a Christian sanctuary, as a sort of human sacrifice to their idea of their god, I suppose. Oh, and my eyes were gouged out, whether before or after I was dead I am not entirely sure. By that time I was watching from a location near the ceiling, so I was probably dead. But there was such an uproar going on during the eye-gouging— such fervour, such zeal, such impatience to be in on it—that I was not able to get a clear view.

In your day they would have taken pictures with their phone cameras: posing and holding up their scarlet clamshells. I am up to date on the latest technologies and practices, as you can see. They would have taken videos of my eyes coming out. One of the gentlemen threw them onto the floor and stepped on them. I was sad about that. I had enjoyed my eyes, they had helped me to observe the heavens, to chart the pathways of the divine spheres. "Goodbye, dear eyes," I whispered.

I can now see perfectly well without them. In this phase of

being, we can see through the eyes of others. I am now seeing through yours.

After the main action was over, my body was dismembered and the pieces of it lugged, or you might say paraded, through the streets to a location outside Alexandria where criminals were taken to be burned. What was left of me was then incinerated.

There was a lot of blood, as you may imagine. Some of these men smeared it on their faces. Some then licked their fingers. People get carried away. How many of them woke up the next day and could not quite remember what they had done? Some of them had wives. Did the wives ask, "What is this blood on your tunic?" Most likely not. A husband with blood on his tunic is liable to be touchy about it. Cloth was beaten against stones in the stream where the washing was done, and my blood flowed down into the river and out into the sea.

A wife should keep it zipped and do the cleaning up of any messes that might prove troublesome. So on the home front lips were pressed together, topics were avoided. "Did you hear about the murder of our respected and beloved wise woman, astronomer, philosopher, jewel of Alexandria, and adviser to the Prefect?" This sentence was not spoken.

The ringleader was a lector. These lectors were educated men: you are not to imagine a rabble of ignorant peasants. In any case, they knew how to read. Or many of them did. Though once the thing got going, all sorts joined in, which is par for the course. When there's something exciting going on, who wants to feel left out?

So that's it. Why did it happen? Political, some have said. A power struggle between the Roman-appointed Prefect and the Christian bishop over who would have the final say in matters concerning Alexandria. Shock and horror were expressed; apologetic though mild reprimands occurred—"That is not the core message of our faith," and so on. A commission was set up to look into it. The bishop's bodyguard was implicated, no surprise there—those bodyguards were a notorious band of thugs and assassins—but no one was ever put on trial. There's safety in numbers. Who gouged out the first eye? And after that, who cared who exactly did what?

In the Afterlife it's a different matter, by the way. There are no more secrets; everything is known. There are trials. Evidence is presented: I proffered my ruined eyes, my wrenched-off limbs. (Such images gave rise to several iconic saints, it was later believed. Saint Catherine of Alexandria, for instance, with her severed head. Saint Lucy, with her eyes on a plate, or, in some images, on a stem with two branches and an eye on each one, like a lorgnette.)

I have never been a vengeful person. I forgave my killers, though the retribution they then faced in this other world was not under my control.

Some have said that my murder was the turning point, that it signalled the end of the so-called ancient world. Certainly a general iconoclasm followed. The incoming Christians destroyed anything that might remind people of the gods and demigods the people had once trusted and revered. Statues, inscriptions, fountains, mosaics, frescoes, vases, scrolls, papyri—all must go. When you dig up the fragments of our shattered world—Artemis minus her nose and arms, Zeus with a broken penis, a nereid with no hands, a dryad with no feet—you rejoice over the treasure you have found. Priceless, you say. And so it will be with your world in its turn. The wrecking ball is already diligently at work, though not in the name of religion, or not as such.

But though old art is destroyed, new art is created, and some of it has been created from me. Over the centuries I have been the subject of many works; noble-browed classical statues prevail, showing me as very much younger and handsomer than I actually was. Do the math: I was at least fifty at the time of my death, and frankly closer to sixty. Since no one could remember what I actually looked like—even my image in the memories of my closest associates had been blurred by their knowledge of my blood-smeared end—the sculptors had free rein, and they'd seized the opportunity. What a lot of hair I have been given! What graceful postures! What becoming drapery! Not that I'm sneering. Ask yourself: Would you rather be memorialized as your actuality, warts and all, or as an enhanced version? Be honest now.

In addition to these statues there have been several paintings of a quasi-pornographic variety, mostly from the nineteenth century—an especially pornographic era, I have observed. What interested these painters was evidently the fact that my clothes were torn off, which allowed them to paint a naked woman in distress, always of interest to a certain kind of man. In several of these paintings the woman's body has no clothes on at all; yet despite my being hauled over the cobblestones in the manner I have described to you, there is not a scratch visible on me.

In the most alarming of the paintings, my body—that of a twenty-five-year-old—is a dead-fish greenish white. It has been gifted with floor-length hair, orange in colour, which it is holding in front of its pubic area with one hand while raising the other hand and arm in a defensive gesture. Ineffectual, as history has so emphatically told us. History is always telling us such things, painters are always painting them, or they did back in the days when they were still painting images of people and incidents instead of wrapping up trees in pieces of cloth and so forth. Napoleon on the morning of Waterloo. The raft of the *Medusa*. The charge of the Light Brigade. Myself, just before being skinned and dismembered. We know how these things turned out.

But now that I've been dead for so long, what is my meaning? To you, that is, in your world, the land of the temporarily living? You might consider me lucky to have a meaning at all: most people who have been dead for as long as I have mean absolutely nothing because no one left knows anything about them at all. They have melted like ice, they have drifted away like smoke.

I, on the other hand, continue to exist among you, but as a multiplicity. Patron of female scientists. Last of the Hellenes. Minor figure in the history of Neoplatonism. Martyr to philosophy. Icon of feminists, though you'd think they'd choose someone luckier. Heroine of several not very good plays and novels, though not yet a film or streamed series. Subject of various bad though earnestly intended poems. And, ironically, example of Christian virtue. Now that should make you think.

But you called me here for a reason. You wanted me to tell you what really happened, and I've done that. Now you're asking another question: Was it worth it? My life. The life I chose to lead. Would I have been happier if I'd never been a respected public figure, if I'd followed the standard path for a woman then— got married, had children? I can't answer that, except to say that once a single choice is made it excludes the alternatives. I would probably not have ended up as a butchers' workout, but you never know. Many obscure women have been done to death merely for existing.

I try to look on the bright side: I did not have to endure the indignities of extreme old age. Which is better, I ask myself, a puddle or a sunset? Each has its charms.

FREEFORALL

✦

It is sometime in the future. Or in a future. Luckily for writers, there are many futures, and few can be explicitly disproven. Let's be vague about exactly when.

In this future, a sexually transmitted disease—or let's say a disease communicable through any sort of moist contact, including kissing—has swept through humanity, which has been forced to adapt in order to survive. The story is told from the point of view of one of the matriarchs in charge of arranging marriages among uncontaminated young people—a thing that must be done to prevent disease and to ensure the creation of microbe-free babies.

Sharmayne Humbolt Grey signed on the line provided. When she was young, her friends had called her Sharm; but her name has been eroded by time, except to old friends (not many of those left)—now, she was mostly just First Mother.

She added the date, which was in the middle of June. She still liked the idea of a June wedding, and though a lot was different now, the orange blossoms had remained. Then she sealed the document with the Least House seal. The image on it was an icon left over from the early days of the House. It showed two figures that looked like old-fashioned keyholes, a knob topping a triangle, one big, the other smaller, two sticks for legs protruding out the bottoms. They were supposed to be a mother and child, though you wouldn't know that if you weren't told.

She'd been there at the beginning, when they'd been cooking up the branding. They'd all sat around the table in what was then the dining room but was now the First Mother's Boardroom, drinking coffee and, in fact, beer, and laughing with excitement. They'd made up the House motto that day too. The Least of These. Too churchy, Sharmayne had thought then, but it had helped to raise money. They'd always needed more of that in those days, when the fabric of society had been dissolving, when the Houses were a bold new initiative, an experiment, an attempt to solve a crucial problem. She remembered with distaste the thick plates and cups, the strictly utilitarian bedspreads, the green garbage bags bulging with donated clothes, some of them none too clean. They'd taken anything they could get, and were thankful for it. Now that the House system was official policy, money was not a problem.

Sharmayne stood up, steadying herself against her desk, and turned to the full-length mirror she'd had them put into her office two years ago, after the day she'd walked into the General Meeting with her skirt caught up in the back and hadn't noticed until some of the young girls had started to giggle. Young girls still giggled, young boys still sniggered; that hadn't changed and probably never would. She didn't want to give them any extra excuses to giggle and snigger, however. If she was looking more than usually ridiculous, she wanted to be the first to spot it.

She checked herself over, starting with the shoes. Bride of Frankenstein shoes, she called them—orthopaedic to the point of despair—but she was well past breaking her neck for vanity. No laces undone; too bad about the puffy ankles, but what could you expect at eighty? Navy skirt where it should be; long sleeves with ruffles at the knuckles, a little bow at the throat, hiding all that uncooked turkey skin; the House seal in silver, on a single string of pearls around her neck. She skimmed over her face—it was a good serviceable face, but worn out by now, of course—pushed back a few strands of hair—darned if she'd dye it like that cow First Mother Mabel, henna red at seventy-nine—and straightened up as much as she could. Today she was a figurehead and needed to look like one, but they didn't just wheel her out for special occasions: she made the most important decisions, those for which her kind of experience was needed. She picked the brides, for instance.

And she'd done yesterday's deal too, though it hadn't been any pleasure. That skinflint hag First Mother Corinna from Sheltering Wings drove a hard bargain. But Sharmayne was no slouch herself—in the old days they'd put her in charge of handling overdraft problems with the banks because she knew how to negotiate.

She had prime stock to trade with; everybody knew it, including First Mother Corinna. Sharmayne had calculated that, despite her bluffing, Corinna would sacrifice at the financial end to get a guaranteed pure product, and that's what she'd done. Least House had a pristine reputation.

No one from there had ended up in the Freeforall for fifteen years, the best record of any of the Houses. Sheltering Wings prided itself on its own record, which was almost as good, as Mother Corinna had emphasized. But Sharmayne had countered with the rumour that Wings were still using turkey basters rather than in-person intimate sessions: so unnatural, almost profane! Corinna had waffled and denied but had turned a satisfying shade of red, caving on the price.

Sharmayne started walking, which was becoming a major project these days. She made her way, left foot, cane, right foot, out the door and along the corridor, pausing to lean against the wall.

Here was the door to the guest suite, for the visiting officials from other Houses. Down the hall—left foot, cane—was the door to the guest-suite nursery, still done in early-twenty-first-century Montessori. Sharmayne favoured antiques; they gave her nostalgia, an emotion she'd brusquely repressed in midlife but now felt free to indulge.

She leaned against the guest-nursery door, looking in, remembering the glee with which they'd selected the toy blocks, the little red and yellow table and chairs, at sale prices of course, gloating over their bargains. Funny, the way the Houses had started back then; shoestring operations, all of them, in the less affluent parts of the cities. They didn't take up three or four blocks each, the way they did now. Homes for battered wives, some of them had been, or shelters for abused teenage girls; a couple of them had begun as lesbian co-ops. All that idealistic stuff, with lumpy porridge and instant coffee. One of the true luxuries of life was real coffee. Sharmayne insisted on it for herself, as her status enabled her to do.

It made her cringe, thinking about how earnest and, to tell the truth, pompous and self-righteous they'd been once, her and her fellow Mothers; but if it hadn't been for them, where would everyone be now? Even the politicians had come to see that the House way was the only way the human race could make it to the next generation. The old hit-or-miss courtship rituals, the lax self-chosen monogamy, just couldn't work anymore: the death rates had become too high.

But most people had taken more convincing. Sharmayne remembered the newspaper headlines: schools and offices closed down, whole towns and suburbs sealed off; the forced testing, the breakdown of the health-care system, the witch hunts, the civil rights cases, first won, then lost again and again as rampant fear took over. Then there had been the hospital riots, the patients from the plague wards dragged into the streets by angry mobs. The ringleaders in asbestos fire-fighting suits; the smell of spilled gasoline and burning flesh.

The new class of diseases had made herpes and penicillin-resistant gonorrhea and R-strain syphilis and AIDS look as innocuous as a runny nose. These viruses spread faster, they killed faster; some mutated so quickly they couldn't even be spotted by testing. Men or women could carry them for years, undetected, spreading them everywhere.

In the end, after the rubber body stockings and the Safe-T-Lips "for kissing with confidence" had been tried and had failed too often, after the virginity certificates had proven susceptible to forgery, after the Gentlemen's Chastity Society had ended in a total washout, there was only one surefire defence: if you couldn't control the diseases, you had to avoid contact, any contact at all. That was when the Houses began to build walls and invest in barbed wire, electric fences, and walls topped with broken glass. They also began to expel rule-breakers. "These are houses of sanctuary, and this is a state of siege," Sharmayne had heard herself saying. "We must think of the children."

Sharmayne, wheezing a little, paused again on the skywalk that connected First House with Second House within the Least House compound. They could have torn down the individual Houses and built some glass-and-steel monstrosity, like that Sheltering Wings carbuncle over in Parkdale, but Sharmayne preferred to have the Houses look like real houses. It was homier that way, though the nineteenth-century brick needed a lot of upkeep.

The skywalk was one of her favourite vantage points. From here she could see the boys' playground, to the left, where the young boys were being taught the rudiments of the War Games. To the right, separated from the boys by a high wall, was the girls' playground. Sharmayne remembered her grandmother's stories about boys' and girls' playgrounds, and how comical she'd once found them.

Down in the girls' playground, the twelve-year-olds were play-ing a game of Freeforall. Each team represented a House; the playground was marked out like a giant Monopoly board, with dollhouse-sized houses. Freeforall was played like Monopoly too, though the rules had been changed to make it fit present-day reality. There were no more hotels; instead, for each House on a property, you got a bride to trade with, and for each four brides a groom. Grooms were more valuable because, as everyone knew, it was harder to find pure ones. Among the Chance cards were cards representing the various strains of disease, and where the Jail square had once been there was now a square marked Free-forall. From what Sharmayne recalled of Monopoly, you'd been able to get out of the Jail square with a special card or several rolls of the dice. But once in the Freeforall, you were in for good, in real life as in the game.

The girls' voices floated up to Sharmayne: young, boisterous with high spirits. "That mouldy cross-eyed failure isn't worth one of my Grade A brides and two Houses! I'll give you a Grade B and one House!" "What, for that reject? Get real!" Sharmayne smiled at them, a little sadly. They had to learn the principles of bargain-ing somehow—one day they might be Mothers—but they were so innocent. They'd seen the propaganda films and been properly frightened, but they had no conception of how bad the Freeforalls actually were.

Each city now had a Freeforall, or even two or three, depend-ing on how many were needed. Toronto had two: one was in a large area to the west that had once been a park; the other was to the north, in a deserted adventure playground, abandoned since the time of the epidemics, when people habitually avoided large groups of strangers. Each Freeforall had electric fences, search-

lights, attack dogs, and guard towers. Food was dropped in daily by
helicopter. There were drone overflights, but for no reason except
keeping count. Fights could break out, murders could take place,
but there was no interference from outside. Who knew what horrors went on in the shadows?

In the Freeforalls, total sexual licence was not only permitted
but encouraged, because that way, it was thought, the inhabi-
tants would finish each other off more quickly; although, it was
rumoured, you could develop an immunity or go into remission,
surviving for years. The babies, if there were any, were considered
doomed. Sometimes people took the fast way out and their bodies
could be seen from a distance, floating in a pond, dangling from a
tree, hanging from the loop of an unused roller coaster that still—
even in its present dilapidated state—appeared to promise some
version of frivolous and unfettered pleasure. Freedom, even; you
could look at it that way.

Sharmayne shivered, thinking how swiftly she herself would
have been consigned to a Freeforall once. Chastity had been out
of style, the old nuclear family was disintegrating, everyone got
divorced at least once, everyone fooled around, or so the pun-
dits declared. When she was twenty she'd listened with smiles of
polite disinterest to the horror stories of the time before the pill—
girls ruined for life, shotgun marriages, back-street abortions on
kitchen tables. She and her friends had done more or less whatever and whoever they'd felt like, taking care to avoid anyone who
looked like a loser or a maniac. There had been a certain amount
of talk about committed relationships, but sex was casual, not
something to get too emotional about. In high school they'd had
to study *Romeo and Juliet,* and it had seemed like something from
another planet. She could still hear the boys, in the halls between
classes, teasing each other in falsetto voices: "Romeo, Romeo,
wherefore fart thou, Romeo?" They'd banned that play from their

own House curriculum years ago. It gave the young people dangerous ideas.

Sharmayne peered at her big-digit watch. She had to stop woolgathering, or one of the others—someone hankering to be First Mother—would start spreading gossip about dementia. On wedding days, now as then, lateness on the part of the groom was not appreciated. The ceremony was in an hour and a half, and she still had to collect poor Tom and his escort of Best Men and get them to the Assembly Hall. They liked to do the weddings as soon as possible after the deals had been done, to avoid second thoughts and pre-empt cold feet. The groom would be told, not asked. One day he'd be playing War Games with his pals, the next he'd be married, and in a different place altogether.

First Mother Corinna would be there on the dot, accompanying Odette, who was Sheltering Wings' side of the bargain, their contribution to the future of the human race. She was a hefty girl, with a case of puppy acne; somewhat foul-mouthed and too rambunctious, as a lot of them were these days. During the interviews she'd asked a lot of questions about height and eye colour and other things that were none of her business. "That's the concern of the First Mothers," Sharmayne had finally told her. "We do the genetic planning around here. He's a good clean boy, that's all you need to know. Maybe a little temperamental, but just go easy with him at first and you'll do just fine." She would have been coached in etiquette—no disparaging remarks about genitalia, no expressions of disgust—but who knows whether she'd follow instructions?

Left foot, cane, right foot, pause. It was the next corridor, or was it the one after that? Then there were some steps: only three up, but even that was getting to be too much. She skipped over the steps in her head and went on to the Groom's Room, where they always had the party the night before, with the senior married men of Least House getting the groom drunk and telling him jokes about women to defuse the terror, and staying with him all night to make sure he wouldn't try to run away. Not that there was anywhere to run, though one unfortunate boy had been found hiding in a laundry hamper.

Later on, when she herself was no longer alive, perhaps the diseases would be extinct, starved out: gone, like smallpox, for lack of carriers. The Freeforalls would be empty. Then maybe none of these constraints and fears would be necessary. The Houses themselves believed all social behaviour was learned, and she hoped the men of those times would be allowed to have some independence, some self-respect.

Maybe this hope was just nostalgia, her secret vice. She knew it was weakness, but nevertheless she felt sorry for the grooms, and sad about trading the boys of Least House away to another House; and this boy Tom was a favourite of hers. She wondered if she should tell him what a great deal she'd been able to make for the Least House because of him. Though better not: it might give him a swelled head, and he'd need to keep his wits and a low profile during his time at Sheltering Wings. There'd been several husband-battering cases there in recent years—dismissed, of course, because you couldn't disrupt the system, but still there was probably something to it.

Just two children, she'd tell him. All you need to generate is two, that's what's in the contract. After you've completed that duty, you'll have a choice: you can stay on at Sheltering Wings and assist in one of their businesses and work your way up to Senior Husband, it's not without perks; or you can ask to be traded to another House and try potluck with another bride, if you've decided that sex is not so terrifying as you'd imagined. Or you can elect celibacy and the War Games. It will depend on what you feel like at the time. But you need to do the two children first.

She wouldn't tell him the truth about the War Games—such a

useful way of eliminating many overly aggressive and problematic males who might otherwise pose a challenge to the rule of the First Mothers. After all, he was only sixteen; time enough for the hard truths later. She'd pat his arm, pinch his cheek, cheer him up, tell him how good he looked: they liked that. She's a nice girl, she'd say, wide hips and not a germ in sight. Hardly even a pimple. No point in granular accuracy; he'd make his own discoveries soon enough.

Then she'd arrange the veil over his face: navy blue for boys, though still white for the girls, it went with the orange blossoms. Veils were obligatory these days. They covered a multitude of sins.

METEMPSYCHOSIS:

OR, THE JOURNEY OF THE SOUL

✦

They were right about the soul: there is one. But nothing else we were told was correct, as it turns out.

You've probably seen those diagrams: a so-called primitive organism, such as a snail, is shown with a globe of light glowing within it. That globe represents the soul. If the snail behaves well, upon its death the soul is allowed to reincarnate in a supposedly higher organism, such as a fish. Hopping from one organic stepping stone to another—or, rather, because the soul's progress is not believed to be horizontal but vertical, from one rung of the ladder on the Great Chain of Being to another—the soul of the well-behaved snail finally arrives at the pinnacle of creation, and—oh joy!—is reborn as a human being. So goes the story.

But I'm here to tell you that very little about this fantasy is true.

For instance, I myself jumped directly from snail to human, with no guppies, basking sharks, whales, beetles, turtles, alligators, skunks, naked mole rats, aardvarks, elephants, or orangutans in between. Nor was I even forced to be conceived, gestated, born, and then raised from infancy, with all the mucus, blood, burping, vomit, urine, rashes, teething, tantrums, pain, and weeping this process entails.

I was demolishing a lettuce leaf, my oval raspy-toothed mouth opening and closing like a flesh valve as I oozed along on my own self-generated glistening slime highway. The lovely green blur all around me, the lacework I was creating, the scent of chlorophyll, the juiciness—it was pure bliss. Live in the moment, humans are often told, but snails don't need to be told. We're in the moment all the time, and the moment is in us.

What happened next? Some guy intent on exterminating me got busy with the environmentally friendly pesticide, which—and I shouldn't be telling you this—was cold coffee in a spray bottle, to which had been added half a cup of salt. *Wait!* I ought to have screamed as the first scalding droplets hit my tender neck. *Spare me! I am part of an ecosystem! I contribute to the eggshells of birds!*

Did I know that then? No. Snails are not focused on their place in the universe. I've researched the bird-shell connection since; it has to do with ingested calcium. (I couldn't have screamed, anyway: snails are notoriously mute.)

I didn't even have time to retract my stalked eyes and withdraw into my protective carapace. My miniature snail soul, a translucent spiral of softly phosphorescent light, shot into the air—the spirit air, you must understand, where the rules are somewhat different—and made its way through the iridescent rainbow clouds and the tinkling bells and theremin woo-woo sounds of that region, then straight into the body of a mid-level female customer service representative at one of the major banks.

I won't tell you which bank. I'm guessing the top brass would be less than pleased to discover that one of their customer service representatives is, au coeur, a snail. Not even an exotic snail. The common garden variety.

"How may I help you?" I found myself saying. My mouth felt stiff; this mouth of a woman was not as flexible as my snail mouth, and its teeth were clumsily block-shaped. Needless to say, I felt

disembodied, also radically unsuited to the work my human casement had apparently been trained to do. This work consisted of
answering calls from distraught members of the banking public
who claimed to have experienced maltreatment. The bank had
lost their money, or some of their money, or had calculated their
interest wrong. The bank had misreported. The bank had failed to
provide cheques in a timely manner, leading to unpaid bills, and
no, digital cheques were not acceptable. The bank had sold them
some banking product or service they did not want. The bank's
anti-hacking defences were crap.

My human casement had been extensively trained to soothe, to
mollify, to reassure. It ran on autopilot, like a flesh robot. It pronounced the word *rectify* a lot.

Curled within the shell of the human woman's skull where our
two souls were space-sharing, I found myself muttering, "Why are
you whining? At least no one sprayed you with snail pesticide."
In fact, these words actually came out through my human mouth
while a customer was still on the phone.

"Snail pesticide? Excuse me?"

People don't want you to excuse them when they say, "Excuse
me." I've learned that. They want you to know you've offended
them. "I'm so sorry," my human mouth said. "We seem to have
had some interference from a radio station. It cuts in on our fre-
quency. It's happened before." The woman-shaped snail refuge
within which I was sheltering had no compunction about lying,
it seemed. But I myself was bewildered: snails never lie, so they
don't recognize lying as a category.

I was shortly to encounter another variety of customer, more
plaintive, more hopeless. These had replied to text messages
purporting to be from the bank that had claimed there was an
irregularity with their account and had then asked them to verify
their details. This they had obligingly done, only to find that the

message hadn't been from the bank at all but from a scammer who'd cleaned out their life savings.

"How upsetting," the woman's face would murmur. "I'll refer you to our fraud squad."

"But what about all my money? Is it gone? Will I get it back?"

"I'm transferring you now."

Snails don't have any money. They don't need money. Yet here I was, forced to witness these irritating conversations about a subject that meant nothing to me.

With considerable exercise of my snail will, I usurped control of our joint mouth and spoke through it as myself. "You replied to the message?" I said to the seventh unwary victim. "You gave them your passcodes? That was certainly effing stupid!"

"Excuse me?"

What was I doing in this uncalled-for body? What force chained me in this room, to this desk, to this phone? My transition from my snail body had been so rapid I didn't even know what this new carapace looked like! Of course, I hadn't known what I looked like when I was a snail either. Snails have no interest in mirrors.

At last the clock said five. My human brain—the thinking-meat part of this foreign body, and let me inform you that the soul is indeed distinct from the brain—this human brain knew about clocks. So I, or perhaps she, could log out and head for the washroom. New torments awaited me there.

We were working from a place that was supposed to be "home," due to something called COVID. (This was a virus. Snails have their own viruses, and also many parasites—let us not even mention rat lungworm—but COVID is not among them.) So the bathroom was "mine," if I may use such a possessive pronoun of a room that, although familiar in a hazy way, felt utterly alien. It was suffused with overpowering aromas. I detected what I would later learn were almond soap, lemon air freshener, and a scented candle: rose petals and orange blossoms. This last was the most tempting. I resisted the impulse to eat it.

Our next act was to look in the mirror. There was a face, a hair-fringed face, a face with an ugly protruding nose in the middle of it, a symmetrical human face I'd certainly seen before, or shall we say my mirror image was a mirage that generated a similar mirage in the brain tissue that enclosed my tiny whorled snail soul. It was a good enough face as they go, I suppose. Humans would find it appealing. There were no large warts on it. I discovered that I could make it smile and frown. I put the face through its motions, to see what sort of range was available. I stuck out its tongue. At last, I thought, a body part I could identify with: moist, flexible, retractable, with chemical sensors on it. Very much like a snail, despite the pinkish colour.

My interest in tongue-manipulating was soon exhausted, and I veered to other matters. Although snails do have eyes, our vision is limited: we examine our surroundings through touch and smell. But although I had a strong desire to get down on all fours and lick the floor, I controlled it. I could not really run my borrowed tongue over everything in this bathroom. I would need to focus. I turned my attention to the fixtures.

There was a sink in this bathroom. In addition, there was a toilet. I did not at that moment know the terminology, although I deduced the purpose. Need I tell you how appalling I found this hard, shiny, water-filled appliance, not to mention the bodily functions it was designed to accommodate? Snails do not give much thought to their excretions, which are innocuous and of a pleasing shade of green. I would have preferred to ignore the whole shooting match, as it were, but I had little choice in the matter. It was the floor, the toilet, or burst. Our body held its breath and availed itself.

In this bathroom there was also a tub with a shower. Human

bodies are very dry on the outside, lacking that luxurious coating of mucus that renders the bodies of snails—apart from their shells—so lithe and sinuous. The thought of immersing myself in water was greatly appealing to me. We shed the sweatpants and the long-sleeved shirt that said This Is Not a Drill—it had a picture of a hammer on it, a joke that at the time I failed to grasp—and slid into the warm water that a twist of a faucet handle had caused to emerge from the tap.

I was soaking in the tub, trying not to look at the daunting expanse of wet mammal flesh extending downward from my neck while feeling my tissues becoming more gastropodal by the minute, when the bathroom door opened. "Hi, beautiful," said a voice.

The word *beautiful* must have been meant for our shared body, as it was the only visible living entity in the room. Nonetheless I was startled. Instinctively I attempted to withdraw into my shell before remembering that I no longer had one. The door opened farther, and another human entered the room. As he was an adult male, his vibrations were alarmingly similar to those of the oaf who had so recently sprayed me with snail killer.

This male was carrying a large paper bag. A nauseating stench of burnt meat permeated the air. Some species of snails are carnivores, but I am not of that ilk.

"I got ribs," said the deeply reverberating voice. This conveyed nothing to me. "I got some cornbread too. I know you like that."

"Great," we managed to quaver. "Ribs."

"And a bottle of Pinot. So when you've got your luscious bod out of the tub, we'll eat, and then maybe . . . Netflix?" He pronounced this last word like a caress.

"Netflix . . . ," we whispered. The hominid brain imprisoning me seemed to recall the term. Was it some kind of food?

The man, whom I now recognized as a sort of quasi-mate, contorted his facial muscles into a lopsided grin and engaged in eye contact, a look I registered as a type of sexual signalling, like the first tentative brush of one tender snail tentacle against another's. "Some like it hot," he said enigmatically as he went out, failing to close the door behind him.

We clambered us out of the tub, then called upon muscle memory for the sequence of movements that followed. We pat-dried our now-wrinkled skin, inspected our toes—how odd to have two feet! Snails have only one—and manoeuvred us into the not entirely clean robe that was hanging on the hook beside the door. It was a sickly shade of pink, like the tongue. Our hair was damp: this caused me to experience anxiety. Snails never have to worry about hair, whereas—as I was soon to discover—humans fret about it constantly. Having it, not having it, arranging it, deriding it when arranged by others, twisting it, braiding it, piling it up, cutting it off, pulling it out . . . In their rummaging through the distant past in search of their prehistoric origins, a thing that obsesses them, humans could do worse than hair as a leitmotif.

We wrapped our hair in another towel and crept cautiously out into the main room. The boyfriend—for such he was—had arranged the ribs and cornbread on two plates, with a side of slaw on each. These were on a small table beside a window. It seemed we lived in a condo, with a view. The view was of other condo buildings, a lake, a sky. Did the human brain remember this view? It did. Was this memory overwriting my snail memories, like a palimpsest? It was. I felt dizzy. It was all too much to take in.

I sat us down in the chair provided. "Is there any lettuce?" I asked faintly.

"I got slaw." The boyfriend grinned, the foreboding grin of an omnivore. How to explain to him that I couldn't eat the slaw? The vinegar in the dressing, which my snail sensors could detect a mile off, might as well have been fire.

The boyfriend was uncapping a bottle of beer. This was better news. Snails love beer; they like the yeast, as it smells like ferment-ing vegetation. Beer, I am sorry to say, is often used to drown us.

"I'd rather have lettuce. I've got some sort of tummy bug. It's easy to digest. Is there some?"

"Dunno," he said. He opened a white door, looked inside. Oh yes, the human brain reminded me. A refrigerator. "Nope. Guess we ate it. There's a carrot."

"I'll have a beer too," I said.

"You? You hate the stuff!"

"Not anymore," I said.

"Anything for you, babe," he said. "Even my beer!" Our mouth took a sip from the proffered bottle: at last, something in this human life I could enjoy.

I toyed with the carrot—it was not rotten, so it was too hard. Then I ventured a small piece of cornbread, but it was too harsh: like sand. The boyfriend, Tyler—his name had appeared in my consciousness as a set of indistinct letters, as if written in mist—gnawed on the ribs, holding each of them in his large paws and wrenching the flesh off the bone with his enormous white teeth. How uncouth was this process—how unlike the delicate rasp-ing motions practised by snails! I watched him, repelled but fascinated.

"Not hungry, babe?" he asked between gollops.

"Not much," I said in my bank service representative voice, smiling in a manner I intended to be agreeable. I hoped the beer contained some nourishment. If I got stuck in this human body for much longer, what was I going to eat? Tomorrow I would take the body shopping. Lay in a supply of pea sprouts and some over-ripe fruit.

"How was your day?" said Tyler. Through what was rapidly becoming a beery haze I eyed him across the table. I could see he was attractive, in the human sense. He had a lot of hair, dark in colour, and some muscles.

"Oh, the usual," I said. "But I think I was rude to a customer."

"You?" he said. "No way!" He barked out a laugh, ejecting small bits of rib. "You couldn't be rude to Godzilla!"

So that was the persona of my woman host, back before she'd had a snail move in on her: she'd been limp, flaccid, a flimsy pushover. Was that why she'd been available to my soul? No inner strength? "I bet they were monitoring the calls. I might get fired," I said. I was hopeful about this rather than otherwise.

"Fat chance," he said. "You're too good for that job. Shit, you're too good for me!" He came around behind and began massaging our shoulders. He would get smelly meat juice on the pink robe. I had a fuzzy mental image of a washing machine: Did we have one? He kissed our neck and gave it an exploratory lick.

This was a courtship move—even among the snails it would have been received as such—and shortly he and our body were engaged in the early stages of a coupling event, which then led with unseemly rapidity to the later stages, with my small green soul enmeshed in the proceedings like a toddler strapped onto a bullet train. How crude are the sexual procedures of humans compared with those of snails! How precipitous! No slow slippery caresses of tentacles, no intertwining, no tantalizingly voluptuous wreathing and writhing. Snails can go on for hours. But not so humans.

How could I explain what I wanted? I couldn't just blurt out, "I'm a hermaphrodite." It would not have been understood. Nor could I tell the boyfriend that I wished to insert my penis into his genital pore—it would have been somewhere near his ear, if he'd had such a pore—at the same time he was inserting his into mine. And I especially could not tell him that I wished to fire a love dart into him, to give my sperm a better chance at fertilizing his eggs. My rational human brain-mind knew that he didn't have any eggs, but sex isn't rational, is it? It's about feelings, and that is how I felt.

I didn't have any love darts anyway. A long steak knife would have made a poor substitute, and might in fact have killed him. I wouldn't have wanted that. But urges are urges. I could barely restrain myself.

"Something wrong, babe? You seemed different," Tyler said upon completion of the act.

"I don't feel like myself." How much could I reveal without being taken for an out-and-out lunatic?

"Like, how?"

"There's something wrong with my body."

There was a pause. By this time it was dark: I could not see Tyler's face. He must have been thinking. The hand that had been stroking my hair withdrew.

"Oh," he said. "You're maybe coming down with something."

"No," I said. "I'm perfectly fine. But this body doesn't feel like mine."

"How do you mean? It's a great body."

"Maybe for someone else," I said. "Just not for me. I ought to be in a different body."

There was a long pause, which I took to be a symptom of thought. "You want to see someone about that?" he said carefully, more as a statement than a question.

"Yes," I said. "I think I should." I noticed that he hadn't asked what sort of body I felt I ought to be in.

Tyler worked as a sound man in the television business, so finding a psychiatrist was not difficult for him. This doctor came highly recommended by a friend, he said. He was used to dealing with unusual people.

"What do you mean by unusual?" I asked.

"Oh, you know. Actors."

It took a couple of weeks to arrange an appointment, during which time I slid further into my human incarnation, as if pulling on a rubber suit. By now, via the neural pathways of my human brain, I had almost total recall of my woman host's days and ways. I knew what was expected of me in this disguise; I mouthed the phrases, I performed the rituals, but I remained convinced that I was really a terrestrial gastropod. At night I would curl up as tightly as I could and pull the sheet up over my head. My dreams would be of leaves, of damp logs, and of other snails.

The psychiatrist was a short man with glasses and a moustache who looked like a child's cartoon of a psychiatrist. He had a notebook. He opened it and asked me what my problem seemed to be. I told him I was worried about having a nose. He tried not to show surprise.

"Ah," he said. "Body dysmorphia."

"No," I said. I'd been reading up on the terms. "I don't want a different nose. I don't want to have a nose at all. I mean, not one that sticks out."

"Have you considered plastic surgery?" This was a ploy called "entering into the patient's delusion." I was ready for it.

"I don't want this body altered," I said. "I want it removed. I'm in the wrong body altogether."

"Ah," he said again. "You are in the wrong body."

"I'm not a man," I said. "If you were wondering."

"Ah." He looked disappointed, but at the same time interested. He fiddled with his pen. Did he sense a peer-reviewed research paper coming on?

"But I do have a penis," I said. "Though it's not a human penis. The real me does."

"Ah?"

"It's near my ear."

He looked confused. He placed his pen on the desk.

"I also have eggs," I said. "And a love dart. I mean, in my real body. The one I'm not in right now."

"A love dart?" His eyebrows went up. "You have a weapon?"

"Not exactly a weapon. It's a gypsobelum," I said. "It's made of calcium. I shoot it into my mate. I mean, I would, if I was in my real body."

"Ah." He was staring at me with some alarm. Not only at me, but past me at the door, which was behind me.

"Not shoot like a gun," I said. "More like a sort of blowpipe."

"I see," he said. "And your real body, you say . . ."

"I'm actually a snail."

There was a silence. "I believe that's our time," he said, though there was at least five minutes to go. "I'll see you next week?"

"I don't think you can help me," I said, gathering up my purse. It had taken me a while to acclimatize myself to this purse. Snails have no use for purses.

I left his office in a state of despair. For what crime am I being punished? I asked myself. What did I do so wrong, back when I was a snail? How long will I be confined to this purgatory? What are the penances I must perform in order to free myself?

Possibly, I thought, it was a religious problem. I began to frequent churches, sidling into them when few people were inside. They were dim and dampish, like the undersides of leaves, and they smelled faintly of mould, a smell I found comforting. I began to pray. *Oh God, or whoever's responsible for this mess, please get me*

*out of here! Let my little soul out of this ungainly giant cage! I don't have
to go back into a snail, though I would prefer that. Maybe a tortoise? A
frog? No, too eventful. Something placid, something vegetarian . . .*

Then I began to have doubts. What if I didn't have the soul of
a snail after all? What if I really was this woman—Amber was her
name—what if I was Amber, and had always been Amber, and was
having a psychotic break? Why had that happened? Should I try
to erase all memories of my snail existence? Would that make
me happier? The mere thought of such a thing drove me frantic.
Should I jump off our condo balcony, put an end to this unloved
body in the hope of reincarnating once again? But I might end up
in something worse. A leech. An eyebrow mite. At the very least,
a slug.

That phase passed, with the aid of some THC gummies procured
for me by Tyler. This was kind of him. I found that if I got sufficiently stoned I could tolerate his form of coupling well enough,
and even enjoy it sometimes. I decided that since I couldn't get off
the bus I might as well appreciate the tour, so I and my purloined
body did our best.

After another two weeks I lost my job as a bank service representative. In truth, I more or less quit. I didn't have the energy for
the work—all those unhappy voices—and I had no interest in anything they said. Who cared about GICs? Not me. "Interest" and
"exchange rate" were inventions that had no relationship to the
real world: they did not eat, breed, or defecate. These fragments
of the human ideosphere swirled around me like smoke, ever-
changing, impossible to grasp in any tangible or satisfying way.

After leaving the employ of the bank I took to snoozing in our
condo, coiled in the beanbag chair, with my tiny spiral soul glowing inside its carnal domicile. When not asleep I dozed, in a liminal
state that felt to me as if I'd been hypnotized. I spent hours gazing
at the hands—the whorls on the fingertips, the lines wandering

over the surfaces of the palms—imagining what it would be like to slide on my slippery tongue-like snail foot along the pathways of my own skin.

Tyler began asking when I would start looking for another job. I assumed he was anxious because I was no longer contributing my share of the rent, but his anxiety left me indifferent. Then he said maybe I had a condition—mononucleosis, was his guess—and shouldn't I see a doctor? I said I was just tired a lot. He said that wasn't normal, plus I was losing weight: I had to eat something more than vegetables. I said I would try, but meanwhile could he get some more lettuce? We seemed to have run out. The farmers' market would be a good place for it, I said. They'd have local produce. Once Tyler had gone off with his reusable shopping bag, I turned the beanbag chair upside down and withdrew under it. So warm and dark, and slightly moist.

As we were eating lunch—a lovely salad, though Tyler's had bacon on it—Tyler found a snail on his romaine. "Proves it's organic," he said. He stood up. "I'll just flush the little fucker down the toilet."

"No," I cried. Or I thought I cried, but no sound came out. I'd lost my voice. Was I speechless with horror? Now that Tyler had been revealed as a murderer, I couldn't possibly stay with him. While he was in the bathroom doing away with my relative, I walked quietly out of our condo and along the hall to the elevator. I was still wearing my sweatpants and T-shirt, with only a light fall coat on over them. Where could I go?

I headed for the nearest park, but it was too open. The bird-filled sky was frightening to me. I found a railway bridge and crouched underneath it, against the dank cement wall. I would stay there, I decided. It was October: I would nudge down into the soil before it froze; I would hibernate. If only I could make my way slowly up the wall to the enticing weeds that I could see through a gap in the ironwork . . . But no, this could not work because I was not a snail. Or was I?

I stuck it out for several hours, crouching, hugging myself, shivering, ignored by passersby. Someone gave me two dollars. I could feel my tissues contracting, shrivelling up. Thirst drove me back to the condo.

"Where did you go, babe?" Tyler asked as I was gulping water in the kitchen.

"Out," I managed to croak. I collapsed into his arms: I must have fainted.

When I woke up, I was in a hospital with an IV line stuck into my arm. Severe dehydration, they said. Also malnutrition. Nourishing soup, gelatin desserts, custards: these were prescribed. I managed to ingest them, although it was an effort. At least they were damp.

Now I'm back at the condo. Tyler is seldom here. He says he goes to the gym, but no one can go to the gym that much. He's avoiding me. In fact, he may be a little afraid of me. Naturally he has another woman he is coupling with—a substitute form of strenuous gym-like exercise for him, no doubt. I can smell her musky perfume on him a mile away. But I don't care: although snails experience passion, they don't understand jealousy. Perhaps this boyfriend-poacher would like to entwine herself with both of us, I speculate idly. Should I suggest it to Tyler? Snails enjoy threesomes. This into that into this into that, a sort of floral wreath of silky but muscular interconnection . . . No, Tyler is at heart a puritan—you can tell by his addiction to the gym—and like all good puritans he is monogamous in his inclinations. Such a pity.

The days pass. I'm biding my time. I'm meditating. Perhaps my understanding of this phenomenon has been upside down. Perhaps I was a woman to begin with—maybe even this particular woman, Amber, with her wardrobe of jokey T-shirts—and I was sent into a snail in order to learn something of deep importance to my soul. But what could that be? To pay homage to the immediate, such as the rich veins and cells of edible greens and the heady, intoxicating scent of decaying pears? To appreciate the simple joys of the universe, such as congress with a fellow snail, or snails? Was that it? What am I missing? It is what it is? I am what I am? What am I?

Why must I suffer? The ultimate puzzle. That is what it is to be human, I suppose: to question the terms of existence.

But it's not all penitential. There are upsides. Snails in their own bodies cannot see the stars, but through these borrowed eyes I have now seen them. The stars are magnificent. Perhaps I will have memories of them when I am a snail again, if I am ever permitted that grace.

There must be a purpose. I must be learning something. I can't believe this is all random.

I must stay positive until my present skin-and-tissue host wears out. Then my small bright spiral soul will rise and fly through the iridescent clouds and minor-key music of the intermediate spirit realm, to embody itself once more. But as what?

Any husk other than this one. Any shell other than this.

AIRBORNE:

A SYMPOSIUM

+

Myrna arrives at Chrissy's house and rings the doorbell. The chimes play, to no avail. She walks in.

"It's me," she calls, or more like yells. "You shouldn't leave the door unlocked! I might be a serial killer!"

"Coming in a minute," Chrissy yells back from somewhere inside.

The pink-tiled hallway is at least cooler. Myrna checks herself in the big oblong mirror—a turquoise wooden frame, a knot of ribbons carved at the top, with an implication of French Provincial. Chrissy can never resist the so-called antique shops, however sham their contents. Other people's leftovers; as, once, Chrissy's taste in men. Really, that thing should be in a bedroom.

"Crap, it's hot," Myrna mutters to herself, pulling off her straw sunhat, pushing back a few limp strands of her overly magenta hair. She shouldn't have let Antonio of the silver scissors have his way. He did apologize obliquely for how it had come out. They could adjust the colour the next time, he'd said, and meanwhile it was certainly dramatic, so enjoy.

Also, she shouldn't have worn this sleeveless dress, for a couple of reasons: one, sunburn; two, flabby triceps. The hand weights have not been enough, though if she'd done more than look at them things might be different. Green is not her colour. Or not this lime green, which makes her skin look jaundiced.

Why so vain? she asks her reflection. It's far too late for vanity. Nobody cares what you look like, not anymore.

She makes her way into Chrissy's living room. The oatmeal-toned carpet feels spongy underfoot, like damp moss: Toronto used to be in a swamp; still is, as far as the humidity's concerned. Everything is as usual: the Mexican vase of dried flowers and branches sprayed mauve and aqua and silver, the throw cushions with embroidered motifs from the women's collective in Bangladesh, the framed blow-up of the rejected cover design of Chrissy's one and only successful book, *Airborne: Women Aloft*. This is the cover Chrissy had longed for, but the one they'd actually foisted on her had been much more basic: orange, with a small image of an ultralight biplane on it. Cover images needed to be crisp, they'd said. They needed to be visible on cellphones.

Airborne was an excursion into cross-disciplinary feminist analysis, or so Chrissy had claimed. (Pseudo-piffle, Myrna had glossed. She considered herself more rigorous.) Chrissy had once taught mythology and folklore at Toronto's third-ranked university; her book had begun as an academic paper on imagined females who denied the laws of gravity.

But *Airborne* didn't stop at Iris, the rainbow messenger of the gods; or the winged and clawed harpies; or the old woman tossed up in a basket of nursery rhyme; or the Flower Fairies of Cicely Barker; or Mary Poppins descending from a cloud with the aid of a magic umbrella; or Tinker Bell, the tiny, sparkly imp in *Peter Pan*; or the well-meaning Benandanti of Italy battling the spiteful witches in the air to save the harvest; or Dorothy of Oz and her little dog, Toto, so frequently aloft. Chrissy had segued from fiction and myth into real life: women shot from cannons, scantily clad lady acrobats falling to their deaths, Amelia Earhart and her mysterious disappearance, and the Night Witches, that band of dauntless Soviet girl pilots in their plywood biplanes who'd rained down death under cover of darkness in World War Two.

What did such flying women mean to those who observed them, either on the page or from below? Chrissy had proposed several theories. Sexual sadism was one—some people might like to watch beautiful acrobats flailing and terrified—and the understandable female desire to escape the constraints of their earth-bound physical bodies was another. What girl hadn't had dreams of liftoff?

Some purchasers had complained: they'd thought they were getting a book about Allied fighter squadrons and found a bunch of fairies. "Fucking fairies," to be precise, thought Myrna, who'd read some of the outraged letters Chrissy had received. Why hadn't they consulted the table of contents? Chrissy had asked plaintively. Why did they say such nasty things? *Stupid feminazi bitch* was not a term you'd employ in a serious academic debate, though *feminazi* had first come from a university professor. And why had two reviewers used the word *frivolous* about her mind, while a third had jeered *airhead*?

"If you publish a book and you've got a C-word body part, you're a hate magnet," Leonie had comforted Chrissy. "Automatic. Happens to us all." She'd added, as she frequently did, "It was worse during the French Revolution. You could get your head cut off for not saying 'Citizen.'" The French Revolution was Leonie's own specialty. She'd taught it at Toronto's second-rated university, back when history still had some cachet.

She too had published a book: *Thermidor!* She'd originally tried the academic publishers, but no dice: the emphasis on sensationalistic violence made it difficult to take the book seriously, they'd said. A medium-sized commercial publisher had seen possibilities, however. They'd removed Leonie's subtitle, which had been "Extra-judicial Political Reprisals and Grudge Killings During the Thermidorian Reaction of the French Revolution, and Their Legacy for Today." Too stuffy, they'd said. They'd added the exclamation mark to make the book feel more dramatic, and used a plain red background, with maroon Belle Epoque lettering based on late-nineteenth-century Toulouse-Lautrec posters. When Leonie had protested the anachronism, there were wide-eyed stares from the editors: It was French, wasn't it? And didn't the colour suggest dried blood? What more could she ask for?

This cover had been a disaster, according to Leonie. Naturally she'd been attacked by a few academic pedants over the ahistorical lettering, but some ordinary bookstore customers had mistaken *Thermidor!* for a seafood cookbook with an emphasis on lobsters—the favourite crustacean of Toulouse-Lautrec—and were upset to be confronted with a drawing of Olympe de Gouges being guillotined for demanding liberty, equality, and fraternity for women, a full-colour painting of Robespierre as he was shot in the face, and an etching of vengeful counter-revolutionaries massacring Jacobin prisoners with sabres, cudgels, and pistols. What sort of bloodthirsty monster was she, to be interested in such depraved material?

Leonie too had received nasty letters. Most of the letter-writers hadn't actually read the book but were reacting to Leonie's photo, attached to the newspaper reviews. There had been a number of reviews, as mass executions and cultural panics were attention-worthy, said the cultural editors. Some of the male letter-writers accused Leonie of having made it impossible for them to get a job; others simply hurled the standard epithets—"Dumb cow," "Ugly pig," "Twisted c__t," and the like—to which had been added, from women, "You must be sick," "Why are you so negative?" and, the coup de grâce, "I was so disappointed."

"Don't mind all this," Myrna had counselled Leonie, who'd been upset and had actually cried. Well, almost cried; real crying was not a thing her generation allowed itself in public. It was too weak and womanish: those stereotypes needed to be stamped out, hard. "A lot of people liked your book."

"Not enough people," said Leonie. "The rest made vulgar comments."

"Vulgar comments are as old as writing. You should see the tavern walls of Pompeii."

"The tavern walls of Pompeii can piss off," Leonie sniffed. "Am I a twisted c__t?"

"No more than most," said Myrna.

"It's history, it's what happened, it's what people did. Why am I getting it in the neck for writing about it?"

"Most people don't want to know what people did," said Myrna. "They prefer to eat lobsters." I'm with them, she'd added to herself. Cut-off heads do not spark joy, so why bother about them? Yes, it happened, but not everyone craves the pure clear glare of Truth.

Myrna had once studied insults and abrasive language as a social and linguistic phenomenon. She still studies them since her retirement from Toronto's top-rated university, though as a private citizen. She's noted the growing use of *disappointed* among critically inclined online females: it has almost replaced *shocked and outraged* as a stealth weapon, much as a faster virus variant replaces a more sluggish rival.

Meanwhile, here is Chrissy's rejected cover presiding over the living room. A pale blue sky, a colourful Victorian hot-air balloon. Three gloved and beruffled young ladies—periwinkle, rose, and mimosa—in broad hats with veils tied under their chins perch in the wicker gondola. They wave happily at the viewer while they sail over trees and rooftops and spires and rivers, risking a little danger, taking in the overview. The sun is setting, or perhaps rising, from or into a froth of pink clouds. Fair weather ahead, or foul? Chrissy has never been definitive on that point.

Leonie has already arrived. She's wasted no time: she has a glass in hand, G and T with lime, her habitual tipple. She's reclining on the cherry velvet chaise longue, stretching out her extensive legs. White patio pants, scarlet platforms, a riotous floral top. Big dangly earrings, orange plastic. She's not wearing a wig today; her off-white hair is wispy, still growing back after the second bout of chemo. She's coloured in her eyebrows. Right after the operation and then the radiation she had a phase during which she painted cat whiskers on her face, but she's over that now.

"Hot enough for you?" Leonie says. A standard opener from forty years ago. Now it would be something with *fuck* in it, Myrna reflects. It's every second word with her teenage grandkids. The littlest ones haven't got there yet, being still at the poo-poo stage.

Fuck used to be unprintable, whereas racial and ethnic slurs were common, but now that has flipped. Myrna takes note of all such verbal mutations, what can't be said having been a leitmotif in human cultures forever. Slanderers and scatologists, form in line here; casual oath-swearers and blasphemers, over there. Taboo words that will bring bad luck, to the rear please. As for *fuck*, she once published a paper on it in *Maledicta: The International Journal of Verbal Aggression*. "'Fuck You' and 'Good Fuck': Negative and Positive Values for a Problematic Word."

"Like an oven," Myrna says. "But give it four months and we'll be moaning about the cold." She could have said We'll pay for it later, an acceptable standard reply. She could have also tried We'll fucking pay for it later, or would that be We'll pay for it fucking later? Or maybe We'll totally pay for it fucking later.

Did she just use *totally* as a modifier? Horrid locution! How easy it is to get sucked down the verbal drain into the bottomless pit of word fashions.

"My God, what happened to your hair?" says Leonie. "Is it beet juice?"

"Run-in with a wizard," says Myrna. "He tried to turn me into an orangutan, but it only half worked."

"It'll grow out," says Leonie. Then, sensing she's been too blunt, she backtracks: "I mean, it does look kind of amazing."

"Thanks. So does yours," says Myrna. Fucking hell, she thinks. Leonie, with a 20 per cent probability of being alive in three months, plus her partner of forty-six years is in a care facility and thinks he's a bomber pilot, and we're discussing hair?

She eyes the impromptu bar Chrissy has set up on a side table: bottles and glasses, ice in a metal kitchen mixing bowl, a smaller bowl with lemon and lime wedges. Cans of Coke and ginger ale, bottles of Perrier. She's so thirsty she could swill the lot. She selects a Perrier, unscrews the top.

"Take two, they're cheap," says Leonie. "Don't worry, I'm going easy on the G this time. Doctor's orders." She laughs, a little raucously. "I overdid it at the last meeting."

The last meeting was almost a year ago, before Leonie's diagnosis. Myrna remembers the overdoing part all too clearly: she'd had to call a taxi, then stuff Leonie into it. No way Leonie should have been allowed to drive; she might have run over some hapless dog-walker. Myrna had had her work cut out, being a mere five three, whereas Leonie is five ten, not counting the platforms.

She shouldn't be drinking at all, thinks Myrna. She should be on nothing but kale juice. And blueberries, a lot of blueberries.

Chrissy hurries in, carrying a fuchsia-and-ultramarine bowl of black olives and a cerulean plate with veggie puffs. She sets the olives and the puffs down on the glass-topped coffee table beside the stack of tiny cutwork cocktail napkins, a pink rosebud embroidered on each. She's wearing a floaty mauve garment that resembles a child's pinafore; her thin, freckled arms are bare, except for a couple of beaded bracelets. Glass earrings shaped like bunches of grapes, lilac in colour, tinkle faintly. Her grey-blond hair is in a ponytail held by an azure scrunchie with—could it be?—a unicorn pattern. It would be impolite to notice the unicorns out loud, Myrna decides.

"You're on time," Chrissy says reproachfully. "Though Leonie was actually early!"

"Sorry, not sorry," says Leonie. "Here we all are, anyway. Gaggle of hags. Except for Darlene."

Gaggle, thinks Myrna. From the German. Denoting a sound made either by a group of geese or a group of women. *Cackle* might seem to derive from the same root, but is actually . . .

"Darlene has bailed," says Chrissy. "I think I need a spritzer."

"Is she sick?" Myrna asks. So many people are.

"No, sorry, I was unclear. I should have said resigned," says Chrissy, manoeuvring a bottle and glass. "From our committee. Says we don't need the controversy."

"What controversy?" Myrna asks.

"Well, she's a dean," says Chrissy. "Also a biologist. Biologists are always getting in trouble, nobody understands them. Probably they shouldn't be deans."

"But we need Darlene! We're a train wreck without her! What *happened*?" says Leonie. "She said all shit stinks, or what?"

"She was on the radio," says Chrissy. "On a panel."

"Panels!" says Leonie. "Kill me first!"

Not all panels are bad, in Myrna's opinion. She'd been on one discussing Anglo-Saxon weather kennings. That had been fun. "What sort of panel?" she asks.

Chrissy drops her voice. "Gender."

"Fuck," says Leonie. "Snake pit!"

"You know Darlene, she's so unsuspecting. She'd been asked to talk about diversity in nature, so she brought up this thing called slime moulds. They're like formless blobs. She said they can solve problems." Chrissy paused. "Also, they have seven hundred and twenty sexes."

"That's about seven hundred too many," says Leonie.

"Exactly," says Chrissy. "That part didn't make anyone happy! Some of the panellists thought she was calling them a slime mould, and the others said she was against women."

"To be fair, slime moulds aren't reassuring," says Myrna.

"Not to those people. They want everything to come in twos, and only twos. Closed boxes. Night and day. Black and white. Men and women."

"Damned and saved," says Leonie. "Very puritanical. Very revolutionary: for or against, off with their heads. So Darlene got put into the damned box?"

"More or less," says Chrissy. "It blew up on Twitter. Only for about one minute, but still. Universities are very sensitive about their images. She had to issue a statement saying she misspoke."

"Darlene never misspeaks," says Leonie. "She's very precise."

"I know," says Chrissy. "I said she *said* she misspoke. That's what deans have to say if they annoy people."

"*Misspoke*," says Myrna. "You might believe that word is an ugly modern concoction, but it's actually fourteenth-century."

"How interesting," says Chrissy vaguely. "I've got a new cheese, from that little shop. It's an ashed goat, it's named after Cinderella. Because of the ashes, I guess."

162 + MARGARET ATWOOD

"A pox on the controversy," says Leonie. "We can handle that. Darlene thinks the three of us never had any controversy before? We want her back on the committee."

"She says she's too polarizing," says Chrissy. "She says she doesn't want to jinx the project."

"Polarizing? Praise the lady lord I no longer toil in the groves of academe," says Leonie. "Reign of Terror in there."

"We went through some of that ourselves," says Myrna. "Back in the day. Remember the fights over *womyn* with a Y?" Not to be confused with *wymmen,* she reminds herself, which is not a modern invention, but a Middle English . . .

"It never caught on, really," says Leonie. "Except among a few sects."

"You have to see Darlene's point of view," says Chrissy earnestly. "She still has a job, unlike us. She's on social media."

"Well, she should get off it," Leonie growls.

"We were polarizing too," says Myrna. "Remember when we started *Great Dames*? 'The Magazine That Frightens Postmen'? Remember the Dykes 'n' Psyches issue, about misogynistic Freudian analysts?"

"We certainly poked the bear on that one," says Leonie. "The hate mail with the capital letters, with red and blue crayon underlining calling us harridans and harpies, and the violent death threats? How inventive they were, some of them! Boobs baked in a pie, as I recall. And look, we're still alive!"

Harridan—now that word's fallen out of fashion, Myrna reflects. Not to mention *harpy. Boobs,* however, is still around.

"So many offers to give us what we needed, which was a good raping," says Leonie. "'Like to see you try,' I wrote back to a couple of them. 'Want a construction-boot steel-toed kick in the nuts?'"

"I never said anything as strong as that," says Chrissy. "Of course, it helps to be on the tall side, like you. You were on the girls' soccer team in college, right?"

"Replying just egged them on," says Myrna. "Not that they ever did anything. But I carried a pointy umbrella and pepper spray, for a while."

"You aren't supposed to shout Help," says Chrissy. "You're supposed to shout Fire!"

"Why?" says Myrna. She remembers being told that the best thing was to throw up but decides not to add this to the conversation.

"Because if you shout Help, nobody will come," says Chrissy sadly. There's a pause.

Are they really that alone? Are people really that frightened and selfish?

"I'd come," says Leonie. "If I heard it."

"I know you would," says Chrissy.

"So would I," says Myrna. "If I had my pepper spray."

"Well then," says Leonie. "Back to Darlene. How old *is* she, anyway?"

"She's younger than us," says Chrissy, twisting the rings on her fingers—a milk opal, an amethyst. "It's different for her."

"Yeah, she's a wuss," says Leonie. She raises her glass. "Here's to polarizing." She tips back her head, pours down a third of her G and T.

"Leonie, be fair! It's not 1972 anymore," says Chrissy, in that preachy tone she can sometimes assume.

"Think I don't know that? If it were 1972, I wouldn't be practically bald, half my friends wouldn't be dead, and Alan wouldn't think he's about to drop a bomb out of a Flying Fortress onto Sunset Lodge. He thinks he's been kidnapped in an airplane. He makes *zoom-zoom* noises, it breaks my heart. It's not as if he was even in the fucking Second World War!" She might be about to cry.

"Oh, Leonie, I'm so sorry, I didn't mean—" Now Chrissy might be about to cry.

Competitive crying: time to deflect, thinks Myrna. "The asphalt out there is literally melting," she says. "I almost dissolved. When I came through your door I looked like the wrath of God."

"That's why I thought we'd stay in here," says Chrissy, grasping Myrna's deflection like the relay-race baton it is. "With the A.C., not that I like it, but sometimes . . . I turned it up high, though it can make me sneeze. I hope it's not . . ."

Myrna gulps her Perrier, scoops up a handful of veggie puffs. "I get these things too, they're made of bean flour. The grand-kids love them. Leave some for your granny, I have to tell them. They're like squirrels!"

"My grandmother used to say that quite a lot," says Leonie, dabbing at her eyes with one of the rosebud napkins. She too is deflecting. Crying can so easily segue into backbiting and rup-tures, thinks Myrna. The schismatic feminist feuds of the 1970s were ferocious and lasted for years, but at their age they no longer have the runway to do a proper, long-drawn-out feud.

"She used to say what?" she asks.

"Wrath of God," says Leonie. "Except she said it more like *roth*."

"And did she?" says Chrissy. She perches her slender bum care-fully on the sofa, deploying her skirt with one hand, clutching her white wine spritzer with the other.

"Did she what?" said Myrna.

"Look like it. The wrath of God," says Chrissy.

"I don't know," says Leonie. "I never knew what 'wrath of God' meant."

"Maybe the landscape after God went over it with a whirlwind," says Myrna. "As was his habit. Broken. Flattened."

"Well, she looked pretty awful at the end," says Leonie. "Of her life. As we all will."

"Not that we don't now," says Chrissy.

"Don't now what?" says Myrna. Why is time slowing down on her? She's having trouble connecting the dots in this conversation, and she's not even drinking. Is this creeping aphasia? If so, how ironic. No, it's the other two jumping around like frogs on a griddle. "Oh, right," she says. "Look awful."

"Yes. It's the neck!" Chrissy takes a swig of her spritzer. "But what can you do? Should I bring out that new cheese and some crackers?"

"Can't hurt," says Leonie. Chrissy goes in search.

"Maybe we should get this show on the road," says Myrna. "What's the agenda?" At this rate they won't reach the main topic till midnight.

"You can have your neck lifted," says Leonie. "I did mine, oh, maybe ten years ago. But you'd never know it now, gravity's taking its toll."

"My mother did too," says Myrna. "Look like the wrath of God. Though once she was actually dead, you'd be amazed how smooth her face was. All those pain and worry lines, just gone. Sort of instant Botox." As soon as this is out of her mouth she feels herself blushing.

"That's morbid," says Leonie, grinning. "Too high a price! I'd rather be wrinkly."

"Anyway, I'm not letting them stick a knife into me," says Chrissy, returning with a primrose-yellow plate, the ashy cheese enthroned on lettuce leaves, surrounded by an oval of seed crackers. "And all those plastic surgeons are control freaks. They think they know what you should look like better than you do."

"A friend of mine got breast cancer," says Chrissy. "She had them both off, then she opted for the implants. She made drawings, she took photos and measurements; she was an A cup, and she wanted to be back the way she was. The implant doctor went, Certainly, of course, don't you worry, and when she wakes up, she's a C! Practically a D! Couple of beach balls. She was so disappointed! Well, more like shocked and outraged."

"Cripes," says Leonie, laughing. "I bet he felt she ought to be grateful!" She's into the black olives; there's a dribble of juice on her patio pants.

White is such a mistake for pants, thinks Myrna.

"Something like that," says Chrissy, wielding a cracker. "Had a fine idea of himself. Tit man to the stars. Why did he think she needed big breasts? She's seventy-five!"

"Never say die," says Leonie. "Or not until you get there."

"Get where?" says Myrna. She eats a cheese-laden cracker. Suddenly she's hungry: it's the talk of death. "This cheese is fantastic," she says to Chrissy.

"Get to the die part." Leonie isn't laughing. She's finished her G and T and is mixing herself another.

"They did save her life," says Chrissy. "Those implants. She tripped and fell down, in the cellar. She would've hit her head on the cement floor, but the fake breasts were in between. She just bounced."

"That's a selling point," says Leonie. "They should put it in the ads."

"She got them taken out again though," said Chrissy. "The big implants."

"I would've too," says Myrna. "Did she have smaller ones put in?"

"No, she just sort of threw up her hands," says Chrissy.

"Like, Why bother?" says Myrna. "I get that." Like, Why *fucking* bother? she adds in her head.

There's a meditative pause.

———

"Okay, I guess it's time to rock 'n' roll," says Leonie. "The clock's ticking. I've got a hard stop before dinner. Lawyer. Will."

"Yeah, we should all do that," says Myrna. "Make our wills." She and Cal have discussed it, but they haven't taken the plunge. It's an easy thing to put off. *Will,* she muses. Such a slippery word. My will. Will of the gods. Will he, nil he. *Willy,* from *membrum virile,* Latin, the *virile* part: V was pronounced W, and the terminal *e* was voiced. Yet one more of the nine hundred and ninety-nine names for penis. "*Penis* is quite a young word," she says, "derived from a word meaning 'tail.' *Tail,* on the other hand, in reference to a woman as a sex object . . ." The others are staring at her. "Oops, inner monologue," she says. "Am I boring you?" She must take care not to free-associate in public places.

"Not me," says Leonie. "Who knew about the tails?"

"I'll get my notes," says Chrissy briskly. She's had enough of penises, in conversation as in life. She stands up and heads toward the kitchen, her draperies fluttering.

"Is it too hot to think about this?" says Myrna. "This whole project."

"No," says Leonie. "We're making progress."

Chrissy comes back with a pink folder, sits down again, opens the folder. "Good news, we're at half a million," she says. "A quarter of the way to our goal."

"That happened fast," says Myrna. "Last time we were only at a hundred and fifty. The initial bequest."

"Well, another old feminist came into money," says Chrissy. "Somebody died. She felt guilty about inheriting from a corrupt mining enterprise in Bolivia and decided to share with us."

"So, dirty money," says Leonie in an amused voice. Chrissy on the crux of a delicate moral dilemma has always amused her.

"All money is dirty," says Chrissy sanctimoniously, "but we'll put it to a clean use."

Leonie snorts a laugh, which Chrissy ignores. "It was Darlene who set this whole thing up for us," she says. "She put so much work into it! We can't let her down, we need to follow through. Maybe now we can hire an executive director."

"Good," says Myrna. "It's time we got someone who knows what she's doing. People with money should die more often."

"Stop talking about the D-word," Leonie says. She pulls herself up, out of the chaise longue. "I find it triggering."

This is possibly a joke. Yes, Myrna thinks, scanning Leonie's face, her impish grin: it is a joke.

"I find *triggering* triggering," says Myrna. Safe ground: they both laugh. "And you're being anti-corpse. Corpses are people too, you know."

"Sorry, sorry. We need to sober down," Leonie says. "By old feminist, do you mean former?" she asks Chrissy.

"No," says Chrissy. "Just old. Our generation."

"Things have changed," says Leonie. She's pouring herself another drink.

"Well, of course they have," says Chrissy. "Nothing's the same! You can't expect it! But the new ones have good intentions!"

"The road to Hell is paved with good intentions," Leonie intones.

"That's not fair," says Chrissy. "People really do mean well, mostly."

"It's partly fair, admit it," says Leonie. "They think their good intentions excuse all kinds of things. They're always accusing, they want heads on spikes. Plus, they're ultra critical."

Chrissy laughs. "That's exactly what my grandmother used to say when I complained! She'd say I didn't know how lucky I was that we had a refrigerator instead of an icebox. Then she'd start in about the war. Rationing, and all that. The meat shortage. Not that I eat meat now anyway; or not as much."

"I only eat seafood," says Myrna. It's nice to have a check mark in a righteous lifestyle box where Chrissy doesn't have one. The truth is that meat now gives Myrna indigestion: her gut biome's no longer up to it.

Leonie eases herself back onto the chaise longue, tinkling the ice in her fresh drink. "I love gin," she says.

"Let's concentrate," says Chrissy. "We write the proposal, setting out the terms exactly—Darlene says that's the next step. Then once we've placed the project at a university, we make an announcement. I thought a virtual press conference, on Zoom."

"Okay, let's go," says Leonie. "What are we proposing, exactly? Pass the goat cheese, it's five-star."

"We can say it's an endowed chair for an emerging female," says Chrissy.

"Which is a contradiction," says Myrna. "An endowed chair should be for a person who's already established."

"You need to add trans," says Leonie.

"Darlene says there should be a chair that appeals to young women," says Chrissy. "They're more than half of the total number of students at universities now, but Darlene says it's still more men at the top. Also, we have to pin down the right university. Darlene's is out, she's tested the waters there."

"Try my old place," says Myrna. "If there's enough money attached, they'd house the devil's grandmother."

"Young women won't like this chair thing, they'll say it's elitist," says Leonie.

"Oh, surely . . ." says Chrissy.

"They don't actually like much of anything," Leonie continues. "Remember what hell it was being young?"

"It was nice at times," said Chrissy. "Though I don't miss PMS."

"Darlene told me that the hormones women have in them when they've got PMS, men have in them all the time," says Myrna.

"That would account for world leaders," says Leonie.

"If Darlene were here, we'd have been done an hour ago," says Chrissy.

"Okay, emerging creative, blah-blah!" says Leonie. "God, I hate *emerging*. Emerging from what? Makes them sound as if they're coming out of a swamp."

"Maybe the metaphor is chicks hatching," says Myrna. "Out of eggs."

"Everyone knows what *emerging* means," says Chrissy. "Please focus. Should it be woman or female?"

"Don't even go there," says Leonie. "I'm getting a headache. Tell me again why we're putting in the time on this."

"We're correcting the gender balance," says Chrissy reproachfully. "Because a lot more male creatives still get the big jobs and win the awards and things. Remember that chart Darlene put together?"

"It's okay, I'm teasing," says Leonie. "I get it. We're laying the foundations for the brave new generation of emerging non-cis-male creatives, and by the way, I hate *creatives* too. They're not a separate class of people. Everyone's creative!"

"We're doing it because we made a commitment," says Myrna. "To Darlene. Anyway, it's not so much for the future, we won't be here by then. It's for the past."

"Sort of like a memorial?" asks Leonie. "I like it. A memorial to the old harridans like us."

"We can't put that in the proposal," says Chrissy. "Certainly not harridans."

"Joking," says Leonie, staring into her glass.

"We have to put in that it's for younger creatives," says Chrissy.

"The ones who want Darlene's head in a basket?" says Leonie. "My head too, I bet, if they ever found out what was inside it."

"So, who's volunteering to write the proposal?" says Chrissy.

"I vote you," says Leonie.

"I'm not good at it. It should be Myrna," says Chrissy. "She's the language expert."

"Myrna? How about it?" says Leonie.

"I'd be too picky," says Myrna. "Obsessive about words. It would take me months. Why don't we hire the executive whatnot and she can do it?"

"Darlene is so excellent at these things," says Chrissy sadly.

"Couldn't we talk her into coming back?" asks Myrna.

"I don't think so," says Chrissy. "She says she feels . . . scorched."

"As in burned," says Leonie. "Some hotshot ladder-climber wants her job, is my guess. Can't they wait decently until she retires, or croaks of natural causes?"

"That's kind of cynical," says Chrissy. "A lot of them really believe—"

"Enlighten me," says Leonie. "'Really believe' seldom comes into it. We're in the middle of a regime change, like the French Revvie. Power struggles! They were always changing the passwords. Wake up one morning, use yesterday's password, off with your head."

"We didn't wait decently ourselves," says Myrna. "As I recall. We defenestrated a few old fogies, one way or another. In retrospect, we may have been cruel."

"But those were men!" Leonie exclaims.

"'Sleeping with the enemy'? Remember that?" says Myrna.

"Yeah, it was fun," says Leonie. "I slept with a lot of enemies. I told myself I was a spy."

"Hypocrite," says Myrna. They laugh.

"Promise me something," says Leonie. "Closed coffin, jokes at my funeral, and lots of gin at the wake."

"Double promise," says Myrna.

"Please don't do that," says Chrissy. "It makes me too sad."

There's a pause.

"Back to Darlene," says Leonie. "She must be feeling battered. We need to give her some ego strokes." She takes out her cell-phone. "Darlene? Leonie here. Fine. More or less fine. I've been better." A pause. "Sorry about the slime mould uproar, or what-ever that was. We live in dangerous times. The Committee of Pub-lic Safety is out to get us." A pause. "Figure of speech."

"Tell her she's essential," Chrissy whispers. "Say we can't do it without her."

"Tell her there's an astonishing cheese," says Myrna. "A new one. She loves those."

"Listen, we're at Chrissy's," Leonie continues. "We need you to come over. Need, need, need." There's a pause. "Yes, it's about the chair for emerging whatever, for female and et cetera creatives, for young . . ." Another pause. "No, you don't have to be an offi-cial committee member, you just have to help us. We're obsolete and uncool, but you can sneak in the back door so no one will see you with us." A pause. "We can't write the proposal by ourselves. We've tried. We get sidetracked. Words fail us." A pause. "It's my dying wish. Anyway, we're drunk."

"Speak for yourself," says Myrna.

"I hope she comes," says Chrissy, clasping her hands.

"In addition to which," says Leonie, "there's a new cheese, ashed goat, unbelievable, and you really have to see Myrna's hair. She screwed up her courage and went to her hair guy, and it came out bright maroon! Limited viewing time only, she's going to change it back, you need to come over or you'll miss it. She got a tattoo as well." A pause. "You're a complete star! Medal in Heaven! We're waiting right here! We're saving you some cheese!" She hangs up. "She's coming!"

"Oh, thank goodness!" says Chrissy.

"Liar," says Myrna. "I didn't get a tattoo."

"Darlene could never resist weird hair," says Leonie. "She's written about it: weird hair as a courtship signal. Though among golden lion tamarins."

"Who would I be courtship-signalling to?" says Myrna, laughing. "The men I know can barely get out of bed!"

"They don't need to get out of bed, you just need to get into it," says Leonie. "With your magenta hair. Shazam! Instant boner, way better than Viagra."

"Now stop teasing Myrna, she didn't intend that colour," says Chrissy.

"I'll defend against hair aggression with an ancient curse," says Myrna. "May the devil fuck you!"

"Wish somebody would. But do your worst," says Leonie. "I'm a tough old hag, I'll simply rise above it. I'm having another G and T. Just a weak one."

"My grandmother always used to say that! Rise above it!" says Chrissy.

"Like sewer gas," says Myrna.

"Like a kite!" says Chrissy. "Like a balloon! Like flying!"

Like the soul leaving the body in the form of a butterfly, thinks Myrna. Like breath.

"Here's to rising above it," says Leonie. "Whatever that means." She lifts her glass. "All together now! Up we go!"

III

—

NELL & TIG

—

A DUSTY LUNCH

✦

T he Jolly Old Brigadier isn't very jolly. He's only called that
behind his back, needless to say, or the J.O.B. for short.
Tig has told Nell how he and his ironic friends cooked up
this title when they were teenagers and therefore heartless—too
young to recognize the Brig's irritating joviality for what it was:
a false front. Or they may have guessed at the falseness but not
understood the reasons for it.

The J.O.B. did try hard at being jolly. He must have put a lot
of effort into it, Nell thinks. In those summers, when Tig would
have a bunch of pals up to the Muskoka family cottage, Tig's father
would get up early, stick a cigarette in his mouth, and set it on
fire with his lighter—a Zippo, Nell has decided. Then he'd pour
himself a cup of harsh percolator coffee, tuck a dishtowel into his
belt in lieu of an apron, mix a batch of pancakes, and fry up breakfast for the boys. He'd even made a sign for this activity—RISE &
SHINE PANCAKE SHACK—and hung it from a tree.

Tig and his friends would be sleeping on the floor of the rudimentary room above the boathouse. They'd be awakened by a
gong, a dinner gong left over from the late nineteenth century,
which was when the cottage had been built. It was nothing like a

modern cottage: there were servants' quarters, not that there were servants anymore. There was a stuffed pheasant under a glass bell. All of this Nell knows from Tig.

The boys would stumble up the granite hill to the rustic outdoor table, still half asleep because you didn't keep the Jolly Old Brigadier waiting, and there he would be, puffing cigarette smoke out of one side of his mouth, flipping the pancakes, grinning in— Nell now thinks—what must have been a heartbreaking way: futile effort is always heartbreaking. But the boys didn't see it, of course not. Possibly Tig's mother saw it, or she would have seen it if she'd looked out the window. Most likely she didn't look out, though. She liked to stay in bed, with her own cigarette and cup of tea and yesterday's newspaper, gathering her strength before the day's onslaught. The newspaper would have been brought by a local man called Norman, who'd fitted oars to a canoe. He was a feature of the place, rocketing around the lake from cottage to cottage, delivering letters and newspapers.

No doubt Tig's mother was trying just as hard as the Brig. They were both performing to the best of their ability, for the sake of the children: Tig and his younger brother. The children must also have been trying hard, though unaware of it. They were all enacting some vision of normality—of what normal family life was imagined to be. It must have been a strain on them, but especially on Tig's mother. What was it like to live with a man who was only half there? The other half was off somewhere else, left behind on the other side of the Atlantic in a ravaged landscape that couldn't be mentioned. Moreover, the Brig would not acknowledge that other half of himself; his double was kept locked away, firmly out of sight, while the visible part of him flipped pancakes and passed the maple syrup and rustled up the bacon, squinting into the smoke from his cigarette and making cheerful small talk. Have a good sleep? Going fishing? Nice weather for it. More pancakes?

It couldn't last, of course. Not for Tig's mother. It was like being married to a psychopathic murderer who's using you for window dressing while keeping a dozen severed heads in the freezer.

When was this? Nell counts on her fingers. It must have been only five or six years after the war—that blank time following a calamity when people are pretending it didn't happen. Whatever it was—the fire, the flood, the plane crash, the house vanishing wholesale into the sinkhole with your entire family, the carpet-bombing, the blitzkrieg, the millions dead—the ashes scatter, the waters recede, the ambulances depart, the earth closes over whatever shards and bones remain. There. It's finished now. Pick yourself up, let's move on, and look! The snow is so white, the grass is so green, the flowers are so blooming, the sun is so shining, we'll have such a picnic lunch, there will be such music, we'll enjoy the moment! They wouldn't want you to mope, would they? Those who didn't make it. Not after all they did for you, even if they did nothing but die, and unwillingly, and not for you. They didn't even know you: you were hardly even born, you were barely a thought. Still, they'd want you to be happy.

An astounding lie, when you come to think of it. Why would they want that—your happiness—in this future they were so brutally severed from? The dead are notoriously resentful. Also notoriously restless, and notoriously hungry. Why would they rejoice to witness your careless picnic? But that lie had been comforting in a minor way: a Band-Aid stuck onto a cut throat.

The cut throat was the war, of course. The War. The war in the middle of the century, the past century. The war that was once now and is now then, and then is very far away, or so you'd think; and Nell does try to think that. But it isn't far away for Tig, and not for Nell either. For them, the war was yesterday. No: it was today—just a little earlier than where they are now in the hours of whatever day they're currently undergoing. It's a middle-of-the-night thing, the war. A waking-up-in-the-dark thing: what year is it, what month is it, what is that siren? they would wonder. Only briefly, because then it will be all right and Tig will be making hot water with lemon in it and bringing some to Nell, and then there will be coffee—real coffee, not like those toasted wheat bran and molasses drinks that had substituted for coffee during the war. Not that Nell drank any of it, she was too young, but she remembers the jar. Instant Postum. You made do with what there was, in the war. You did not complain.

There you go again. The War. They can somehow never get past it.

So here is the Jolly Old Brigadier, many years later, a remnant. Military surplus. Returned from the wars, as they used to say—returned, like a package that wasn't wanted. He's sitting in the big stuffed maroon velvet chair in the living room, the same chair Santa sits in to eat the cookies and drink the glass of Scotch left out for him, having a little rest because he's so tired from carting around all that joy.

It's the day before Christmas, and the Jolly Old Brigadier always turns up then, or he has so far. The children—the grandchildren—tiptoe around him with wide eyes. He's been in the war, but they don't know what the war is, except that people's voices drop lower when it's mentioned. He's a solemn object, the J.O.B., perhaps even sacred: to be gazed at but not touched. Holiness is a form of monstrosity, so perhaps, underneath his wrinkly shell of a semi-benign old man, he's something horrible. Something possibly dead. Something covered with blood.

He's getting frail now, veined, crumpled. Nell has trouble

matching him up with the black-and-white photos of him taken in the 1940s: so dashing in his uniform—the wide leather belt, the handgun in its holster, the tallness and thinness, the ramrod posture, the dapper moustache—looking at a map with several other moustached officers, in berets or hard peaked officers' caps; or, in another view, riding in a jeep, a cigarette in his gloved hand; then again, standing beside a tank; then making a speech to a happy-looking crowd in a town just liberated, the women with kerchiefs tied under their chins as was the custom, the men with cloth caps or fedoras.

Nell brings the Jolly Old Brigadier a glass of Scotch—splash of water, no ice—and, on a little white plate, a cheese shortbread in the shape of a fir tree. She puts the glass in his hand, sets the plate on a side table. He looks at her as if he doesn't quite know who she is. The fire crackles, the decorated tree winks and glitters, coziness casts its deceptive glow over the room. Tig is in the kitchen, just through the double doors, getting his own drink. It could all be swept away in an instant. A billowing of smoke, shards of their life hurled through the air. *Kaboom*, a hole in the ground. This is the effect the Jolly Old Brig has on her.

"Thank you," he says. He's always courteous. He's wearing a tweed jacket, and a tie that is most likely military. He still manages to tie it himself, despite his tremulous hands. A little silver pin of some kind in his lapel, its meaning unknown to her. The moustache is white now, with yellow edges from the cigarettes. It could use a trim. His hair is impinging on his collar. She must speak to Tig about that.

The Brig has buried two wives and is living alone, in an old-fashioned apartment, with a cleaner who comes in twice a week. Is that enough help? Who's feeding him? What's he doing for company? Is it time to start talking about a retirement home, with extra care? He would hate that: even admitting to the need for physical help would be humiliating. He refuses to wear the old-folks monitor button—press it if you fall down—that they've supplied. Tig routinely searches for this button, and just as routinely finds it hidden in the Brig's handkerchief drawer.

Should they endow him with a cat? Probably not, he would trip over it.

He sometimes phones Tig, always at night. If Nell answers, he hangs up; only Tig will do.

People are appearing in his apartment, he has confided: sometimes people he knows, sometimes not, sometimes alive, sometimes not. They sit in his easy chair and he brings them cups of tea, but they won't speak to him. What is to be done? He wants them to go away or at least acknowledge him, but they pay no attention.

Tig unchains his bicycle, pedals over there in the dark—a worry to Nell, as he might get hit by a careless or drunk driver, as has happened once before, despite the reflective strips on his jacket, though nothing was broken. At the apartment, Tig finds notes the Jolly Old Brigadier has written to these unresponsive people. *Why are you here? Why won't you talk to me?* In the daytime the J.O.B. admits the people aren't actually there. But still, they are very solid. You can't see through them.

"How real are they?" Tig has asked him.

"As real as you." In some sense that's true, thinks Nell. It's us—Tig and me—who are mist creatures. For him our existence is tenuous.

A couple of weeks ago he called after midnight, in a panic. There was a dead man hanging in the shower. "Keep calm," Tig said to his father. "I'm coming." And he went.

What's causing these phenomena? "It's because he's so alone," Nell says.

"It's more than that," says Tig. Unsaid is: How many men do

you think he actually saw hanging from trees, from lampposts, from telephone poles? It's no wonder that at least one of them, with purple face and swollen tongue, has now turned up in the shower.

"Would you like an olive?" Nell says, proffering the dish. No reply. The Brig is possibly a little deaf. He gazes past her into the fire. What is he seeing? Where has he gone? How far back?

Nell knows something of his story, but only because Tig has told her. The Brig himself has said nothing much about his life, or not to her.

He was born long ago, in 1908, before World War One, which at the time was called the Great War; there were not yet two of them. He was almost seven when the Great War broke out, and he must have remembered it; especially the later phase—the men coming home minus limbs or minds, the uniforms everywhere, the sad or frightened adults, the prayers in churches, the parades. Then, right after the armistice, the Spanish flu, a huge and chaotic tsunami of yet more deaths. People fell over on the streets, blood spurting from their ears; young soldiers died within hours, turning blue from lack of oxygen, their lungs destroyed; unburied corpses piled up. Had the Brig himself undergone this illness as a twelve-year-old? Unknown, but likely.

The Brig's father had been a well-to-do lawyer. He'd once owned the land at the corner of Yonge and St. Clair in Toronto, imagine that! Pity he'd sold it, Tig used to say. He was born in 1866. There's a photo of him among the Brig's papers, aged six or seven, stuffed into a tight, dark, truly ugly mid-Victorian boy's outfit, with knee britches and high buttoned boots; he's scowling ferociously. As a grown man he'd been a pillar of what they once called rectitude: a strategic churchgoer, a practitioner of discreet but sturdy three-piece suits, a close relative of a Commissioner of Penitentiaries—a brother? An uncle? Nell has forgotten. He'd voted in every election, and had even had himself carried to the polling station in a chair when he was ninety-eight. Nell interprets Tig's grandfather as having been cold and self-righteous, but Tig seems to have been fond of him, and had been in the habit of playing chess with him, or was it checkers, or both? The grandfather was a shark, according to Tig. Hop, hop, hop, hop, queen, checkmate!

This old chess or checkers player had had the same secretary for fifty years and had never once called her by her first name. What else do you need to know? thinks Nell. But she's being too judgmental: it was another time, not one that went in for first names, not for the help. When the Brig had moved into his cramped little apartment after the death of his second wife—who'd been pissed that she was dying first, she'd wanted to inherit—Tig and Nell had been gifted with far too much Victorian silver. *Gifted* is a euphemism: *stuck with* is more like it. This silver has to be polished, worse luck, and it can't be given away. It's a fetish: to dispose of it would be sacrilegious. Nell's family did not have those kinds of ancestors—they were more inclined to be backwoods peasants, though she does have some of her maternal grandmother's fragile, flowery china, her grandmother having been the only one with a pedigree and corsets, however modest. Nell feels guilty about this china—if she uses it, will it break?—and hides it in a sideboard.

Tig's ancestral silver is teapots, coffee pots, sugar sifters, salts and peppers, engraved trays. The cutlery is in an oak chest on legs, with three drawers—knives, forks, spoons, extras such as napkin rings—and the original receipt, from Mappin Brothers Ltd., Silversmiths and Cutlers, in London, England. All the items are listed in elegant longhand, with the prices, and the date: October 16, 1883. Objects fallen from use: game carvers, fish carvers, fish knives, a cake basket. A cake basket? What kind of cake?

All this would usually have been acquired at a wedding: it was the kind of stuff you were once supposed to have. But it couldn't have been the wedding of the stern lawyer's parents: they were already married by 1883. Nell seems to remember they were prosperous grocers. No, the lawyer's parents were farmers; it was his wife's parents who ran the edible-goods business, and had done well, said Tig. Tea imported from England, no doubt.

The name on the receipt is Burgess, the maiden name of the lawyer's wife. Maybe the original Burgess purchasers had died and the silver had moved sideways into Tig's family through his grandmother. Or was it gifted to her at her wedding? Had she been pleased about the silver, or about anything? Silence. There are no pictures, no letters. All Tig remembers about her is that everything in her dining-room cupboards was labelled. He too, though an impromptu and untidy cook, is a labeller; though not of table services.

The cake basket is no longer in evidence. At some point during the years it has disappeared. Where it is now? Lurking in an antiques shop, in a flea market? A message from the past, waiting for someone to decipher it; but waiting vainly, like most such messages. Nell pictures it as a time capsule, shot into the future, a future of aliens; aliens of which she is one. What have we found here? the aliens wonder. A rare artifact! Does it predict the weather? Is it for small-animal sacrifices? Is it a god?

Into this cake-basket-inheriting family the Jolly Old Brigadier was born. Nell counts from 1908. She counts like this for everyone she meets, wanting to know what they might have lived through before she met them. When were they ten, when fifteen, when thirty?

The Brig was seventeen in 1925, the height of the jazzy 1920s, so he'd been a flaming youth: he'd danced a mean Charleston even in his fifties, according to Tig. He must have worn wide-legged Oxford bags, narrow lapels, knitted vests; broad pale suspenders, all the rage once upon a time. Spectator shoes, with white uppers and dark toes. Had this youth played golf or tennis, those sports of the leisure classes? Nell can't picture it, nor football or hockey, though she can see him at a card table. Bridge or poker? Unrecorded, though probably both.

As a university undergraduate he'd taken up smoking cigarettes and drinking this and that, such as Scotch and martinis, and writing poetry, and drawing cartoons, and acting, and working for the student newspaper, and skipping classes. Not surprisingly, he'd flunked out, which must not have gone down well with his stiff-collared lawyer father. The family found this dancing wastrel a position in a stockbroking firm, just in time for the financial crash of 1929. The Brig then did what one did if one could: he went into the army. He'd already got his commission through the Reserve Officer Training Corps—inspired perhaps by a distinguished military uncle from the Great War—so the army was a natural choice for him.

Then all of a sudden it was the 1930s and things were very different. Much less elegant, much more earnest. Angrier. Foreboding. But despite the general strikes and bread lines and Communists and the Spanish Civil War, the Brig had risen through the ranks in and around Wolseley Barracks in London, Ontario, with a couple of training stints in England, and had married and procreated—thus Tig and his brother—and was a captain by 1939, when war was declared.

In August 1940, he went "overseas." You wouldn't say "overseas" now, but the other side of the Atlantic was much farther away then. It was away, away, away over there, with a vast sea in between. There were no real transatlantic passenger planes, so it was the sea that had to be crossed, in ships. The Brig would have left Toronto from Union Station in a train for Halifax, most likely a troop train. He would have boarded a ship docked in the enclosed basin of Halifax Harbour—already morphing into the huge staging area for men and materials it was shortly to become—and set sail with his regiment.

They were probably in a convoy, probably in a merchant ship, probably with a corvette escort: U-boats were already active. They would have moved slowly out of the harbour and along past McNabs Island, watching the land recede, then spent approximately six or seven or eight days crossing. In rough seas there would have been considerable rolling. There was probably a lot of drinking and also vomiting, but that's how you had to get across.

So many *probablys*, thinks Nell.

Once in England, the Brig would have waited, undergoing training at Camberley in Surrey, studying logistics, observing or supervising military exercises. Outmoded exercises, as armies typically rehearse for the last war, not the one they are about to fight. Digging foxholes, shoring them up with sandbags? Firing rifles, not the latest models? Trying out a few creaky tanks? Marching the men around. Inspecting their uniforms. Writing uninformative letters home, with funny drawings in the margins, for the children, a skill left over from his callow cartooning days. Then more waiting.

Poland had already fallen. So had France. So had Denmark. So had Norway. Churchill had just become prime minister, and was popular due to his handling of the Dunkirk evacuation. The bombing of London had begun. America was not yet in the war.

Rationing was in effect. The mood was grim.

Still, there were parties. There was dancing. Nell imagines the Brig, on a break from training, having a cigarette, then swinging out onto the dance floor with an unknown girl, kicking up his heels, cashing in on his Charleston skills. Would he have done that? Of course he would. He was barely thirty-two.

By 1941 the J.O.B. was a major, and a brigadier by early 1943, at the age of thirty-four: the youngest in the Canadian Army. He went up through Sicily with the British and the Canadians, and then across into Italy as the Germans retreated north, blowing up towns as they went, leaving wreckage and starvation in their wake. He and his brigade went past Naples, fought at Ortona, crossed the Moro River. Then came Monte Cassino, one of the most vicious battles of the war. Even so it was early days. Worse was to come.

After the Brig's death—after everyone's death, Tig's included—Nell found a curious letter among his papers. It was from Martha Gellhorn, the well-known war correspondent. The Brig had kept this letter, tucked into a folder with his official war record, with write-ups of military operations he'd been involved in, with the texts of speeches he'd made after the war and over the years.

What people preserve, what they discard: this has always been of interest to Nell. The Brig had not only kept the letter, he'd treasured it. There were several copies of it, here and there in his papers, in one folder or another, among newspaper clippings, photos, and citations.

My favourite Brigadier

I hope you will like this article. It is terribly unpleasant to read articles typed out on tissue paper and it is unpleasant to read them as they are sent via cable. But anyhow, perhaps it will please you. It does not say anything about the beloved brigade in person, simply because what I write has to be so general. You see, it comes out weeks from now, and is written for 3 million people who probably read Colliers only when riding in subways, and it is meant to be a sort of sweeping picture shall we say. I think this is the last story of a battle I shall write, because I believe the war will be over in a month. Anyhow, pray to God for same.

Am leaving tomorrow for France and simply do not know what will be doing afterwards. I may easily come back this way, and if so will hope to see you. And if not here, somewhere.

Thank you for your great kindness. You were angelic to me and I had a lovely time with you boys. Please give Roscoe and Alan and the handsome colonel, and all of them my love. And the best luck to you all, always.

Yours,
Marty

Sunday

"Angelic" how, exactly? Nell wonders now, rereading this letter. What was the "great kindness," or was the phrase merely a standard politeness? When was this? Which Sunday? Maddening of her not to say. It would have been in the spring of 1944—before D-Day. Where was Martha Gellhorn when she wrote this letter? How was it delivered? "Leaving tomorrow"—leaving where? She must still have been in Italy.

Nell has seen pictures of her at that time: long blond hair in a 1940s style, cigarette in hand, sometimes in a trench coat, at other times wearing a forage cap. Slender but not skinny. A little tall for a woman then; just as well, in case of unwanted advances. There were bound to have been some of those. Wanted advances too, judging from her letters. Some of these have been collected in a book that Nell has read, though the letter to her favourite brigadier was not among them.

What were the adjectives you might use for her? *Practical, sentimental, tough, empathetic, determined. Fearless,* though no one is fearless really; more like a calculated risk-taker.

In other, far earlier times, this sort of girl might have helped run a Midwestern farm, as daughters did then. She'd have milked cows, broken colts, put up with no nonsense, then married and had eight children; rolled up her sleeves, got it done, whatever it was. But by the time young Martha came along, her family had money, and she was sent to Bryn Mawr. She left before graduating: the only thing she wanted to do, she told her grandmother, was to write novels.

Then the era swept her up and she was off to the wars—the Spanish Civil War, the world war that followed it—talking herself into places that women, most women, were not allowed to go, as they were considered too fragile. Martha was not fragile; she made a point of that. No sobbing, collapsing, fainting, or throwing up.

In Italy she would have sat at an improvised table somewhere, typing on onionskin paper. Shortly after sending her letter to the J.O.B., she got herself to the D-Day landings by sneaking onto a Red Cross ship and locking herself in the bathroom. She wasn't a credentialled war correspondent at that point—her papers had been stolen. Once the brass hats figured out she was there, she was plucked away from the front and disciplined for her rule-flouting; but to hell with them, she'd got her story.

The letter to the Brig was attached to the manuscript of an article on the breaking of the Gothic Line by the assembled Allied forces—Poles, Australians, Canadians, South Africans, New Zealanders, and Indians, among others. It was written in the peculiar telegraphese made necessary by cable transmission: no capital letters, and the punctuation needed to be spelled out.

> gothic line paragraph the gothic line from where we stood
> was a smashed village an asphalt road and a pinkish brown
> hill stop on this dusty mined lane leading up to the village
> the road and the hill the infantry was waiting to attack
> stop they stood single file well spaced apart and did not
> speak and their faces said nothing either stop the noise of
> our artillery firing from the hills behind us never stopped
> stop no one listened to it stop everyone listened to sudden
> woodpecker beats of german machine gun fire ahead
> and everyone looked to the sky on the left where german
> airbursts made dark loose small clouds stop

It's very modernist, this kind of writing, Nell thinks. The terse short-story writers, the poets who never capitalized or punctuated—they came into existence via the telegraph, and now that the telegraph is done with, that sort of writing has mostly vanished too. But stumbling over the typescript among the Jolly Old Brig's papers, Nell feels an electric current. The writing is so fresh, so immediate, it's as if she's looking over the shoulder of this person in a light shirt, with short sleeves because it was hot weather, didn't the boys go swimming once they'd reached the Adriatic, while the young woman reaches for the right words, how to say it, how to say the unsayable because how can this be described at all, how can it be understood, anything so extreme, the smells no the stenches, the choking smoke, the noises no the shattering booms, the stupid sudden deaths, the beauty, the utter confusion, *bam bam bam* on the typewriter, a manual typewriter of course em dash most likely a Remington em dash on the makeshift

table comma and one more cigarette and some awful coffee with
tinned milk if lucky before bashing on with it stop

> there it was the gothic line carefully planned so that every
> fold of the earth was used to conceal death and the young
> men were walking into it and because they have seen so
> much and done so much they walked into it as if it were part
> of the day's work comma a hellish day but still just part of
> the work stop paragraph it was the canadians who broke this
> line by finding a soft place and going through stop it makes
> me ashamed to write that sentence because there is no soft
> place where there are mines and there is no soft place where
> there are spandaus and no soft place where there are the
> hideous long 88 guns and if you have seen one tank burn on
> a hillside you will never believe that anything is soft again
> stop

Her account of the battle grinds forward, with roaring and
explosions and heat and dust and blood:

> paragraph a battle is a jig saw puzzle of fighting men
> bewildered terrified civilians noise smells jokes pain fear
> unfinished conversations and high explosives stop [...] the
> dust lay in drifts a foot thick and whenever you could get up
> a little speed the dust boiled like water under the wheels stop
> everyone's face was greenish white with dust and it rose in a
> blinding fog around the moving army and lay high over the
> land in a brown solid haze stop [...] paragraph we watched
> the battle for the gothic line from a hill opposite sitting in
> a batch of thistles and staring through binoculars stop our
> tanks looked like brown beetles semicolon they scurried up a

hill streamed across the horizon and dipped out of sight stop
suddenly a tank flamed four times in great flames and other
tanks rolled down from the skyline seeking cover in the folds
of the hill stop the desert airforce cabrank the six planes which
cavort around the sky like a school of minnows was signalled
to bomb a loaf shaped hill called monte lura stop [...]

Cabrank? thinks Nell, pondering this. Oh. *Cab rank.* That's what
they did then: kept planes in the air like taxis waiting for fares,
switching them around so some were always available and no time
would be wasted while all of them refuelled. Things were moving
so quickly; the planes queued, circling until told what to do from
the ground command. Able Baker Charlie. Over and out. Like an
old radio drama.

monte lura went up in towering waves of brownish smoke
and dirt stop our artillery dug into the gothic line so that
everywhere cotton balls of smoke flowered on the slopes
stop our own airbursts now rained steel fragments [...]
stop the battle looking absolutely unreal tiny chrystal clear
spread out before us stop but there were men in the tanks
and men in those trees where the shells landed and men
under those bombs stop the noise was so exaggerated
that nothing like it had been heard since the movies
stop paragraph we had all been awake and roaming the
countryside since five o'clock when our first giant artillery
barrage started stop we were hot and hungry by now and we
went to eat lunch in a tent about fifty yards from our own
gun positions stop the blast of the guns shook the tent and
we could only talk between salvos stop all that day and the
next the noise of our guns was physically painful stop

There's an interlude: a young Canadian brigadier entertains the lunch-eaters by describing a garden party he will give after the war for guests who want to know what it was like, complete with screaming tank sound effects, dust from a Hollywood dust machine, and clouds of flies released over a spread of bully beef, beans, and hardtack with jam, washed down with lukewarm coal-black tea.

The amusing man performing this skit must have been the Jolly Old Brig: Nell detects a shadow of the high-spirited cartoonist and heel-kicking Charleston dancer he must once have been, and in some ways continued to be. At least he'd been able to wring a little fun out of life, back then in the middle of the barrage. When he was flipping pancakes for the boys at the summer cottage with the stuffed pheasant, is this what he was thinking about?

Then the lunch was over and that particular slice of the Gothic Line had been breached, and Martha Gellhorn filed her Monte Casino story and went travelling—first back to North America to try to patch up a failing marriage, then to D-Day and Normandy despite every obstacle. Meanwhile, the Brig was slogging on through Italy, in command of the 2nd Canadian Infantry Brigade. They were making their way laboriously up the Adriatic Coast, from one town to another, across one swollen river after another. Enemy resistance was heavy. Mile by mile they went, hill by hill, gully by gully, death by death.

A battalion of the Brig's 2nd Infantry was the first unit to break through the Gothic Line in this region, and the Brig got his Distinguished Service Order by staging and leading a "brilliantly executed night attack" that captured the Fortunato Ridge. (Nell has looked this ridge up on a map, which like all maps is flat, and not informative about the texture of the actual terrain.) The Brig did what you were supposed to do, and what he did was described by the *Canadian Gazette* in the kind of language you were supposed to be described in if you did such things. He "led his brigade in a skilful manner, inspiring confidence in all ranks of his command, often under enemy fire which he disregarded without thought for his own personal safety."

Who decided on the words? Nell wonders. How did they know what he did? The account Nell has found is dated April 28, 1945. It was typed out by Tig, and attached by him, with a note, to a copy of Martha Gellhorn's Monte Casino letter. *She sounds like a charmer,* he has written. When did Tig do this note-writing and attaching? It could only have been after his father's death.

So Tig did understand something about the Jolly Old Brig after all, Nell thinks. Not just an out-of-date pancake flipper, his dad.

Shortly after the capture of Fortunato Ridge, the Brig and his infantry brigade were pulled out of Italy and sent with the 1st Canadians into Western Europe, via Antwerp, which had already been captured. That was in the fall of 1944. Then they had to move up into Germany.

Following the story, shuffling through the J.O.B.'s papers—which she has inherited from Tig, like the Victorian silver, and which she similarly cannot throw out—Nell makes a surprising find. It's a folder labelled *Father's poems.* The handwriting on the label is Tig's.

Tig had read these poems written by his father, then. What had he thought? Reading them herself, Nell can't really imagine. A discovery of buried treasure? An invasion of privacy? There's always something duplicitous about it, this spying on the dead.

The poems are amateur, as poems. But that is hardly the point.

There aren't many of them. They all appear to have been written between March 1945 and May of the same year. The last one
is dated May 9, the day after VE Day, when the war in Europe
was finally over. Insofar as it has ever been over, Nell adds to
herself.

The poems begin during the Battle of the Reichswald, a grue-
some and desperate affair: mud, blood, and death in the booby-
trapped forest; flooded lowlands, dank bone-chilling cold, misty
fields, comfortless. The 7th Canadian Infantry, the Brig's new
command, was in it up to the neck, often literally. But there is the
J.O.B. in the middle of it, somehow writing poetry.

How did he do that? Did he scribble into notebooks and then
type the poems out later? Because they are all typewritten. The
typewriter must have been for writing up reports: there are a number of such typewritten reports in his papers. He must have had
a manual typewriter, and a portable command post—some field
tent or other, or a vehicle; a space or level surface that could hold
the typewriter; something. Nell knows very little about how such
things were actually managed.

THE REICHSWALD

There is a moon, shaded with mist
A cloudless sky, and 'neath the pines
I stand and listen.
This was a place where lovers kissed
In silent rapture.

No silence reigns, no peace to-night
The din of guns and roar of planes
Herald tomorrow's dawn.

Beneath the moon, bathed in it's light
Quietly we wait.

Far on ahead, the dense barrage
Covers the men who grimly fight
On German soil.
And they can see the bright barrage
For which they strive.

These graceful pines, the misty moon
Unruffled by the grief of war
Are mute to-night.
For well they know amid the gloom
Right will survive.

To-morrow with sad bloody beams
The sun will rise, and sorrowful
Behind the clouds of war
The moon will drift away in dreams
Of lost romance.

Germany, March 1945

It's sketchy, this poem, thinks Nell. The pines that are so certain of a rightful outcome—what Edwardian children's book are they from? Not to mention the dreaming moon. What are the lovers doing in this forest, let alone this poem? What lost romance? What was the Brig getting at? And the waiting—that was presumably for the next order, the signal to advance into the meat grinder that was going on up ahead. The waiting is quiet, the ongoing battle is not. It is, as they say, raging.

Then comes an even more curious poem:

A WISH

A kiss—a glance that does not hide
The ache and sorrow—or a smile
So bravely given. For inside
The heart is riven.

Such was our parting. If and when,
My darling, we shall meet one day
Then in meeting, give again
A lover's greeting.

Years have passed since we were parted
Pleasures lost that were our own.
Yet such sorrow, sadly started
Fades tomorrow?

Germany, March 1945

The poem is on half a page: the bottom half has been torn off. (Not cut, Nell notices.) There's the mere suggestion of what must have been typed below: the very top of a first word, which looks like *The*. "A Wish" seems to have been written about the same time as the first one. Is it connected to the moony, vanishing romance of "The Reichswald"? Who is the girl, or woman? It isn't the sort of poem that chimes with "wife"—with Tig's mother, toughing it out for six years with her two boys back in Toronto, writing anxious but steadfast letters, expecting any day to get the black-edged telegram that so many women—so many military wives she knew—had already received. While the Jolly Old Brig, not yet old at all, stands in a dark wood with explosions going off all around him and dead men or parts of them bleeding into the pine needles, and remembers a lost love.

Who could she have been? Nell wonders. A college sweetheart? "Years have passed" would suggest that, but time moves both quickly and slowly in a war: decades can be condensed into a week. Could it have been Martha Gellhorn? Did they have a moment—as people used to say—back in Italy in 1944, with the hot tent and the dust and flies and bad tea and horrible rum? Nell hopes so. Those who feel they may be about to die are liable to snatch at life; not that she herself has ever been in that position. She wouldn't blame the Brig at all, nor Martha, whose own marriage must have been very nearly over by that time.

On second thought, unlikely. There wouldn't have been time. It would have been too dusty; also deafening. Their minds would have been on other things. Some light flirting between one explosion and the next; a few courtesies; some jokes. Shared horrors. Martha Gellhorn was very good at being a comrade, Nell has concluded from reading about her. But a lover? Not so interested, not in the purely sexual part. Though the Brig's poems aren't sexual, as such.

What about the question mark at the end of the poem? Is it a hope that the sorrow will fade, or a fear that it will?

And what had Tig made of this, if anything? When he'd come upon the poem after his father's death—and he had, there's the testimony of his own handwriting on the folder—was he annoyed that the Brig had been having unfaithful thoughts, or had this discovery enhanced his understanding of his father? There had been friction between them, once the J.O.B. had returned from the rubble of Europe. There had been mutual contempt, of the kind that arises between idealistic adolescents rejecting stuffy, outmoded parental values and fathers who view them as ignorant, arrogant, and above all ungrateful. There had been resentment on both sides. But now here's the Brig, in later life so buttoned up on the outside, writing wistful poetry; revealing his sentimental core.

Sorrow is in the poem twice. It's an old word, almost Victorian. The Jolly Old Brig, then: *Sorrowful. Lost. Bravely.* Those were the key words as he waited in the misty forest for the command to move forward.

The next poem is titled "Breakout," and is subtitled "The Rhine." It's not signed—none of the poems are—but it's dated: "Germany (The Rhine) March 1945." By that time the First Canadian Army, or the Brig's own brigade at any rate, must have been heading to the river, with the objective of crossing it. Nell knows from old photos in books she's read—inherited from the J.O.B., some of them—that there was practically a traffic jam on the route, so many vehicles were involved.

> *No longer bursting shells break the hush*
> *So ominous, that tells*
> *Of danger lurking there*
> *Quiet lonely fields, where silence spells*
> *A warning in the air.*
>
> *Now the traffic's roar, steady and harsh*
> *Echoes amid the trees. A score*
> *Of tanks roll by in haste.*
> *Men, trucks and guns. In war*
> *There is no time to waste.*
>
> *Busy, laughing men stop a while,*
> *Racing raucous motors, and then*
> *Shouting or cursing go*
> *Along the crowded road again*
> *Within the traffic's flow . . .*

The poems are all typed on the same typewriter. The paper is thick enough so that the pages haven't crumbled; there's almost no yellowing. They aren't carbons. There are a few grammatical errors—*it's* rather than *its*—and quite a lot of missing punctuation. There's one annotation in pencil, a reversal of *one day* and *again* in the poem about the parted lovers, so the Brigadier had read them over at least once after typing them. He'd gone to some trouble.

What was the Brig intending to do with these poems? Possibly nothing. Possibly they were like journal entries, notes to self. On the other hand there had been soldier poets before, quite a few of them when you add them up—Sophocles, for one; he was a vet. King David of the Psalms. Then Lovelace, Owen, Brooke, McCrae, lots more; and the Brig had been a writer during his artistic years at university. Did he envisage a slim volume?

In any case, he kept these poems with him during his laborious and potentially fatal progress through Europe. Each had been folded in half, then in half again, suggesting that it had been carried in a pocket. Then it was unfolded and stowed flat, and filed among his papers: his silent witnesses, the voice of some deeply hidden part of himself. Had Tig's mother come across these poems later? Had there been questions about—for instance—that parting kiss? Was there jealousy? *Who was she? Was it that Martha woman? I know she was there with you in Italy, I found her letter. Just tell me.*

Nell suspects there might have been a discovery of some kind, about the woman and the kiss, or about other women and other kisses. The marriage hadn't lasted; but then, few marriages begun before the war and picked up by returning soldiers had lasted, according to Tig. He'd witnessed the marriages among his parents' military set crumbling and falling apart, like slow-motion explosions. It had happened unless there was a postwar child, he'd said;

sometimes even then. The one who'd gone—the man, 95 per cent of the time—and the one who'd stayed behind—the woman, also 95 per cent—could no longer understand each other. What was it like to believe you might die the next day, the next hour? What was it like to stand looking up at the stars, fearing that your beloved on the other side of the world might then—right that minute!—be bleeding into a swamp, gasping for his last breath? And to do that day after day and month after month and year after year—almost six years, because they didn't send soldiers home on leave then, it was too dangerous and expensive. Waiting and waiting, stretched thin as a rubber band, with nothing but censored letters and messages sent through radio programs, with no exact location given. *I'm okay, all my love, somewhere in Italy.*

Then the return, the joy, the embrace, the gradual awakening to the fact that the two of them might as well have been from different galaxies.

Talk to me!

I can't. (Head in hands.) I'm sorry. I just can't.

Please, tell me what it was like. (Trying hard.)

There's no way of describing it. (You wouldn't understand.)

I love you. (Trying hard.)

(Silence. A little too long.)

I love you too. (Dead voice.)

We can get through this. You'll feel better in . . . well, soon.

(A pause.) Yes.

(A pause.)

Cigarette?

They'd both smoked like furnaces, the Brig and his wife. They drank a lot too. Taking the edge off because everything was too sharp. Too cutting. Too cut off.

She'd died when she was just over fifty, of throat cancer; though Tig said it was a broken heart. Many things get broken in a war. The Brig lasted quite a lot longer. He'd had a couple of life-threatening illnesses; he'd recovered, but pneumonia got him in the end. It was right after that Christmas when he'd been sitting in the Santa Claus chair with his tree-shaped shortbread and his glass of Scotch, no ice.

"I'm tired of this," he'd said to Tig during their drive to the hospital. Four days later he was gone. At least the two of them had had a little time to forgive each other. The postwar period hadn't been easy for them, with Tig no longer a tearful six-year-old hugging beloved Daddy goodbye, but a surly adolescent in league with his resentful mother. The Brig had been shunted off to peacetime babysitting, a headquarters here, a headquarters there, a defence attaché in Washington decorating cocktail parties, but for what? Soldiers in peacetime are superfluous: celebrated once a year for something they once were, avoided in the here and now for what they have become.

The Jolly Old Brigadier, past his prime too early, flipping pancakes for the boys.

Nice weather. Going fishing?

Mist and moonlight. Sorrow and pain. Brave smiles.

No more poems in March 1945; things must have been very busy around that time. The Rhine was eventually crossed; then the Canadian Army was given the task of clearing Holland. Nell has looked up these clearing operations in the massive red-bound official-history volumes once belonging to the Brig and annotated in blue ink here and there, most likely by him. The books cover—in detail, with dates and maps—the movements of the Canadian battalions and regiments during the war.

Clearing Holland. A lot of flooding. Miserable weather. Wallowing in cold mire. Temporary bridges, amphibious vehicles, villages and towns heavily damaged, houses cautiously probed, first with grenades. How many killed, how many wounded, how many prisoners taken: all of it listed in the red books. Jubilation among the citizens; also privation.

By that time it was April. The Brig was liberating the town of Deventer, on the River Ijssel. There was a critical bridge; it needed to be taken, and eventually it was, though with many dead.

Quite a lot about this is known by Nell, because there had been anniversaries, there had been ceremonies, bagpipes had been played, wreaths laid. Speeches had been made, commemorating the liberation, remembering the food brought in to help the civilian population, which by then was starving. Nell and Tig and the grandchildren had attended several times. On one of these occasions, the main street was named for the Brig. Tig helped with the unveiling of the plaque. People shook his hand: he looked so much like his father, they said. People cried.

The first time they made the trip, an old man who had smuggled a map to Tig's father was still alive. The map showed the positions of the Germans, so the J.O.B. was able to do the clearing more efficiently, without bombing the city to pieces. This man had been very young during the occupation; like many young people he'd been in the Resistance. He'd also been a baker, so he was allowed to drive around in his little delivery car, and to be out in the early morning before curfew ended. He'd never been suspected because everyone thought he was stupid. But his brother had been caught, and shot.

He took Tig and Nell and the kids to a large house surrounded by dark trees: this was where Tig's father had stayed while directing the operations, he said. The same house was where the SS had done their torturing. Seven murdered young people had been found buried in the garden, his friends. Nothing had grown on that spot since.

The Resistance hiding places in the woods, the scenes of discovery and betrayal, the camouflaged location of the buzz bombs targeting England—he showed them all of it. That time was the present for him; he was still living in it. Still in anguish.

Along the river, the positions of the enemy machine-gun nests. According to Tig, who'd heard that much from his father, they'd contained boys. Twelve-year-olds, given ammunition and liquor and ordered to stay put until both were gone. The Brig's battle-hardened troops found they were shooting children, but fanatical children with deadly weapons. It was a heartbreaker, but what could you do?

The last visit that day was to the Canadian war cemetery with its rows of gravestones, the name and the regiment on each one. There was a white rose on every grave, placed there by the town's schoolchildren, for Easter. "More than they do at home," Tig murmured to Nell.

An old woman had joined them by then; she'd served in the Canadian canteen and helped with the nursing. She stood in the middle of the cemetery, her arms spread wide, tears running down her face. "These are my boys," she shouted to the sky.

Not *were*. *Are*.

"This is where your father was," the old man said to Tig. "This is where."

The Brig wrote another poem right after Deventer. It's the first one that has both a month and a day: April 18, 1945. On that date—Nell has checked the records—a large number of German soldiers surrendered. Thousands of them. There are pictures, black and white: long lines of men, dirty, tattered, shuffling along, hands sometimes behind their heads, flanked by guards with rifles.

THE WEHRMACHT 1945

In shadows of despair,
The dark door of defeat
Closes in silence.
No hope of triumph's glare
To hasten flagging feet.

Gone are the glorious hopes
Which, nurtured in conceit
Killed man's compassion.
The warrior sadly gropes
The way to judgments seat.

18 April 45

No gloating, no peacocking. Silence and dark doors clos-ing; diminuendo. After all the adrenalin, a letdown, for winners and losers alike. Nell has read memoirs: she's heard this mood described. Now what? Now living with it, with whatever you'd done, for whatever reason you thought had once justified doing those things. Some hadn't lived with it, on both sides. There had been suicides. You couldn't kill and kill and see the results of your killing and the results of the killing done by the others and just forget it. The images got inscribed on you too deeply, there was no way of erasing them. You could think you'd shoved all of it out of your skull but it was still there, waiting for you. People came in the evenings and sat in your chairs, and wouldn't speak to you. Some of those people were dead.

———

What came next? The army went north. The Brig was command-ing the 2nd Canadian Infantry when it liberated Westerbork, a transit pen where Jews were parked en route to the death camps. The liberation was shocking to those doing the liberating, accord-ing to reports. Though they might have been given a general alert, they seem to have been unprepared for the actuality. How could such places exist? Who could have imagined them?

The Brig reached Bergen-Belsen, days after the British had taken charge of it, and that was even worse.

No poems arose. Nor did the Brig ever speak about these expe-riences, to Tig's knowledge. Not until the end of his life, and then not to Tig, and then not much.

Soon after that, another explicitly dated poem:

"CEASE FIRE"

Our war is over. Men live
In fields where others died.
Pain is now forgotten? We recall
Friendship, nonsense, foolish laughter
With regimental pride.

No wild frivolity, our joy
Lies deep within our heart.
As an ardent lover curbs his love,
So we face today and smile
For fear that tears will start.

Germany, 9 May 45

The ninth of May was the day after the end of the war in Europe. Again, the ambiguous question mark: Pain is now forgotten? As in: *Think again.* Here's the ardent lover, appearing this time only as a simile, but again associated with a superficial smile and an inner sorrow. There is a fear of tears.

The Brig had just turned thirty-seven. Now would come the rest of his life.

Is that it? No more poems? Nell goes through the pages again to see if she has the sequence right. But look: she's missed something. On the back of the half-page containing "A Wish," there's another poem. This one—only this one—was typed on a different machine. Unlike all the others, it has a lower-case title.

the awakening.

The cold gray haze, the rising sun
With clear all-seeing eyes,
Watches the fleeting darkness run,
Truth stands naked, without guise.

The moon was clever, the clouds had skill
They blended well to gild the scene.
And now my eyes their sadness spill.
Sorrow lies where joy has been.

No date. What was going on here? Nell wonders. And which poem was written first? Is it the same woman or a different one, or is it even a woman? "Joy" would point to a romantic encounter—not, for instance, a battle scene—but the cold grey haze and the shadowed moon are like the landscape in "The Reichswald." "A Wish" seems to allude to events of sometime past, whereas "the awakening" is more immediate; but they're on the same piece of paper.

What was the history? No one left to ask. But what business is it of hers, anyway? None, except that she's inherited it, like the silver teapot, the sugar sifter, the fish knives. Objects move from hand to hand, things get forgotten about, their meanings evaporate.

What to do with the poems in their tidy folder? What to do with the parade sword leaning in a corner with the canoe paddles, or the Distinguished Service Order, which is in a cardboard box on a shelf in the cellar, or the silver pins and official buttons, shrouded in velvet and still in Tig's chest of drawers? What about the silent people, some alive, some dead, who sit in armchairs but aren't really there, and the man hanging in the shower? Because they are part of it too.

Then there's Martha Gellhorn's letter, the tiny piece of her journey that had touched the Brigadier's own story for an instant. "War is always worse than I knew how to say," she'd told a friend toward the end of her life. "Always."

Why am I so obsessed with all this? Nell asks herself. So entangled? Reading the letters of the dead. Snooping around in their heads. It was almost eighty years ago.

What is she doing, wandering around the house in the middle of the night, in the middle of this one condensed slice of past time in which so much is happening but so much is obscure? Pawing through the rubble, a brick here, a shard there, fragments of lives; trying to understand things that can't be understood, or not by her. Pieces of paper, folded in a pocket. The Brigadier saved these words up; he guarded them; he must have wanted someone to read them eventually. Otherwise he would have destroyed them.

I should give up. I'm the wrong person, Nell thinks. The wrong reader for you. I'm sorry. All I can say is: I hear you. Or I hear something. Or I'm trying to hear something. Yes?

WIDOWS

✦

Dear Stevie:

Thank you for your letter. I hope your health remains good.

It seems we must now begin a letter this way, with a Victorian tip of the hat to physical well-being: it's become a social prerequisite, as leaving calling cards once was. And we must end by saying, "Keep safe." What a ridiculous concept! There is no "safe." At any moment the fragile thread by which we dangle may break, and we may plummet into the unknown. "Safe," the word, ought to be outlawed. It gives people false ideas.

Sorry. I'm becoming cranky about language, a thing you don't do unless you're past a certain age. For youngsters, things were always called what they are called right now, but for oldsters, not. We notice the gaps, the chasms. And the jokes of former decades have ceased to be jokes, while new jokes have arisen, jokes that are not always understood by us. Joking happens less frequently in the puritanical moment we are passing through— not that I wish to sound judgmental—but a few laughs are still permitted, it seems.

Though each generation's catchphrases die on the vine as a matter of course. What did "twenty-three skidoo" mean? I said it as a child, but it was old even then and conveyed nothing to me except as part of a skipping rhyme. A sinister skipping rhyme, now that I think of it: a number of robbers have broken into a lady's house—grown-up women were called "ladies" then—and are giving orders to her, such as turning around and touching the ground. No good would come of this: there were twenty-three of the robbers and only one of her. But "skidoo" was this lady's exit line, so maybe she ran away.

What fun we used to make of death! Hallowe'en was a chance to put on a sheet and pretend to be a ghost, or to fill a bowl with peeled grapes, blindfold our little friends, and guide their hands to the bowl. "Eyeballs," we would say in sepulchral tones. "Ewww!" was the expected reply. Next would come a chant about dying, being buried, becoming worm-infested, and turning green. All hilarious, to us, then. But how many of our once large basket of impish children are left? Not many. Gone, and with them the vestiges of the grape eyeballs and the green decaying bodies. A few old cronies clinging onto the cliff's edge, having tea and cookies in the sun and spilling crumbs and milk on their not entirely clean T-shirts, or distressing their neighbours by trying—slowly, ponderously, slipping dangerously on the ice—to shovel the snow off their walks. Here, let me do that for you. Oh no, I can manage, thank you. Beetles near the end of their life cycles, still gamely making their way up the once familiar flower stalk. Where am I and what am I doing here? the beetle might be wondering. How long can they go on? the neighbours muse. Surely not much longer.

Oh, don't suppose for an instant that we don't know what they're thinking. We thought it all ourselves, once. We still think it.

But none of this is happening to you, dear Stevie. You are much younger, although you don't think so now. If you live another thirty years—which I sincerely hope you will, and more, depending on your condition by then, of course—if you live another thirty years and are still enjoying it, or most of it—if anyone will be enjoying, or indeed living, considering the huge unknown wave that is already rolling toward us—I expect you will look at a picture of yourself as you are today, supposing your personal effects have survived flood, fire, famine, plague, insurrection, invasion, or whatever—and you will say, "How young I was then!"

But that's a long digression. You asked me how I was doing, another social pleasantry. No one wants an honest answer to that one.

What you mean is how am I managing to cope, now that Tig has died. Am I lonely? Am I suffering? Is the house too empty? Am I checking all the boxes of the prescribed grieving process? Have I gone into the dark tunnel, dressed in mourning black with gloves and a veil, and come out the other end, all cheery and wearing bright colours and loaded for bear?

No. Because it's not a tunnel. There isn't any other end. Time has ceased to be linear, with life events and memories in a chronological row, like beads on a string. It's the strangest feeling, or experience, or rearrangement. I'm not sure I can explain it to you.

And it would alarm you unduly if I were to say to you, "Tig isn't exactly gone." You'd jump immediately to ghosts, or delusional states on my part, or dementia, but none of those would apply. You will understand it later, perhaps, this warping or folding of time. In some parts of this refolded time Tig still exists, as much as he ever did.

I don't intend to share any of this with you. I don't want you calling my younger friends and relatives in a state of concern and telling them something must be done about me. You were always a well-meaning busybody. I don't fault you for it—you have a kind heart, you are filled to the brim with good intentions, but I don't want any casseroles or oblique, probing questions, or visits from professionals, or nieces talking me into buying an assisted-care condo. And no, I do not wish to go on a cruise.

Meanwhile I'm hanging out with a clutch of other widows. Some of them are widowers: we have not yet got around to a gender-neutral term for those who have lost their life partners. Maybe TWHLTLP will appear shortly, but it hasn't yet. Some are women who have lost women or men who have lost men, but mostly they are women who have lost men. More fragile than we'd thought, those men: that much has made itself clear.

What do we talk about? The curious folding nature of time, the phenomenon I have just described to you: that has been experienced by all of us. The quirks and preferences of the lost ones. What they would have said—or are indeed still saying—on any given occasion.

The death scenes. We are a little obsessive about those: we share them, we revisit them, we edit them, arranging them to make them, perhaps, more tolerable. Which dwindling was the worst? Was it better to have witnessed a lingering fadeout, with pain but with lots of time to say goodbye, or on the other hand was a sudden stroke or heart failure preferable, easier for him, harder for you? *I could tell this was it. I left the room for five minutes and he was gone. We knew it was coming. Ten years? That must have been terrible.*

The tidying up. There's a lot of that. So much accumulates, year after year. Then there's a mini-explosion, and all the items that have been gathered together—the letters, the books, the passports, the photos, the favourite things kept in drawers and boxes or on shelves—all of this is strewn in the wake of the departing rocket or comet or wave of energy or silent breath, and the widows must sweep and sort and donate and bequeath and discard. Pieces of a soul, scattered here and there. The widows are thoroughly engaged by this task, and are being driven crazy by it in equal measure. We phone one another, all in a hand-wringing dither, and say, "What am I possibly supposed to do with . . . fill in the blank?" We offer lots of suggestions, none of which solves the central problem.

We talk about our regrets too; or some of them. *If only I had known. If only he had said. If only I had asked. I should have been more* . . . fill in the blank. *If only we had* . . . fill in the blank. There are a lot of blanks.

We're bad luck, of course, we widows. We know it. Awkward silences occur around us. People tiptoe. Should we be invited to dinner, or will we cast a pall? We certainly try not to cast palls: palls are unpleasant.

It used to be worse, in other places and in other eras. We'd get buried alive with the dead king, or we'd join him on his funeral pyre. If we escaped sharing his death, we'd have to wear black, or else white, forever. We had the evil eye. Black widow spiders, venomous enough to kill, were named after us. People crossed themselves and spat to avoid contamination by us. Or, if we were not decrepit—if we still had some blood left in us—we'd be merry widows, off the leash, looking for a little unbridled sexual action. An older man actually hinted at this to me at a party. (We do still go to parties. We paint our toenails red, though we put shoes on our feet so no one will see our flashy toes. We know this toe enhancement is absurd, but we do it anyway. A tiny dead-end pleasure.) I'd just met the man. No sooner were the introductions over than he gave the ghost of a leer and said, "So, are you dating?" Meant as a joke, though possibly not. Widows are thought to be wealthy, and also susceptible.

I answered, a little sternly, "I'm a widow. Tig just died."

"So, you're hunting?"

It was a form of geriatric flirting on his part, I believe. People of our age can flirt like that without it being seriously inappropriate, because both parties know nothing will come of it. Or, more precisely, nothing *can* come of it. Flirtation Village, that's where we live. If I'd had an old-fashioned fan, I would have tapped him with it, archly, as in some grotesque Restoration comedy. *Oh, you are so naughty!*

I could not have said, "Don't be silly. Tig is still here." Instant gossip would have resulted: "She's turned the corner into bonkersland." "Well, she was always a little odd." And the like.

So we keep such notions to ourselves, we widows.

✦

Needless to say, dear Stevie, I will not be sending you this letter. You are on the other side of the river. Over where you are, your beloved is still in tangible form. On this side, the widows. Between us flows the uncrossable. But I can wave to you, and wish you well, and that is what I will do. Thus:

✦

Dear Stevie:

Thank you for your letter. I hope your health remains good. It's nice of you to ask how I'm doing. Quite well, I'm pleased to say. The winter dragged on, as it did for everyone, but now it's spring and I'm busy in the garden. Already there are snowdrops, and the daffodils are sending up their first shoots. I have my eye on some oriental lilies that I intend to plant in the front border. I used to have them years ago but the lily beetles got to them before I noticed. I'll be ready for those beetles this time: forewarned is forearmed.

The children are fine. The grandchildren are full of beans. I'm thinking of adopting a kitten. Not much other news. Let me know when you're coming this way and we'll grab lunch.

Stay safe.

Fondly,
Nell

WOODEN BOX

✦

Nell shambles around, up and down the narrow stairs, in and out of rooms. Not aimlessly: she's looking for a book she wants to read. *Maigret Sets a Trap*. She's read it before, but she's forgotten what kind of trap. This time she won't peek at the end, this time she'll allow herself to be enticed. She can go slowly, she doesn't have to race through, she has enough space in her life for that now. Now that Tig.

There are portals in space-time, opening and closing like little frog mouths.

Things disappear into them, just vanish; but then they might appear again without warning. Things and people, here and then gone and then maybe here. You can't predict it.

One day not so long ago, Tig lost his upper bridge. That was what it was called by then, not false teeth, as in earlier centuries. They looked and looked but it was nowhere. Then pop, back it came, on top of the tall bookcase where Nell would not ordinarily have been able to spot it because she couldn't see up there. They'd searched everywhere else, so she'd reached the stepladder phase. Surprise! Why had Tig put it there? He never had before. Or had he put it there? Maybe it had been sucked into one of the portals. In here, out, then back up there, in quite a different place. So maybe Tig is somewhere now, instead of being simply gone.

Maigret Sets a Trap—here it is, in the laundry hamper. Where else?

Nell props herself against the kitchen counter and opens the book. She'll read while she's eating what passes for dinner: a piece of cheese, some leftover soup heated in the microwave, a day-old baked flour specimen that was supposed to be a croissant, cut into slices and browned in the toaster oven. It's like being a student again: the same disorganization and fecklessness and sudden bursts of intention, the same formless anxiety, the same bare-bones meals. How easily she has slipped back sixty years, give or take: grazing, dubious leftovers, no ceremony.

Tig liked table settings, he liked wineglasses. Cooking special recipes. Toasts to this or that memory, this or that person or cause. Occasions. Celebrations.

The people who made the croissant have evidently never seen a real one, Nell thinks, chewing. Flaky, not doughy, she broadcasts to them silently, whoever they are. What if she could have control over one of the frog-mouth portals and drop things into it? Away would go all the bad croissants.

Tig would just have thrown this doughy croissant out. Why eat food if you disapprove of it? he'd say. If you don't like the road, don't go. He'd laughed at her for being so frugal. I'm fighting waste, she'd say. Which was ridiculous: Why was it less wasteful for a croissant to go through her digestive system than through the compost pile? It was not.

The trap Inspector Maigret is setting is designed to catch a man who's been murdering women. He murders them in a particular neighbourhood, but for no special reason that Maigret can discern. The women have nothing in common, although it hasn't escaped him that they are all brunettes. Men get murdered too, only not quite so much; not in the Maigret books. Or is that just Nell's impression? Is it that she notices the murdered women more? How many of each, altogether?

She could count them. It would be a project.

It seems to her that most of what she's done in her life has been of this ilk. Projects, ultimately inconsequential. Who have they helped?

This scene or thrown-together dinner or reading interlude takes place in a cottage, or a sort of cottage. A second house that she and Tig had bought on impulse because it was there and they were there, and it was cheap, and it was in a wood, and why not, and it was a period of their life when they were still open to adventures. What they liked was the secluded location, the birds.

The house itself was in a sad state. It wasn't even finished: only the subflooring was in place, there were no baseboards—leaving a gap through which spiders, pill bugs, and millipedes came and went—and there were mushrooms growing out of one of the walls, due to high levels of humidity. They soon discovered that the water-filtration system discharged into the rudimentary basement: not a good plan. There were two bees' nests, a population of mice, and a screech owl living between the external wall and the plasterboard; and a family of starlings behind the soffit; and several squirrels in the crawl space under the roof, who were getting in through a hole made by flickers. It was lively in that house, at first.

Little by little they'd dealt with these inconveniences. Tig had finally ejected the squirrels, who might have burned the place down by chewing through the electrical wires. After several unsuccessful efforts involving the banging of pots and pans and the playing of rock 'n' roll, he'd climbed up on a stepladder and sprayed the crawl space full of cayenne pepper. The squirrels had staggered out, rubbing their eyes, and Tig had nailed a piece of tin over their entrance hole. After that, every time they'd seen him, they'd screamed at him.

To defeat the summer heat, Tig and Nell had added on a screened porch. Later, a downstairs work room, a shower, and an entranceway for taking off muddy or sandy boots after their wind-swept, rain-washed hikes. They'd stocked the kitchen with their favourite cooking doodads, they'd furnished the rooms with items scrounged from lawn sales and the local dump, they'd reroofed. How they had enjoyed all of it!

That was the active period. Then there had been the slow-down; an accumulation, as in sluggish rivers. Things ended up in this house that hadn't been needed in their city life but that they couldn't simply throw out. Layers of sediment, over thirty years of it, had sifted in during springs and summers and falls and springs and summers, and now Nell must dig down through these layers, excavate them, as if the house has been buried under the ash from a volcanic eruption. Will there be treasures perfectly preserved, as at Pompeii? Or a more fitting metaphor: an ancient tomb dis-covered in a desert or jungle, furnished with objects put there to assist the journey of the soul and its continued existence in the afterlife. A magazine rack—where had that come from, and when did they last use it? The magazines in it are at least a decade old. A disarticulated shotgun. A pewter stein with a cracked glass bottom.

Under the bathroom sink, a welter of pills and tubes and small bottles. Painkillers, long past their expiry date. Cough syrup, con-gealed. Toothpaste hard as wood.

At the very back, an ancient mug containing a wizened shaving brush and a shrunken, cracked plug of soap. The soap smells of nothing, it's that old. Similarly the shaving brush. No vestige of Tig remains on it, unlike his hairbrush, which still evokes him. She has tucked the hairbrush away into a little shrine in a night-table drawer, surrounded by a small flashlight, a couple of pencils, half a box of cough drops. If the children should come across this assemblage, will they think it's morbid? Yes. They will.

It is morbid, says Tig silently. But it's kind of funny too.

Oh great, thinks Nell. I have an imaginary friend who's a dead person. In this she is not the first.

When was it that Tig had habitually shaved? Except for the moustache. When had he stopped shaving at all, opting for the whole beard? So difficult to remember such details, although they'd made an impression at the time. There's a picture record—Kodachrome slides—but Nell isn't up to sorting them out just yet.

The mug is pre-Victorian, she guesses. The colour scheme is mauve and black. Inside a wreath of what may be olive leaves, there's a verse:

REMEMBRANCE.

The sun shall lose its splendour,
The tides shall cease to flow

And tyrants' hearts grow tender,
And melt at others' woe,

Thy frosty breath December,
Shall blight the flower of May

Ere I cease to remember
The freuds now far away!

It's *freuds* rather than *friends:* someone doing the printing—how? A stencil of some kind?—had left out an *i* and got the *n* upside down. How long had it taken for anyone to notice? Not very long, Nell guesses, but by that time the batch of mugs would have been fired, and there was no way to correct a typo on a glazed mug, and they wouldn't have wanted to waste them, and anyone who complained could have been given a correctly spelled one from the next batch. That would have been the thinking of anyone operating close to the bottom line, as the mug-makers must have been: it was a cheap mug.

On the other side of the mug there's an image. Three barefoot children: a boy in ragged britches holding several tree branches, an older girl carrying a toddler. In the background, a house with a thatched roof. A couple of dark blobs that might be stones, or possibly animals. In the far distance, a pointed mountain. A title: "Young Cottagers." It's a bad copy of a well-known painting by Gainsborough, sometimes called *The Wood Gatherers;* Nell remembers it from various art history books. The mug manufacturers reversed the image from left to right, added the house, and tidied things up considerably from the down-at-heels original, which was a study in rural poverty.

What do the young children have to do with the absent freuds? Nell wonders. And where did Tig get this mug, which she can't recall having seen before, even though it must have been under the sink for thirty years? Did he pick it up in some flea market in England, before her time? Had he found it droll? Was it a gift, and if so, who was the giver? Perhaps it had been a kind of joke—an ironic wink at sentiment. Freuds. Someone in his group must have appreciated the Freudian slipware: Freud was much in vogue back then.

"Not funny, you asshole," she says out loud. Not to Tig: to the unseen trickster who slid this mug into her own timeline, hiding it. Planting it for her to find, now that Tig.

Look: she's crying again. "Oh stop it," she says. But she does not stop.

It was Tig who liked Inspector Maigret the most. He didn't much care about who got murdered. He just wanted to be in France, in the 1930s if possible, or possibly in the 1950s, when he himself had first gone there. He wanted the same zinc-topped bars, the same seedy hotel rooms, the same mean-eyed concierges, the cafés in provincial towns where everyone has something to hide; he wanted to be sitting in the sunlight with a glass of white wine while nervous locals told him lies. He wanted to listen in on Maigret's ponderous trains of thought, get drenched in the same dark pouring rain while wearing the mandatory belted trench coat and muffler. He wanted to eat in Maigret's habitual bistros, warm himself at Maigret's ogre of a wood stove that would cause clouds of steam to rise from damp clothing, smoke Maigret's pipes— a comfort after he'd no longer been able to smoke his own pipes, although he'd kept them, all lined up in a pipe stand, old friends. He appreciated the fact that Maigret sometimes let the murderer go because he saw that the murder had been a kind of accident, or felt that the murdered person had it coming. Tig would have done the same.

A year before he died—or was it less?—Tig stopped being able to read. He was losing names too. Once, at supper . . . Suppers became a whole other story, frantic improvisations that Nell would throw together as best she could, not having cooked much for years, since Tig had liked to do that. Cans of clam chowder and frozen peas became her fallbacks. Once, at supper—a can of chicken noodle soup she'd doctored with cream and a handful of parsley . . .

"This is delicious," Tig said, as he often did now. The old Tig would have viewed these slapdash measures with disdain, he'd liked to make everything from scratch . . .

Once, at supper, Tig paused, spoon half lifted, and looked out the window. "He sometimes let them go," he said.

Nell knew exactly who he meant, and what he meant. He meant Maigret. You can recognize whole songs, whole symphonies, from just a few notes, if you know the music well.

The house is a problem. Of course it is. Everything that was effortless back when Tig was functional is now part of an obstacle course Nell must run. Correction: walk.

The house is a storey and a half: cathedral ceiling over the ground-floor living area, bedrooms above, with a balcony running along the access hallway. They'd installed skylights to keep the house from turning into an oven in summer; these must be opened and closed with rod-like devices that require one hand to hold on to them while the other hand twists, but Nell can't quite reach them. They're too high—though not too high for Tig—and she has to stand on something. A little wooden stool, bought at a junk sale many years ago. It's tippy. One misstep and will she go headfirst over the balcony railing, fall onto the tiled floor below, and break her neck? The narrow painted stairs are slippery and too steep. If she topples down them, she'll be all but finished; a broken hip at the very least.

The awnings that must be rolled in when it rains and out when it blazes are a workout in themselves. She and Tig had installed them as a substitute for air conditioning, which would have been moderately useless anyway: they would just have been cooling the great outdoors. It's a cottage, after all; it's a sieve; and anyway global warming and so forth, they'd known about it back then, thirty years ago, when it hadn't been too close or too late. They'd done their cooling with fans, and with air flow: opening and closing the windows, rolling the awnings in and out. If the awnings were already out when it poured they filled with water, and sagging and breakage could result. One time they forgot, and had to rush outside with brooms and push the awnings up from underneath to expel the water, with the thunder booming around them. They'd got drenched.

Now she has to tend to all of this by herself. Run here and there. Correction again: walk. Walk mindfully, or it's down the stairs with you, break your neck, she tells herself. In recent years the stairs had worried her on Tig's account: if he fell down them she wouldn't be able to pick him up. But now the worry is about herself.

"Fuck it, Tig," she says out loud.

Take it slow, he replies soundlessly. You'll be fine.

"When?" she asks him. "When will I be fine?"

Nell and Tig sit side by side on a bench in the cool evening air, watching the sunset. They've had a sauna in the little shack Tig designed and built for the purpose, back when he was first feeling arthritic, back when he thought such a thing as a sauna might reverse time. No such luck, but anyway here they are.

They're holding hands. They're wearing white terry-cloth bathrobes like those in spas, bought by Nell when white terry-cloth bathrobes were a thing, when spas were a thing. Maybe both of these are still things; Nell hasn't checked. Keeping up with the times has lost its appeal. Strings of cotton thread dangle here and there from their bathrobes: it's a problem with terry cloth. Nell makes a note to cut them off.

Tig would never have gone to a spa. He preferred cigars. The bathrobe is too small for him, the arms are too short. His wrists and forearms extend from the sleeves like those of Frankenstein monsters in old films. So like a mad scientist: to cut up corpses and stitch brains and body parts together while paying no attention to the clothing size that might fit the finished product.

The declining sun is orange, then red: fair day tomorrow.

"We've had a good long run," Tig says.

"Yes, we have."

"We've been very lucky."

"Yes, we have."

"We did some good stuff."

"Yes, we did."

"Thank you."

Tig is saying thank you a lot these days: too much for Nell. She pushes it away, this unaccustomed gratitude. She doesn't want it. She wants the old Tig back, the more careless one, intent on his own trajectory, rollicking through life while paying scant attention to what he might owe, to her or to anyone else; including, for instance, credit card companies or tax collectors. Nell, a conscientious bill-payer, had found this feature of Tig alarming, but also obscurely thrilling. She doesn't like it that he is now balancing some unspoken spiritual account. How to respond to these thank yous?

"Thank you too," she says. That seems more or less right.

There's a pause. Silent words are said and heard. I'll be leaving soon. No! Don't go! Will you help me get out of this when the time comes? Yes, but not yet.

"I want to still be me," says Tig.

"You still are you," Nell says.

"So far," says Tig.

Another pause. "We'll get through it," says Nell.

"Yes, we will," says Tig. They squeeze hands.

It's not the first time they've had this conversation. It will not be the last. Nell, for instance, is having it now, in the middle of the night. Where is Inspector Maigret when she needs him? He'd follow the clues, he'd figure it out. Aha, he would say, or something similar, but French: Tiens!

Quick, open the book, she orders herself. Step into it. Tiens! The trap Maigret is setting is a policewoman, a brunette, pretending to be a potential murder victim. Sometimes you cut it too close, she scolds him. What if this decoy really does get murdered? But she won't, and neither will Maigret. He'll live on forever, drinking his beers in his cafés, smoking his pipes, eating in his bistros, setting his traps.

Nell is cleaning the refrigerator, another time-filling nocturnal project. It's quite a new refrigerator; the previous one had to be discarded after there was a power outage when they were away and the fridge didn't come back on, and the package of frozen shrimp that was in the freezer went bad. There is almost nothing smellier than rotting shrimp. They were always careful about leaving the freezer empty after that.

Out must go the half-jars of pickles, the suspicious ketchup remnants, the no longer possible mayo, the Crisco, designed to last almost forever but there are limits. The cans of tonic water may stay; also the small bottle of lime juice, as it hasn't been opened.

On one of the door shelves there's a jar of marmalade. The name on it is Tig's, the date is a year and a half ago. It's from the last batch he'd made. They'd made.

When they'd begun—another enthusiasm, plunged into with gusto, with a marmalade kettle acquired for the purpose—Tig had done almost all of it himself. He'd bought the Seville oranges, he'd cut them up, he'd weighed and measured. He'd copied out a special recipe that involved tying up orange pips in a cheesecloth bag and soaking them overnight. He'd sterilized the jars, he'd boiled and boiled, he'd refrained from stirring.

Nell, once an accomplished jelly-maker—apple, jalapeno, wild grape, when was that?—was called in only at the end, because she was thought to have the secret of jelling: the waving around of a hot, syrupy spoon, the blowing on it, the depositing of a blob onto a cool white plate, the close observation to see if it was runny, or wrinkly, or set. All this with the aid of a candy thermometer; but it wasn't infallible, she'd still needed the spoon and the plate. Once or twice she hadn't waited long enough and they'd had to dump the contents of the jars back into the kettle and boil the marmalade some more, but only once or twice.

Tig loved making the marmalade. He'd labelled every jar, dated each one, signed them with his name. Marmalade lovers among their friends had been gifted, though of course Tig and Nell had kept enough for themselves. Tig piled his marmalade onto brown toast, added ground pepper. He didn't like things that were too sweet.

Over time, Nell's role had grown. Things had become a little tense. Tact was required. Tig could still cut up the oranges, but Nell had to decode the special recipe since Tig could no longer read his own handwriting. She'd had to do the measuring. It was a close-run thing, but they'd managed to turn out that one final batch.

Nell had taken a picture of it: the jars set out on newspaper, neatly labelled—she'd done the writing, though with Tig's name; Tig sitting at the kitchen counter, behind the array. In the picture he has a rueful expression, almost like a shrug. Does he feel like an imposter? Is he sad, remembering his former marmalade prowess? Is he happy they've at least fulfilled the ceremony? Hard to decipher.

Now here's the jam in the refrigerator, the last jar ever. The last half-jar. Should she eat it or not eat it? Either one seems like a violation.

Go to bed, she tells herself. Go to sleep. In the morning it will just be marmalade.

"I'm not much interested in *them* anymore," Tig said, shortly before he. Before.

"Them?"

"All that."

"You mean politicians," Nell said.

Tig had once been very interested in them and all that. He'd listened to the news every evening, adding commentary, uttering brief shouts, and also swearing.

"Yes. Them."

The year before, he would have said, "Fuckpigs." The year before that it would have been, more elaborately, "One a penny, two a penny, fuckpigs all."

Though he'd approved of some of them, once. Public health care: he'd approved of that.

Nell found herself wondering about the word. *Fuck* and *pig* could both be insults, but the juxtaposition equalled more than the sum of its parts. Was it the pig who did the fucking, or the other way around?

"I just like to watch the trees now," Tig said. "They aren't very interested in all of that either."

Then, after a pause: "They don't know what to do." He doesn't mean the trees, he means the fuckpigs. "Nobody knows."

"The mess we're in? The mess the planet's in?"

"Yes." And, after another pause: "It isn't only them. It's us. It's all of us."

"You mean humans?"

"Yes. Us." A pause. "Not on purpose. But nobody knows."

He liked thunderstorms too. In addition to the trees.

Strange markings began appearing on Tig's arms. He pointed to them. At first Nell couldn't see. Was he imagining things? No, there were faint bruises, deep down, as if underwater. Mottling. Somewhat later, more alarmingly, small cracks in the skin, beaded with blood. But he hadn't bumped into anything, he hadn't cut himself. Or had he? How was she to know?

"Does it hurt?" she asked him.

"No."

This was somehow worse.

Tig took to sleeping a lot. He slept too much during the days, until Nell discovered that he'd got the medication bottles mixed up and was taking the night-time pills in the morning. She ought to have checked the labels earlier. Once she got the pill bottles straightened out, he slept too much at night. He went to bed before Nell could. She had to prowl around, turning lights off, turning heat down, checking the doors. Tig used to do those things.

Then she would creep into bed beside him. What if she woke up in the morning and he wasn't breathing?

She would hold on to him while he slept. "Don't go, don't go," she would whisper. She only said that when he was asleep. If she were to say it when he was awake, what answer could he give? Neither of them had any control over it, this gradual departure of his. He would only feel guilty at abandoning her.

It's an optical illusion, the retreating figure dwindling, growing smaller and smaller and then disappearing in the distance. Those retreating stay the same size. They aren't really diminished, they aren't really gone. It's just that you can't see them.

One year, Tig and Nell decided to spend the month of March in this house. It's on an island, reached by a ferry, but not from December to April: in those months the only way on and off is by small plane. On the first of April that year, the ferry was scheduled to start again. They would fly over in March, then they would cross back on the ferry in April and rejoin their car. That was the plan.

At the beginning of March, the lake was still ice-covered. So were many of the island roads. The temperature was sub-zero. Theoretically their house was winterized, but as usual there was a gap between theory and real life. The baseboard heaters were inefficient and expensive. The wood stove worked fine as long as you kept putting wood into it, which meant they went to bed warm and woke up freezing. There were extra blankets, there were hot-water bottles; one of them burst and had to be discarded. There was long underwear.

Tig loved all of this. He found it energizing. He split wood with his various axes and thrashed around among the trees, cutting things with his chainsaw. The two of them walked on the gale-swept beaches, devoid of people at that time of year, sand blowing into their faces. They roasted dinners in the oven, which was folly in the summers. They read murder mysteries in the evenings, with the fire blazing in the stove and one of Tig's favourite CDs playing.

He was in a lieder phase then: Elly Ameling. Either that, or Waylon Jennings, or Stan Rogers. His tastes were eclectic.

But at the beginning of April there was no ferry. It had had an accident and was in for repair. Meanwhile, the plane had stopped flying. They were marooned. Not only that, supplies were low at the only grocery store on the island, which had been counting on the ferry to deliver the spring orders. All they had in the way of fresh fruit was bananas. Luckily there were several recipes for bananas. They tried all: fritters, fried with brown sugar, made into bread. They were running out of butter, however. That might be harsh.

Nell counted the dry goods on hand. Macaroni, rice, noodles. They would definitely survive, though life might get starchy. By this time most of the snow had melted on what passed for their lawn. They had let the weeds grow one year just to see what would happen—more butterflies, perhaps?—but the dried plants were a fire hazard, so they'd gone back to mowing. Nell went outside with a knife and a bowl to dig up spring dandelions as a vitamin-rich supplement to all the white things. Pissenlit was the French vernacular for dandelion: piss your bed, dandelions being a well-known diuretic. Madame Maigret would doubtless have prepared them in season—she was a formidable cook, unlike Nell—but being gently spoken, she would have used the more elegant dent-de-lion. Lion's tooth.

Nell poked in the earth with her knife, digging up the pissenlits. The plants were the right age: after the buds began to open they got too bitter. While she was doing this, crouched down near the ground, a wave of the spring vulture migration passed overhead. The vultures kept a sharp lookout for any living thing that might be ill and possibly close to expiring. They got a glimpse of Nell, circled around, then settled in the trees near the house, eyeing her hopefully.

Once her bowl was full of dandelion greens, she stood up. There was a flapping. "Not today," she said to them. "We're still alive."

Vultures are always right eventually, she thinks now. After all, they were gods once. Protectors. Eaters of the outworn.

Nell gave away most of Tig's clothes, but she kept three shirts. All of them were blue, with small bright patterns: shirts of a kind Tig had worn for decades. Her idea had been that she would wear them herself on casual occasions, with the sleeves rolled up because of course they were much too big for her, over jeans or summer pants, and she would have the sensation of Tig wrapping his arms around her and hugging her gently. It would be comforting, she'd thought.

This hasn't happened. The three blue shirts are not comforting.

They hang in her closet, to the left of the pink and white linen tops that she wears in summer. She's pushed them to the side, into the corner, as far as they will go. She can neither look at them nor put them on.

What next? It's a standoff. They're just cloth, she tells herself. She refuses to be reproached by three pieces of fabric. Reproached, implored, intreated; and they won't even say what they want.

One day she'll take them off the hangers, all three at once, and drop them on the table, and plunge her hands and face into them as if into a pool. Washing, baptizing, drowning? Some kind of miserable ritual.

On Tig's desk there's an accumulation. Bottles of ink; a mixed heap of paperclips, copper pennies green with tarnish, picture-hanging hooks and wires, dried-out rubber bands, bent thumbtacks; files of old documents having to do with the pond Tig made, back in the woods, for the benefit of frogs and snakes; withered receipts; used tickets.

On one side of the desk, an oblong box, ten inches long or so. Handmade; not very well, an amateur effort. It's wood, with a dark varnish. Tig's name is stamped or embossed on one end of it, probably with letters of metal that you hit with a hammer, one by one: the spacing is uneven.

It looks like a high-school project, something Tig would have made when he was thirteen or fourteen in a class called Shop— short for wood shop. You were supposed to learn the uses of edged tools and blunt instruments—saws, gouges, screwdrivers, drills—by turning out towel racks, spice shelves, and other items that could be presented to mothers on holiday occasions, when they would be admired more than was merited.

Girls did not take shop classes then. They were not supposed to know about hammers. Instead, they cooked. Harvard beets, whatever they were; Nell seems to remember they had orange rind in them, or was it vinegar? Blancmange, vanished from memory. Floating Island, archaic as the pyramids.

Pans of brownies. At least those are not gone.

A picture in a magazine: two teenage girls, long hair parted to the side and held in place with barrettes in the shape of bows, oven-mitted, dark-lipsticked, with dimpled smiles, holding out their pans of brownies toward two appreciative teenage boys in shirts and jackets and ties, hair slicked down with water, also smiling. Very polite, the four of them. The kids who'd posed for the shot must be dead by now.

Girls cooked treats for others. Boys made wooden items for others. That's how it used to go.

Tig had made the box for himself, however. He'd kept it all those decades. What treasure was he hiding in it?

Nell opens it. Two large darning needles and a skein of braided

wool, different colours, of the kind for darning socks; Tig being
of a generation that would have learned how to do that, at Boy
Scouts perhaps, and who would have been taught that socks ought
to be darned. Nell had never known him to darn any socks—if he
needed something sewed, he gave it to her—but here is the proof
that it was always a possibility. Self-sufficiency: a worthy aim. A
fellow had to know how to look after himself. Socks were important, they kept you from getting blisters if you needed to go on a
long march. To escape, for instance. To evade the enemy. Also,
you never knew when you might find yourself on a desert island,
where such a skill would be valuable. Or Tig never knew. At any
moment a dangerous accident could occur.

A pair of glasses, with owlish round lenses, minus one of their
arms. Those were from before Tig's cataract operation, which had
turned the world full-colour again, at least for a short time.

Three large brown-leather braided buttons, from no garment
that Nell can recall.

How long had it been since Tig had looked inside that box? Had
he forgotten all about it?

Or had he left the box for Nell? Is it a trap, like the shaving mug?
One more ambush, hidden under a sink or camouflaged as daily
background, poised to leap out at her suddenly before she's in any
way ready.

"How could you?" she says to him.

He's puzzled. What did I do?

"Your wooden box," she says. "Why did you leave it behind like
that? For me to find?"

Why are you crying? he says. It's just a box. Thank you. We had
a good long run. You'll be fine.

OLD BABES IN THE WOOD

✦

P ants or dead leaves?" Lizzie says.

"My guess is pants," Nell says. The two of them stand on the dock in their age-inappropriate bathing suits and stare at the dark patch under the water.

An hour earlier, Nell was toasting her laundry on the dock, which was the best place to dry it: it had been the best place for seventy years. But she didn't put rocks on top of her cotton yoga pants, though she ought to have known better, and then she went back up the hill to the house, through the sighing and rustling trees. The pants are lightweight, and they seem to have blown away. Logic dictates that they must be somewhere in the lake. Other pants she might have kissed goodbye, but she's fond of these.

"I'll go in," she says.

"Maybe it's not pants," Lizzie says dubiously. Waterlogged leaves accumulate on the sandy, rocky lake bottom. Their older brother, Robbie, sometimes rakes them out as a courtesy to others, along with the tiny water weeds that grow if allowed, and puts the resulting sludge into a large zinc washtub, after which its fate is unknown to Nell. The rake and the tub are leaning against a tree, thus he must have done this recently. Though only on the other side of the dock. So it might still be leaves.

Nell sits on the edge of the dock, then gingerly eases herself down, conscious of possible splinters. She and splinters have a long history. Splinters in the bum are especially bad because you can't see to pull them out.

Her feet hit sand. The water is up to her waist.

"Is it cold?" Lizzie asks. She knows the answer.

"It's been colder." This is always true. Did the two of them really once hurl themselves off the end of the dock into the freezing, heart-shocking water, laughing their heads off? Did they cannonball? They did.

Nell has a flash of Lizzie at a much younger age—younger even than the cannonballing—two or three. "A pider! A big pider!" she was saying. She couldn't yet pronounce "spider." Pider. Poon. Plash. Nell herself had been what, at that time? Fifteen. A seasoned babysitter. It won't hurt you. See, it's running away. Spiders are afraid of us. It's hiding under the dock. But Lizzie was not reassured. She's remained that way: beneath every bland surface there's bound to be something with too many legs.

"Am I aimed right?" Nell asks. Her feet move tentatively, encountering soft tickles, oatmeal-textured gunk, tiny sharp stones, what feels like a stick. She's up to her armpits now; she can't see the dark patch because of the angle of reflection.

"More or less," Lizzie says. She slaps at her bare legs: stable flies. There's a technique to killing them—they take off backwards, you have to sneak up with your hand—but it requires focus. "Okay, warmer. Warmer. A little to the right."

"I see it," Nell says. "Definitely pants." She fishes around with the toes of her left foot and brings the pants up, dripping. She can still fish things up with her toes, it seems: a minor accomplishment, but not to be sneered at. Enjoy the moment, it won't last, she comments to herself.

Tomorrow she might tackle the wide strips of grey paint, or stain, that have flaked off the dock and are lying on the lake bottom like sinister sci-fi fungus growths. It was Lizzie who painted the dock; it was Robbie who'd wanted it painted. He thought it would preserve the planks, keep them from rotting, so they wouldn't have to rebuild the dock yet again. How many times have they done that? Three, four?

Wrong about the paint, or stain, as it turned out: the dock is peeling like a sunburn, and water gets under the remaining patches, softening the wood. Still, they may not have to rebuild the dock themselves; this one could last them out. The younger gen will have to do it, assuming they're up to it.

That was the kind of thing their mother used to say about her clothing. I don't need another sweater. This one will last me out. Nell had hated it at the time. Parents ought not to die; it's inconsiderate.

Pants in hand, Nell wades back to the dock. She has a brief moment of wondering how she's going to clamber back up. There's a decaying makeshift step on the other side, made of two boards and covered with mossy growth, but it's a death trap and ought to be removed. A sledgehammer would do it. But then there would be a couple of lethal rusty spike heads sticking out of the huge log the step is attached to. Someone will have to go at the step with a crowbar, but it won't be Nell. All she needs is one of those spikes popping out suddenly and backwards she'll go, into the shallows, and brain herself on the annoying pointed white rock they keep meaning to dig out but haven't got around to.

On second thought, better to hammer the rusty spikes in, not pull them out. Now who, exactly, is going to do that?

Nell flings her sopping-wet pants onto the dock. Then, placing her feet carefully on the slippery logs of the underwater crib that holds the dock in place and gripping the nearest wooden tie-up cleat, she hoists herself up. You old ninny, you really shouldn't be doing this, she tells herself. One of these days you'll break your neck.

"Victory," Lizzie says. "Let's have tea."

Having tea is sooner said than done. To begin with, they're out of water, a problem they've anticipated by bringing a pail down the hill. Now they must wrestle with the hand pump. It's creakier than ever this year, the flow of water is diminished, and there's a pronounced iron tang, which probably means that the sand point far underground is clogging up or disintegrating. *Ask Robbie about sand point,* Lizzie has written on one of the numerous lists she and Nell are endlessly making and then either losing or throwing away.

The choices are: dig the thing up, a nightmare; or sink a new point, also a nightmare. They'll end up with one of the sons, or grandsons, or two of them, being called upon to do the actual sledgehammering. No one can expect old biddies of the ages of Nell and Lizzie to do it themselves.

No one, that is, except the two of them. They'll start, then they'll injure themselves—the knees, the back, the ankles—and the younger gen will be forced to take over. They will do it wrong, of course. Of course! Tongue-biting will be in order from Lizzie and Nell. Or, better, they'll say they have headaches so they won't have to watch, then they'll wander up to the cabin and read murder mysteries. Lizzie has the family's accumulation of flyspecked and yellowing paperbacks arranged by author on a shelf in her room, ever since a large mouse nest was discovered behind its former location.

They take turns with the pump handle. Once they've got a pailful—or a half-pail, because neither one of them is up to lugging a full pail, not anymore—they stagger up the steep hill, which is inset with tripping hazards in the form of steps made of flat rocks, switching the pail back and forth until they arrive at the top, breathing heavily. Heart-attack city, here I come, Nell thinks.

"Why the fuck did he have to put it at the top of this fucking hill?" Lizzie says. *He* changes its referent depending on what they're talking about; right now, *he* is their father. *It* is the log cabin he built, with axes, crosscut saws, crowbars, drawknives, and other tools of Primitive Man.

"To discourage invaders," Nell says. This is only partly a joke. Every time they see a boat trolling unpleasantly close to them—their sandy point is a known spot for pickerel—they have the same reaction: Invaders!

They make it in through the screen door of the cabin, spilling only a little of the water. "We need to do something about the front steps," Lizzie says. "They're too high. Not to mention the back steps. We've got to get a railing. I don't know what he was thinking."

"He didn't intend to get old," Nell says.

"Yeah, that was a fucking surprise," Lizzie says.

They all helped build the cabin, once upon a time. Their father did most of the work, naturally, but it was a family project, involving child labour. Now they're more or less stuck with it.

Other people don't live like this, Nell thinks. Other people's cottages have generators. They have running water. They have gas barbecues. Why are we trapped in some kind of historical re-enactment TV show?

"Remember when we could do two pails?" Lizzie says. "Each?" That wasn't so very long ago.

It's too hot to have the wood stove on, so they heat the water on the ancient two-burner propane-cylinder camping stove. It's rusting out around the intake pipe, but so far there have been no explosions. *New propane stove* is on the list. The kettle is aluminum, of a type that has surely been outlawed. Just looking at it gives Nell cancer, but an unspoken rule says that it must never be discarded. The cover will fit only if placed just right: Nell marked the position years ago, with two circles of pink nail polish, one on the lid, a corresponding one on the kettle itself, which must be stored upside down so that mice won't make their way down the spout and starve to death and make a horrible smell, plus maggots. Learn by doing, Nell thinks. There have been enough dead mice and maggots in her life.

The tea in the lidded 1940s enamelled roasting pan labelled "Tea" is practically sawdust; they keep meaning to throw it out. Lizzie has come prepared, with her own tea bags in a plastic ziplock. Bags are easier to discard than soggy tea leaves, even though everyone knows that tea bags are made from floor sweepings and mud. In the days of Tig, he and Nell had always used loose-leaf, which he bought at a little specialty shop run by a knowledgeable woman from India. Tig would have derided the tea bags.

The days of Tig. Over now.

High up on the wall, above the wood stove, hangs the flat oblong griddle that Nell and Tig bought at a farm auction forty-odd years ago, and on which jovial sourdough pancake fryings often took place, Tig doing the flipping, back when largesse and riotous living and growing children had been the order of the day. Coming up! Who's next? She can't look directly at this griddle—she glances up at it, then glances away—but she always knows it's there.

My heart is broken, Nell thinks. But in our family we don't say,

"My heart is broken." We say, "Are there any cookies?" One must eat. One must keep busy. One must distract oneself. But why? What for? For whom?

"Are there any cookies?" she manages to croak out.

"No," Lizzie says. "But there's chocolate. Let's have some." She knows that Nell's heart is broken; she doesn't need to be told.

They take their cups of tea and their treat—two squares of chocolate each, salted almond—and sit at the table that's out on the little screened porch. Lizzie has brought the current list so they can update it.

"We can scratch off 'Boots and shoes,'" Lizzie says.

"Yippee for that," Nell says.

They spent the previous day going through the plastic bags hanging from nails in Robbie's old bedroom. Each contained an ancient pair of shoes and a mouse nest. The mice liked nesting in shoes; they filled them with chewed-up bark and wood and fabric threads they'd filched from the doorway curtains and anything else that suited their purposes. A mouse had once tried to pull out some of Lizzie's hair during the night.

The mice had their babies inside the hung-up shoes and pooped into the bottoms of the plastic bags, when they weren't pooping on the kitchen counter or around the sink in the washroom, leaving tiny black seeds everywhere. Lizzie and Nell habitually set a trap for them, which consisted of a tall swing-top garbage pail with a blob of peanut butter strategically placed on the cover. In theory, the mouse leaps onto the cover to get the peanut butter and falls into the pail. Usually it works, though sometimes the peanut butter is gone in the morning and there is no mouse. The trapped mice make a sound like popcorn as they jump up, hitting the top of the container. Nell and Lizzie always put some raisins in the pail and a paper towel for them to hide under, and in the mornings they canoe the mice across the lake—they'd come back otherwise, they'd seek out their nest smell—and release them on the far shore.

Robbie is more severe. He uses mousetraps. Nell and Lizzie believe that this practice is detrimental to owls, as owls prefer to hunt live mice, but they don't say this because Robbie would laugh at them.

Yesterday Nell and Lizzie lined up the mouse-nest shoes, plus a rubber boot with an epic nest in it, took pictures on their phones, and sent the pictures to Robbie: Can we throw these out? He replied that they should leave all footgear until he himself came up; he would then decide what should be saved. Fair enough, they said, but no more hanging shoes in plastic bags: mouse-nesting was a crime of opportunity and must be discouraged.

"Write 'Snap-top container for Robbie's shoes' on the list," Nell says. Lizzie does so. Lists procreate; they give rise to other lists. Nell wonders if there's a special therapy for excessive list-making. But if the two of them don't make lists, how will they remember what they need? Anyway, they like crossing things off. It makes them feel that they are getting somewhere.

After supper, which is pasta—"Write 'More pasta,'" Nell says— they walk out to the sandy point, where they've set up two camping chairs, the folding kind with a mesh pocket in one arm to put a beer can in. One of the chairs has a hole in it, eaten by mice, but it's not a major hole. Anything you don't actually fall through is not a major hole. The chairs face northwest; Nell and Lizzie sit in them every evening and watch the sunset. It's the best way of predicting the next day's weather, better than the radio or the different websites on their phones. That plus the barometer, though the barometer isn't much help because it almost always says "Change."

"It's a little too peach," Lizzie says.

"At least it's not yellow." Yellow and grey are the worst. Pink and red are the best. Peach can go either way.

They stay out there as the clouds fade from peach to rose, and then to a truly alarming shade of red, like a forest fire in the distance.

Sure enough, when they make it back to the cabin, a trip they can both do in the dusk, which is just as well because they forgot the flashlight, the barometer has moved up slightly, from the *a* to the *n* in "Change."

"No hurricane tomorrow," Lizzie says.

"Hallelujah!" Nell says. "We won't go to Oz in a tornado."

There actually was a tornado here, in the days of Tig. It was only a little one, though it snapped off some tree trunks just like matchsticks. When was that?

Once it's truly dark, Nell puts on her headlamp and takes a flash-light and shuffles her way to the dock. She used to walk around at night without lighting—she could see in the dark—but night vision is one of the things that go. She doesn't want to hurtle down the hill, crippling herself on the pieces of geology that serve as steps or were stashed here and there by her father for some arcane purpose, forgotten now; nor does she want to step on any small toads. These come out at night and hop around, bent on adventures of their own, and are slippery when squashed.

She's going to the dock to view the stars, out over the lake, with no treetops obscuring them. It's a clear night, no moon yet, and the constellations have a depth and brilliance you'd never be able to see in the city.

Tig used to do this. He'd go down to the dock to brush his teeth and stargaze. "Amazing!" he would say. He had a great capacity for being amazed; the stars gave him such joy. There may be some falling stars: it's August, the time of the Perseids, which always coincided with Tig's birthday. Nell would make him a cake in the wood-stove oven—scorching it on the top, sometimes, but that part could be scraped off—and decorate it with cedar cones and tufts of club moss and whatever else she could find. There might even be a few strawberries, left over from the patch that had grown in what used to be the garden.

She makes it to the bottom of the hill without mishap, an achievement. But, once she's on the dock, she can't follow through. She's not feeling any amazement or joy, only grief and more grief. The old griddle hanging on the wall above the stove is one thing— easy enough for the gaze to avoid it—but the stars? Will she never be able to look at the stars again?

No stars, not for you, not ever, she mourns. And in the next breath: Don't be so fucking maudlin.

She hauls herself back up the hill, guided by the light that has now come on inside the cabin. She half expects to see Tig in the evening lamplight, uttering whoops of enthusiasm over whatever he might be reading. Not half. Less than half. Is he fading?

In the olden times, which are numerous, Nell and Lizzie and Robbie used kerosene lamps, which had to be treated with the utmost caution—the wicks or mantles were prone to flare up or carbonize—but the modern age has taken its toll and now they have a marine battery, recharged by a solar panel during the day, into which they plug an electric lamp. By the light of this lamp, Nell and Lizzie set out to do a jigsaw puzzle. It's one they did before, thousands of years ago—a wetland with a lot of bulrushes and waterbirds and vine-infested vegetation—and, as they work on it, Nell begins to remember its fiendish intricacies: the root clumps, the patches of sky and cloud, the deceptive spikes of purple flowers.

It's best to solve the edges first, and they do make some headway. But there are two edge pieces missing—has somebody lost them? Some member of the younger gen, invading Lizzie's hoard of sacrosanct jigsaw puzzles? "How irritating," they mutter to each other, though Lizzie discovers one of the keystone pieces stuck to her arm.

They give up on the puzzle eventually—the underground clumps of roots are too daunting, after all—and Lizzie reads out loud. It's a Conan Doyle mystery story, though not a Sherlock Holmes one, about a train that's diverted off its tracks and into an abandoned mine by a master criminal, in order to destroy a witness and his bodyguard.

While Lizzie reads, Nell deletes photos from her computer. Many of them are pictures of Tig, taken in the last year, when they were making a valiant effort to do the things Tig wanted to do, before—before what was not said. Nor did they know the exact timing. But they both knew that this year they were moving through with at least a minimum amount of grace was quite soon before. They didn't think it would be as much as two years. Nor was it.

The photos of Tig that Nell is throwing out are sad ones. In them he looks lost, or empty—Tig on the wane. She doesn't want to remember him looking like that, or being like that. She keeps only the smiling ones: when he was pretending that nothing was wrong, that he was still his usual self. He did pull that off a lot of the time. What an effort it must have cost him. Still, they managed to squeeze in some happiness, from hour to hour.

She throws out photos until Lizzie reaches the end of the story, where the megalomaniac criminal who planned the disappearance of the train is crowing over his perfect crime: the two doomed men, stuck on a train hurtling into an abyss, their faces looking aghast out the open train windows, as they watch their fate approach, the yawning blackness of the mine's mouth, the precipitous drop, the plunge into oblivion. Nell is afraid this story will give her nightmares; it's the kind of thing that does. She's never liked heights or cliff edges.

The dream she has that night isn't a nightmare, however. Tig is in it, but he isn't empty and sad. Instead, he's quietly amused. It's a spy story of some kind, though a leisurely one; a Russian named Polly Poliakov is involved, though he isn't a woman, so his name shouldn't be Polly.

Tig isn't an action hero in this dream—he's just there—but Polly Poliakov doesn't seem to care about Tig's presence. He's very anxious, this Polly. There's something that Nell urgently needs to know, but he has no luck at all explaining what it is. As for Nell, she's happy that Tig's in the dream; that's what she's mostly focused on. He smiles at her as if enjoying a joke they're sharing. See? It's all right. It's even funny. It's idiotic how reassured she feels, once she wakes up.

The next day, after they've found the last missing piece of jigsaw on the floor, after they've had breakfast and relocated the night's trove of mice, chewed-up paper towel, gnawed raisins, and mouse poop to a hospitable decaying log, and while they're making a pretense of going for a swim—"I've changed my mind," Lizzie says—Nell whacks one of her toes on the pointed white rock under the water. Of course she does. She was bound to injure herself sooner or later; it's part of the grieving process. Barring bloodletting and clothes-rending and ashes on the head, a person in mourning has to undergo a mutilation of some kind.

Has she cracked a toe bone, or is it only a bruise? It's not a major toe; she can still more or less walk. With a pirate Band-Aid decorated with skulls and crossbones left over from a layer of children—hers? Robbie's? grandkids?—she tapes the offended toe to its neighbour, as instructed via her cellphone. Not much else to be done, according to the websites.

Dig up white rock, Lizzie adds to their list. Her idea is that they will wait until autumn, when the water is lower, or else spring, when it may be lower still, and then go at it in a sort of exorcism, with shovels and pitchforks and the inevitable crowbars. The vampire white rock must go!

How many times have they made such a plan? Many.

The week proceeds. They wend their way through time as if through a labyrinth, or that is what Nell feels; Lizzie, possibly not so much. Nell's injury is good for a few distracting conversations. They both examine the victimized toe with interest: how blue, how purple, will it become? Such observations of the wounded body are cheering: you don't get bruises or pain unless you're still alive.

"Or mosquito bites," Lizzie says. They both know from their murder books that mosquitoes ignore dead people.

You have been mistaken in the time of death, *mon ami.* How so? There were no mosquito bites upon the corpse. Ah! Then that means . . . but surely not! I tell you it must be, my friend. The evidence is before us, it cannot be disputed.

"Small mercies," Nell says. "You don't have to be dead *and* itchy."

"I'll take Option B," Lizzie says.

———————

Others have been through this particular time labyrinth before them. The whole cabin is strewn with instructional signage left over many years. Labels, prohibitions. In the kitchen, *Put No Fat Down Sinks:* this in their mother's handwriting. The cookbook always kept up here has tiny remarks in pencil, also by their mother: *Good!!* Or: *More salt.* Not exactly the wisdom of the ages, but solid, practical advice. *When feeling down in the dumps*—What, exactly, were these dumps? Who still knows?—*go for a brisk walk!* This isn't written; it just hovers in the air, in their mother's voice. An echo.

I can't go for a brisk walk, Nell tells her mother silently. My toe, remember? You can't fix everything, she wants to add, but her mother is well aware of that. Sitting in the hospital while he was possibly dying—*he* again referring to Nell's father, once of the axes, once of the crosscut saws, once of the crowbars—her mother said, "I won't cry, because if I start I'll never be able to stop."

The day before Nell and Lizzie are due to leave for the city, Nell comes across a note written by Tig, long ago, when the two of them installed mosquito nets over the beds as a communal service. The mosquitoes can be thick as fur on the outsides of the screens, especially in June; they can squeeze through the tiniest cracks. Once inside, they whine. Even if you've got repellent on, they can ruin your night.

Large mosquito netting: At the end of the bug season the large netting should be packed in this bag. The wooden frame, once collapsed, is inserted in the inner compartment of the green bag—Thanks.

What green bag? she wonders. Probably it got mildew and someone discarded it. In any case, no one has ever followed these instructions of Tig's; the mosquito netting is merely left in place and tied into a bundle when not in use.

She smooths out the piece of paper carefully and stores it away in her suitcase. It's a message, left by Tig for her to find. Magical thinking, she knows that perfectly well, but she indulges in it anyway because it's comforting. She'll take this piece of paper back to the city, but what will she do with it there? What does one ever do with these cryptic messages from the dead?

ACKNOWLEDGEMENTS

✦

My thanks first to the many readers of these stories—both pub-lished and unpublished—over the years.

Thanks to my sister, Ruth Atwood, and to Jess Atwood Gibson, earliest readers and editors, for their very useful comments and notes; and to the indispensable Lucia Cino, who also read and helped.

Thanks to the magazine editors who wrestled with my peculiar-ities of style, including but not limited to Amy Grace Loyd, Susie Bright, Deborah Treisman, and Kjersti Egerdahl.

Thanks to my book editors on both sides of the Atlantic, whose thoughtfulness and enthusiasm have been so encouraging. This group includes Becky Hardie of Chatto/Penguin Random House UK, Louise Dennys of Penguin Random House Canada, and Lee Boudreaux and LuAnn Walther of Penguin Random House USA. Heather Sangster of Strong Finish again acted as the demon copy editor who picks every nit, including those yet unhatched. Special thanks to Todd Doughty of PRH USA for his boundless positive energy, as well as to Lindsay Mandel of PRH USA for marketing; to Jared Bland of McClelland & Stewart, a calm presence; to Ashley Dunn of PRH Canada for cheerfulness and overall splendour no matter what; and to Priya Roy of PRH UK for her attentive focus and professionalism.

And thanks to my tireless agent, Karolina Sutton of Curtis Brown; and to Caitlin Leydon, Claire Nozieres, Sophie Baker, and Katie Harrison, also of Curtis Brown, who so deftly handle business and foreign rights. Also to Ron Bernstein of ICM (now CAA), who handles film and television rights with admirable zest.

Thanks once more to my now-retired agents, Phoebe Larmore and Vivienne Schuster, who have always been terrific supports.

To those who keep me trundling through time and who remind me what day it is, including Lucia Cino of O.W. Toad Limited and Penny Kavanaugh; to V.J. Bauer, who designs and tends the website; and to Mike Stoyan and Sheldon Shoib, to Donald Bennett, to Bob Clark and Dave Cole.

To Coleen Quinn, who makes sure I get out of the Toronto Writing Burrow and onto the open road; to Xiaolan Zhao and Vicky Dong; to Matthew Gibson, who fixes stuff; and to the Shock Doctors, for keeping the lights on, and to Evelyn Heskin, Ted Humphreys, Deanna Adams, and Randy Gardner, who help make the Writing Burrows habitable.

And as always to Graeme Gibson, who was with me for many but not all of the years in which these stories were written, and who is still very much with me, although not in the usual way.

Some of these stories first appeared in the following publications:
"Impatient Griselda," The Decameron Project, *New York Times Magazine*, July 7, 2020.
"Morte de Smudgie" (San Francisco: The Arion Press, 2021).
"Old Babes in the Wood," *The New Yorker*, Apr. 19, 2021.
"Two Scorched Men," Scribd, Aug. 4, 2021.
"The Dead Interview: George Orwell," *INQUE*, Oct. 1, 2021.

"My Evil Mother" (Seattle: Amazon Original Stories, 2022).

A much earlier version of "Freeforall" appeared in the *Toronto Star* newspaper in 1986.

Thanks to Alexander Matthews, the executor of Martha Gellhorn's estate, for permission to use unpublished material by Martha Gellhorn; and to Janet Somerville, editor of *Yours, For Probably Always* (Richmond Hill, ON: Firefly Books, 2019)—a collection of Gellhorn's letters—for sharing background information, and for her enthusiasm.

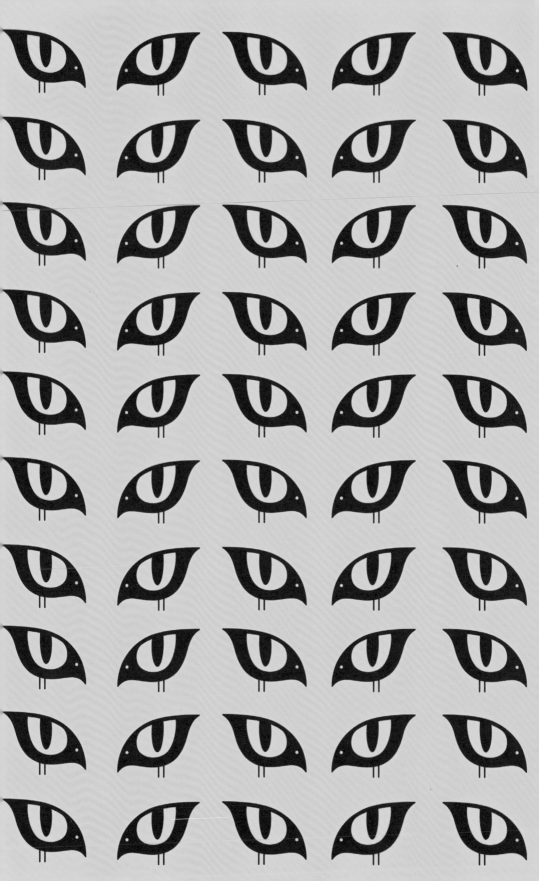